CREATURE!

NOVELS BY BILL PRONZINI

The Cambodia File (with Jack Anderson)
Labyrinth
Night Screams (with Barry N. Malzberg)
Twospot (with Collin Wilcox)
Acts of Mercy (with Barry N. Malzberg)
Blowback
Games
The Running of Beasts (with Barry N. Malzberg)
Snowbound
Undercurrent
The Vanished
Panic!
The Snatch
The Stalker

ANTHOLOGIES EDITED BY BILL PRONZINI

Creature!
Mummy!
Voodoo!
Werewolf!
Shared Tomorrow (with Barry N. Malzberg)
Dark Sins, Dark Dreams (with Barry N. Malzberg)
The End of Summer: Science Fiction of the Fifties
(with Barry N. Malzberg)
Midnight Specials
Tricks And Treats (With Joe Gores)

A CHRESTOMATHY OF "MONSTERY"

CREATURE!

EDITED BY **Bill Pronzini**

ARBOR HOUSE
NEW YORK

Library of Congress Catalog Card Number: 80-70221

ISBN: 0-87795-310-4   cloth
         0-87795-321-X   Priam trade paperback

Manufactured in the United States of America

10 9 8 7 6 5 4 3 2 1

The following page constitutes an extension of the copyright page. The
author gratefully acknowledges permission to include from the following:

ACKNOWLEDGMENTS

"The Terror of Blue John Gap" by Sir Arthur Conan Doyle. Published with the permission of the copyright holder of the Sir Arthur Conan Doyle literary estate.

"Creature of the Snows" by William Sambrot. Copyright © 1960 by William Sambrot. First published in *The Saturday Evening Post*. Reprinted by permission of Curtis Brown, Ltd.

"Waziah" by Joe R. Lansdale. Copyright © 1981 by Joe R. Lansdale. An original story published by permission of the author.

"Barney's Bigfoot Museum" by Richard Laymon. Copyright © 1981 by Richard Laymon. An original story published by permission of the author.

"Survival Exercise" by Talmage Powell. Copyright © 1981 by

CONTENTS

CREATURE!

INTRODUCTION

They only come out at night.

If you are a wilderness traveler, whether on land or sea or other body of water, you must always remember this. Especially on dark nights, late, when the forest or the mountains or the water is hushed and no moon shines in an ebon sky. Especially if there are no other human beings close by, no one to hear a cry for help.

For no matter what the species—Yeti, Sasquatch, swamp beast, sea serpent, or other creature strange and wonderful—they only come out at night . . . and they come out to go a-hunting.

No, they seldom actually prey on human flesh; some are not even carnivorous. They make every effort, in fact, to avoid contact with the race of man. But they are not afraid of man, nor are they unwilling to attack if provoked or frightened. Some are huge, with the strength of a hundred, a thousand puny humans; and all possess a cunning far greater than any in the mind of *homo sapiens*. They can be dangerous: when they are on the prowl for food for themselves and their young they must be avoided at all costs. If aroused, their wrath may be almost as great as God's—and in a confrontation between man and creature, man almost never wins.

Or survives.

So be careful, traveler, and be vigilant. If you must walk by night, walk soft and wary. Otherwise remain in your camp with a high hot fire burning through the dark hours, or in your boat with all lanterns lit. Stay clear of caves and bog holes and dense swamp thickets. Do not sail into uncharted waters or too near unknown shores. Do not investigate cries or rustlings or other strange sounds in the darkness.

Mark the words of Coleridge's Ancient Mariner, if you mark no others:

> *Like one that on a lonesome road*
> *Doth walk in fear and dread,*
> *And having once turned round, walks on,*
> *And turns no more his head;*
> *Because he knows a frightful fiend*
> *Doth close behind him tread.*

Fiend—or creature—remember these words well. And remember, too, that most important fact of all. You will receive no other warning, and if you fail to remember, if you fail to heed, the consequences are frightful indeed:

They only come out at night . . .

There have been sightings of land and water creatures for thousands of years. On every continent, on every sea and inland body of water, man has encountered and often done battle with beings of myriad type and description. Every race, civilized as well as primitive, has its creature legends; and every race has its believers, its worshipers. This is as true today as it was a hundred or five hundred or five thousand years ago.

Creatures, monsters, *do* exist.

Until the last century, that was a claim only whispered, if spoken at all. Fear and superstition precluded open discussion, much less a sustained scientific interest in such phenomena. The advancement of modern civilization, and the shrinkage of the world that came with it, brought the question of creatures into the open. And people began to speak of the unspeakable.

In 1887 Lawrence A. Waddell, a major in the medical corps of the British Indian Army, found a series of large tracks in Sikkim and caused something of a stir in England by attributing the tracks to "a creature, not a man" in his 1899 book *Among the Himalayas.* In 1902 British Indian officials stringing the first telegraph wire between Kalimpong, in northern India, and the capital of Tibet, Lhasa, filed a report stating that a dozen native workers had vanished near a place called Jelep-La on the Sikkim–Tibet border, and that during a search for them a huge hairy creature was found asleep under a rock and summarily killed by soldiers. (What happened to the body no one knows.) In 1915 a British forestry officer named J. R. O. Gent wrote in a letter to scientific explorer H. J. Elwes, who himself had seen a creature some years before, that he had found evidence of a "big monkey, or ape perhaps—if there were any apes in India" near Phalut in the outer Himalayas.

These are just three of dozens of early reports from India, Tibet, Sikkim, and Nepal of the creature known variously as the *Metoh-Kangmi,* the Yeti, and the Abominable Snowman (ABSM for short). The majority of these reports, whether made by Westerners or Tibetans, Sherpas, and other natives of the region, coincide in their descriptions of what the creature looks like: four to ten feet tall when erect on its hind legs (several different species have been theorized by scientists); massive body covered with dark brown or occasionally lighter colored hair; long arms; oval head pointed or ridged at the top, with an apelike face only sparsely hirsute. It is said to possess great strength and a peculiar whistling call like that of a seagull, and—survivors say—to fear the light of a fire.

Later scientific investigation has evidently established the fact that the term "snowman" is a misnomer: the creature is not human, nor does it live in the snow. Its habitat is the impenetrable forests below the Himalayan snowline, where it sleeps by day in a hidden lair and goes foraging at night. In the forest it may move on all fours or by swinging apelike through the trees; in the open it walks upright in a rolling, somewhat unsteady fashion. The reason it treks up into the snow regions, according to speculation, is that it craves certain lichens, found on the rocks of the moraine fields, which are rich in vitamin E and minerals.

Until 1954 the world at large knew relatively little about the Yeti. In that year, spurred by reports of creature tracks and sightings by famed mountaineer Sir Edmund Hillary, among others, the *Daily Mail* of London organized the first expedition aimed at finding an ABSM. This expedition was led by a reporter, Ralph Izzard, and included a zoologist among its members, and although it uncovered little new information (and no ABSM) on its year-long trek through the Himalayas, it served the dual purpose of publicizing the Yeti phenomenon and pointing the way to serious scientific attempts at solving the enigma.

Several other expeditions followed, notably three led by a prominent Texas researcher named Thomas B. Slick; most of these found and photographed Yeti tracks, and some ABSM were sighted in and out of the snow regions. These additional discoveries added fuel to both public and scientific interest. A number of ·ABSM books—some scholarly, some sensationalistic—began to appear. More expeditions were organized, and continue to be organized, by men searching for more specific data.

But to the date of this writing no one has succeeded in capturing (or in killing) a Yeti, or even in locating one of its hidden forest lairs. The true nature of the beast remains a mystery.

The Sasquatch, or Bigfoot, of North America is believed by many to be either a western hemispheric cousin of the Yeti or a breed of ABSM which migrated to a warmer climate from Asia across the Bering Sea and down the Pacific coast. In either case, the central domain of Sasquatch appears to be British Columbia, Washington, Idaho, Oregon, and northern California. Its habitat may range as far east as the Dakotas, as far north as the Alaskan interior.

Reports of huge hairy creatures that walk on two legs—of "wild men of the woods"—have emanated from the Northwest since the early 1800s. One of the more interesting of these appears in a book entitled *Wilderness Hunter* (1893), written by Theodore Roosevelt in his pre–White House years. It relates a story told to Roosevelt by a grizzled old mountain hunter named Bauman.

In his younger days Bauman had gone trapping with a partner in Idaho, and,

> not having much luck, he and his partner determined to go up into a particularly wild and lonely pass through which ran a small stream said to contain many beaver. The pass had an evil reputation because the year before a solitary hunter who had wandered into it was there slain,

seemingly by a wild beast, the halfeaten remains being afterwards found by some mining prospectors who had passed his camp the night before.

The two men found much more than they bargained for. Twice in the next two days their camp was visited while they were out setting traps, their things rummaged through, and the lean-to they had built (and then rebuilt) torn down. The ground was marked up by tracks which Bauman swore were made by a creature walking on two legs, a creature that could not have been a bear.

On the third day he and his partner determined to leave the area. They spent the morning retrieving all but three of their traps, feeling the while as if they were being followed. Bauman set out after the remaining traps while his friend returned to the camp to make their packs ready. When Bauman himself returned he found

the body of his friend, stretched beside the trunk of a great fallen spruce. Rushing towards it the horrified trapper found that the body was still warm, but that the neck was broken, while there were four great fang marks in the throat.

The footprints of the unknown beast-creature, printed in the soft soil, told the whole story. . . . It had not eaten the body, but apparently had romped and gambolled round it in uncouth, ferocious glee, occasionally rolling over and over it; and had then fled back into the soundless depths of the woods.

In British Columbia alone more than one hundred and sixty Sasquatch incidents have been documented, ranging from sightings and the discovery of tracks to attacks on human beings. Most of the eyewitness accounts agree that

Bigfoot is similar to Yeti in appearance: seven to ten feet tall, long dark brown (or in some cases black) hair, weight in the neighborhood of three hundred pounds, with pointed head and apelike face. The females sighted are said to have huge, pendulous, hair-draped breasts.

(There exists a film of one such female, taken by Roger Patterson, head of the Bigfoot-oriented Northwest Research Association, while exploring "Bigfoot Country" northeast of Eureka, California, in 1967. Rounding a bend on horseback, Patterson and a companion came upon the creature opposite a shallow stream some one hundred yards distant; Patterson managed to load his movie camera and to shoot several feet of film as he chased the creature into the woods. Dr. John R. Napier, director of Primate Biology at the Smithsonian Institution—and later author of a superior book called *Bigfoot: The Yeti and Sasquatch in Myth and Reality*—was among those who viewed the film. His comment is significant: "I observed nothing that, on scientific grounds, would point conclusively to a hoax. I am satisfied that the walk of the creature shown in the film was consistent with the bipedal striding gait of a man. The bodily proportions of the creature, as far as could be seen, appeared to be within the normal limits for man. The appearance of the high crest on top of the skull is unknown, but given a creature as heavily built as the subject, such a biochemical adaptation to an exclusively fibrous raw vegetable diet is not impossible.")

In May of 1967 the evident *corpus delicti* of a Bigfoot-type male went on exhibit in a refrigerated van attached to a traveling show in the Midwest. Eminent ABSM authorities Ivan Sanderson and Dr. Bernard Heuvelmans learned of this and, wary of a hoax, subsequently examined the creature in December of 1968. They found it to be shaped like an adult human male, some six feet tall and covered with dark brown hair several inches in length. The skin beneath it was a pale white. The hands were almost human except for overlong thumbs; the feet measured eight inches across the toes and were covered with thick hair. The face was large and pugged, more like a Pekingese dog than a gorilla or a man, with large circular nostrils, wide mouth with no visible lips, and small teeth dissimilar to those of either ape or human. Around the mouth were folds and wrinkle lines which Sanderson found to be "absolutely human . . . like those seen in a heavy-jowled, older white man."

Where did this creature come from? Who had killed it? (It had been shot to death.) The man who had put it on exhibit, a Mr. Hansen, claimed not to be the owner, that he had been led to it in a deep-freeze plant in Hong Kong and there made arrangements to export it to America for a fee. He refused to say anything more about it. Many scientists, and the Smithsonian Institution in particular, asked for permission to X-ray the creature; Hansen declined. Later he exhibited a wax or latex-rubber model of the beast and the whole matter was denounced in the press, as well as officially by the Smithsonian, as a hoax. The fate of the original creature, which Sanderson and Heuvelmans (both of them scientists and both experienced hoax-debunkers) had examined and certified as real, is unknown to this day.

Sasquatch, like the Yeti, is still as much a mystery as it ever was.

The so-called swamp creature, of the type popularized by the film *The Creature from the Black Lagoon,* may also be a relation of the Yeti and/or Bigfoot. Sightings have been reported in most of the United States, Canada, Burma, South America, and other locales—usually in swamps or boggy areas of some size. Most of these creatures resemble Sasquatch, with the primary difference being that their hair or fur is wet and matted from the swamp water, thus making the stench which surrounds them noxiously foul. Others have been described as scaly (*The Creature from the Black Lagoon* again), deformed, shapeless blobs with bushy heads, and having luminescent greenish eyes; all of these, too, are evil-smelling—"like the stench of stale urine," as one eyewitness put it.

But no one has caught or killed a swamp creature yet, either.

The Loch Ness Monster—or Nessie, as she has been dubbed—has also been sighted on a great many occasions (three thousand responsible citizens claim to have seen her since 1933), and indistinctly photographed and filmed several times as well. Rumors of her existence date back hundreds of years, but it was not until 1933 that she began to appear with enough frequency so that reports of sightings were taken seriously and documented.

Nessie has been described in various ways, but most often as a serpentlike creature between thirty and forty feet in length, with a huge black body containing at least two large humps, short flippered legs, a neck from eight to twelve feet long, and a smallish horselike head. She appears capable of making growling (or similar) noises, and of swimming at great speed while churning the water to a froth with either flippers or a tail.

A number of people believe the creature to be a plesiosaur—a suborder of Mesozoic marine reptiles with dorsoventrally flattened bodies and limbs modified into paddles. But zoologists do not believe that plesiosaurs could have survived from the Mesozoic Age, particularly in such cold water as that of Loch Ness, and paleontologists are of the opinion that the most recent reconstructions of plesiosaur fossils do not fit the descriptions of Nessie. Others have suggested that she is the mollusk known as a giant sea slug, a distant relative of the kraken (giant squid); a form of manatee, or sea cow; an enormous seal; a gigantic and grotesque salamander or newt; or a monstrous, thick-bodied eel. But there are numerous scientific grounds on which to negate each of these explanations as well.

Nessie is by no means alone among sea creatures. Hundreds of others have been reported throughout the world, in oceans and lakes, salt water and fresh water. Water-horses (beasts similar to Nessie) are said to inhabit other lochs in the Scottish Highlands. Snakelike animals have been seen in several Irish lakes. Lake Storsjö, in the mountains of central Sweden, contains a creature thirty to forty feet in length, with slimy skin dark green to brown in front, yellowish gray in back, and capable of moving through the water as if propelled. In Lake Okanagan in British Columbia there is a creature which the local Indians call Naitaka, "the monster spirit of the lake," and which the white man calls Ogopogo; it has a goatlike head, a long neck, and appears to be covered in scales. In the United States, water creatures have been seen off the coast of New England, in Lake Erie, in several Wisconsin lakes, in Silver Lake in upstate New York, in Utah Lake south of Salt Lake City, and in Lake Payette in Idaho (this one is called "Slimy Slim" because it has a sleek twenty-five-foot-long black body with no visible sign of fins or flippers).

Dr. Bernard Heuvelmans, in his carefully researched book *In the Wake of Sea Serpents,* has broken down the probable types of sea creature into nine categories. Two are obscure; the other seven are: (1) marine saurian—a primitive sea-going crocodile; (2) super-eel—serpentlike animal, limbless, a kind of fish; (3) super-otter—long-tailed mammal that looks like a giant otter; (4) many-finned—long jointed mammal with rows of triangular fins; (5) many-humped—long mammal with a blunt head, short neck, a single pair of flippers, and a series of humps along the back which move with a rippling effect; (6) long-necked—tailless seal-like animal with a very long neck and back humps; (7) mer-horse—an animal similar to that above except that it possesses huge eyes, whiskers, a mane, and may also have a tail. It is Heuvelmans's opinion that most of today's sightings, including those of Nessie, are of long-necked mammals in the last two categories.

But neither he nor any other investigators have been able to prove their theories, or to disprove any other. No one has captured Nessie or any other water monster so far.

A great many other creatures have been sighted and are believed to exist in remote, and not so remote, sections of the world. Globsters (shapeless sea things covered with short hair, the first of which washed ashore in Tasmania in 1960); the "mothman" (a manlike being with wings, seen several times in West Virginia); cat-beasts (giant gray-and-black-striped creatures, with catlike heads, which have killed sheep and frightened humans in New Zealand); even fifteen-foot-tall penguins (sighted in Florida, of all places, and by several different witnesses). But none of these, either, has been caught or killed.

The skeptic, of course, will say that no creature has been captured and authenticated because none, in fact, exists. He will shrug off the sheer staggering number of sightings and reports, from people of different races, different religions, different intellects and attitudes. They can be attributed, he'll say, to misinterpretation, hallucination, delusion, or hoax. And he will dismiss any suggestion that this is even more improbable than the presence in our world of creatures with more instinctual cunning, and a greater ability for survival, than our own.

One can't persuade a skeptic with words or eyewitness acounts or even scientific argument. He remains aloof; he

knows what he knows and that's that. And what he knows is
that there are no such things as monsters.

For his sake, let us hope he never meets one . . .

Of the dozens of nonfiction books about creatures, the
majority deal with the Yeti and/or Sasquatch and with sea
serpents (Nessie in particular). And the bulk of these have
been published during the past four decades, as a result of
scientific investigation and a renewed general interest in the
occult and the unknown.

Three books on the Yeti appeared in the early 1950s; all of
them are well worth reading: Ralph Izzard's account of the
London *Daily Mail* expedition of 1954, called *The Abominable
Snowman Adventure;* C. Stonor's *The Sherpa and the Snowman*
(1955); and Sherpa guide Norgay Tenzing's autobiographical
Tiger of the Snows (1955). A remarkable book titled *Jadoo*
(1957), by John Keel, tells of a series of the author's hair-
raising "personal experiences" with mystery and magic
throughout the East, one of which involves a lengthy search
for, and a sighting of, an ABSM in northern Nepal. But it was
not until 1961 that the first (and perhaps best) of the scholarly
studies of the ABSM was published; this book, Ivan T.
Sanderson's *Abominable Snowmen: Legend Come to Life,* is a work
of expert historical, bibliographical, and personal research
into the subject of land creatures and is fascinating for its
insights as much as for its documentation. The same may be
said for two subsequent books of similar intent and success:
Bernard Heuvelmans's *On the Track of Unknown Animals* (1965)
and John R. Napier's *Bigfoot: The Yeti and Sasquatch in Myth and
Reality* (1972).

Books which deal solely with Sasquatch have begun to
proliferate in recent years. A privately printed volume by

Roger Patterson, mentioned earlier—*Do Abominable Snowmen of America Really Exist?* (1966)—contains several fascinating articles and eyewitness accounts. Also worth reading is John Green's well-researched *On the Track of the Sasquatch* (1973). But the Sanderson, Heuvelmans, and Napier books remain the best sources of ABSM facts and lore.

One of the earliest and best books on Nessie is R. T. Gould's *The Loch Ness Monster and Others,* published in 1934. Later entries of note include Maurice Burton's *The Elusive Monster* (1961), Nicholas Witchell's *The Loch Ness Story* (1975), and Gerald Snyder's *Is There a Loch Ness Monster?* (1977)—and in particular, for its documented list of sightings to that time, Constance Whyte's *More Than a Legend* (1957). But the strongest books in this category are those which consider Nessie's worldwide counterparts as intently as Nessie herself: Tim Dinsdale's *The Leviathans* (1966), Bernard Heuvelmans's *In the Wake of Sea Serpents* (1968), and Peter Costellos' *In Search of Lake Monsters* (1974). The last-named title is especially well-researched and includes material on fiction and films, as well as an extensive bibliography.

A few books, all of them paperback originals, are devoted to other-creature reports and seem mostly to be Fortean in design; that is, they are anthologies of unexplained phenomena similar to Charles Fort's *Wild Talents* and *The Book of the Damned.* The most intelligent and authentic of these "collections" are by serious writers already mentioned: Ivan Sanderson, with *"Things"* (1967) and *More "Things"* (1969), and John Keel, with *Strange Creatures from Time and Space* (1970).

A considerable amount of fiction has been devoted to creatures over the past century or so, beginning with Jules Verne's two famous novels, *Journey to the Center of the Earth*

(1864) and *Twenty Thousand Leagues Under the Sea* (1873). These early works, and a number of others by other authors which followed, involve "lost worlds" populated by prehistoric creatures and men, as well as other strange beings. Sir Arthur Conan Doyle's *The Lost World* (1912) is probably the best of these; others of note are the Pellucidar, and some Tarzan, novels of Edgar Rice Burroughs (e.g., *The Land That Time Forgot, Pellucidar, Tarzan at the Earth's Core*).

The Yeti and Sasquatch seem to have been "discovered" by fiction writers only in recent years. William Sambrot's 1960 short story, "Creature of the Snows" (which appears in these pages), is one of the earliest, and no doubt the finest, Yeti tales. Only a few novels deal principally with the Abominable Snowman, the best of these by default being Norman Bogner's *Snowman* (1978) and Josef Nesvadba's science fictional *In the Footsteps of the Abominable Snowman* (1970). The same is true of Bigfoot, although the qualitative pickings are somewhat better: Thomas Page's excellent and chilling *The Spirit* (1977), which combines Sasquatch with Indian legend, and Walter J. Sheldon's imaginative *The Beast* (1980).

Nessie was the subject of a novel earlier than either the Yeti or Sasquatch—*The Rival Monster* by Compton MacKenzie, a humorous tale of the Scottish Highlands, published in 1952—but has been badly neglected since. Only one other (and rather bad) novel, Peter Tremayne's *The Curse of Loch Ness* (1979) can be said to deal primarily with Nessie. And only one short story: Leslie Charteris's dandy Saint adventure, "The Convenient Monster," which also appears here.

Novels about other types of creatures are much more prevalent. Vercors's superior *You Shall Know Them* (1953) deals with the discovery (and subsequent murder) of the missing link in New Guinea; John Lutz's *Bonegrinder* (1977) involves a legendary Ozark lake creature; a trio of horror thrillers by British writer Guy Smith concern giant crabs *(Killer Crabs, Night of the Crabs)* and a swamp creature *(The Slime Beast)*. There are also two film novelizations of note in this category: *King Kong* by Delos Lovelace and *The Creature from the Black Lagoon* by Carl Dreadstone.

A few good—and a large percentage of bad—films have been made about creatures, beginning with probably the best of them all, *King Kong,* in 1933. At the front rank of the Yeti films by far is *The Abominable Snowman of the Himalayas* (1957), starring Forrest Tucker and Peter Cushing—an effective and intelligent, if B-styled, Hammer film made in England. Sasquatch, alas, has yet to be brought to the screen in anything except low-budget clunkers *(Snowbeast, The Curse of Bigfoot, Bigfoot, The Mysterious Monster)*. The only Nessie film to date, rather curiously, is *The Secret of the Loch,* made in 1934 by a Scottish film company and starring Scots actor Seymour Hicks. (She did make a brief appearance in Billy Wilder's *The Private Life of Sherlock Holmes,* but only as a hoax to be debunked by Holmes.) Other sea-creature films of some quality and/or notoriety are *The Creature from the Black Lagoon, The Beast from 20,000 Fathoms,* and the original *Godzilla.*

In addition to *King Kong,* other creature films worthy of viewing are *Them* (giant ants), *Valley of the Gwangi* (prehistoric monsters), and *Tarantula* (giant spider). Conversely, creature films to be avoided at all costs—these don't even offer unintentional laughs; just boredom—are *Man Beast* (Yeti), *Monster from the Surf* (sea creature), and *Trog* (prehistoric beast—not, it should be noted, Joan Crawford, who nonetheless does walk and sometimes lurch through the film).

As with novels and movies, a substantial amount of short creature-fiction has been published over the years but relatively little of it is of quality. The best and most unusual of these stories dealing with the ABSM, Nessie, and other types of land and sea creatures have been gathered together here. And where no appropriate story has previously been published, as was the case with Bigfoot, original material has been commissioned.

The land creatures featured in the following pages are the subterranean or "lost world" beast ("The Terror of Blue John Gap" by Sir Arthur Conan Doyle); the ABSM (William Sambrot's "Creature of the Snows"); Bigfoot ("Waziah" by Joe R. Lansdale, "Barney's Bigfoot Museum" by Richard Laymon); and the swamp creature (Talmage Powell's "Survival Exercise"). The watery creatures are Nessie ("The Convenient Monster" by Leslie Charteris); sea serpents (William Hope Hodgson's "A Tropical Horror," Stephen Vincent Benét's "Daniel Webster and the Sea Serpent"); and a being from another dimension (Robert Bloch's "Terror in Cut-Throat Cove"). Other creatures strange and wonderful are a changeling ("Notes Leading Down to the Events at Bedlam" by Barry N. Malzberg); a creature born of straw ("In the Straw" by Edward D. Hoch); a duppy (Avram Davidson's "Where Do You Live, Queen Esther?"); a worm (John Lutz's "Wriggle"); and frogs ("The Pond" by Nigel Kneale).

These stories, as you'll soon see, offer a little something for every taste. But not just yours; not just the reader's.

The *creatures'* taste as well . . .

Is it night as you are reading this? A dark night, prehaps—hushed, moonless?

If so, make sure your doors and windows are locked before you begin any of the stories which follow. See that all your

lights are on, and that your telephone works in case of an emergency. For the warning is the same to the exploring reader as to the wilderness traveler: be watchful, be vigilant, as you enter the domain of the monster. And remember—
They only come out at night.

—Bill Pronzini
San Francisco, California
September 1980

PART I

LAND CREATURES

THE TERROR OF BLUE JOHN GAP
BY SIR ARTHUR CONAN DOYLE

As mentioned in the introduction, an abundance of novels in the late 1800s and early 1900s (and in the years since) have dealt with "lost races"—uncharted islands, primitive jungle plateaus, undersea colonies, subterranean worlds extending to the earth's core inhabited by any numbr of strange and/or prehistoric creatures. The famous King Kong, as you may recall, is a member of just such a lost race. And so is "The Terror of Blue John Gap."

Most lost-world creatures seldom make journeys into the populated areas of the earth's surface, either by accident or authorial design. But this one, "a great shaggy mass, something with rough and bristling hair of a withered gray color, fading away to white in its lower parts, the huge body supported upon short, thick, curving legs," does appear in a populated area at the turn of this century—and a populated area in that most civilized of countries—England—at that. During its nocturnal prowls it terrifies several Derbyshire residents, as well as a visiting

London physician named Dr. James Hardcastle; it may also terrify you . . .

Born in 1859, Sir Arthur Conan Doyle began his literary career in the 1880s with the creation of his famous detective, Sherlock Holmes, and with a number of excellent fantasy/horror stories. He was so prolific and his work so well-received that he abandoned a lucrative medical practice in 1892 to devote his full time to writing—a pursuit which he energetically followed, with time out for service in the Boer War, until his death in 1930. He was deeply interested in the occult and wrote six books on spiritualism, including the definitive two-volume work, History of Spiritualism *(1926). Among his many novels is the superior lost-race tale,* The Lost World, *which was published in 1912.*

THE FOLLOWING narrative was found among the papers of Dr. James Hardcastle, who died of phthisis on February 4th, 1908, at 36, Upper Coventry Flats, South Kensington. Those who knew him best, while refusing to express an opinion upon this particular statement, are unanimous in asserting that he was a man of a sober and scientific turn of mind, absolutely devoid of imagination, and most unlikely to invent any abnormal series of events. The paper was contained in an envelope, which was docketed, "A Short Account of the Circumstances which occurred near Miss Allerton's Farm in North-West Derbyshire in the Spring of Last Year." The envelope was sealed, and on the other side was written in pencil—

Dear Seaton—

It may interest, and perhaps pain you, to know that the incredulity with which you met my story has prevented

me from ever opening my mouth upon the subject again. I
leave this record after my death, and perhaps strangers
may be found to have more confidence in me than my
friend.

Inquiry has failed to elicit who this Seaton may have been.
I may add that the visit of the deceased to Allerton's Farm,
and the general nature of the alarm there, apart from his
particular explanation, have been absolutely established.
With this foreword I append his account exactly as he left it.
It is in the form of a diary, some entries in which have been
expanded, while a few have been erased.

April 17.—Already I feel the benefit of this wonderful
upland air. The farm of the Allertons lies fourteen hundred
and twenty feet above sea level, so it may well be a bracing
climate. Beyond the usual morning cough I have very little
discomfort, and, what with the fresh milk and the home-
grown mutton, I have every chance of putting on weight. I
think Saunderson will be pleased.

The two Miss Allertons are charmingly quaint and kind,
two dear little hard-working old maids, who are ready to
lavish all the heart which might have gone out to husband
and to children upon an invalid stranger. Truly, the old maid
is a most useful person, one of the reserve forces of the community. They talk of the superfluous woman, but what would
the poor superfluous man do without her kindly presence? By
the way, in their simplicity they very quickly let out the
reason why Saunderson recommended their farm. The
professor rose from the ranks himself, and I believe that in his
youth he was not above scaring crows in these very fields.

It is a most lonely spot, and the walks are picturesque in the
extreme. The farm consists of grazing land lying at the bot-

tom of an irregular valley. On each side are the fantastic limestone hills, formed of rock so soft that you can break it away with your hands. All this country is hollow. Could you strike it with some gigantic hammer it would boom like a drum, or possibly cave in altogether and expose some huge subterranean sea. A great sea there must surely be, for on all sides the streams run into the mountain itself, never to reappear. There are gaps everywhere amid the rocks, and when you pass through them you find yourself in great caverns, which wind down into the bowels of the earth. I have a small bicycle lamp, and it is a perpetual joy to me to carry it into these weird solitudes, and to see the wonderful silver and black effect when I throw its light upon the stalactites which drape the lofty roofs. Shut off the lamp, and you are in the blackest darkness. Turn it on, and it is a scene from the Arabian Nights.

But there is one of these strange openings in the earth which has a special interest, for it is the handiwork, not of nature, but of man. I had never heard of Blue John when I came to these parts. It is the name given to a peculiar mineral of a beautiful purple shade, which is only found at one or two places in the world. It is so rare that an ordinary vase of Blue John would be valued at a great price. The Romans, with that extraordinary instinct of theirs, discovered that it was to be found in this valley, and sank a horizontal shaft deep into the mountainside. The opening of their mine has been called Blue John Gap, a clean-cut arch in the rock, the mouth all overgrown with bushes. It is a goodly passage which the Roman miners have cut, and it intersects some of the great water-worn caves, so that if you enter Blue John Gap you would do well to mark your steps and to have a good store of candles, or you may never make your way back to the daylight again. I have not yet gone deeply into it, but this very day I stood at the mouth of the arched tunnel, and peering down into the black recesses beyond, I vowed that when my health returned I would devote some holiday to exploring those mysterious depths and finding out for myself how far the Roman had penetrated into the Derbyshire hills.

Strange how superstitious these countrymen are! I should have thought better of young Armitage, for he is a man of some education and character, and a very fine fellow for his station in life. I was standing at the Blue John Gap when he came across the field to me.

"Well, doctor," said he, "you're not afraid, anyhow."

"Afraid!" I answered. "Afraid of what?"

"Of it," said he, with a jerk of this thumb towards the black vault, "of the Terror that lives in the Blue John Cave."

How absurdly easy it is for a legend to arise in a lonely countryside! I examined him as to the reasons for his weird belief. It seems that from time to time sheep have been missing from the fields, carried bodily away, according to Armitage. That they could have wandered away of their own accord and disappeared among the mountains was an explanation to which he would not listen. On one occasion a pool of blood had been found, and some tufts of wool. That also, I pointed out, could be explained in a perfectly natural way. Further, the nights upon which sheep disappeared were invariably very dark, cloudy nights with no moon. This I met with the obvious retort that those were the nights which a commonplace sheep-stealer would naturally choose for his work. On one occasion a gap had been made in a wall, and some of the stones scattered for a considerable distance. Human agency again, in my opinion. Finally, Armitage clinched all his arguments by telling me that he had actually heard the creature—indeed, that anyone could hear it who remained long enough at the gap. It was a distant roaring of an immense volume. I could not but smile at this, knowing, as I do, the strange reverberations which come out of an underground water system running amid the chasms of a limestone formation. My incredulity annoyed Armitage so that he turned and left me with some abruptness.

And now comes the queer point about the whole business. I was still standing near the mouth of the cave turning over in my mind the various statements of Armitage, and reflecting how readily they could be explained away, when suddenly, from the depth of the tunnel beside me, there issued a most extraordinary sound. How shall I describe it? First of all, it seemed to be a great distance away, far down in the bowels of the earth. Secondly, in spite of this suggestion of distance, it was very loud. Lastly, it was not a boom, nor a crash, such as one would associate with falling water or tumbling rock, but it was a high whine, tremulous and vibrating, almost like the whinnying of a horse. It was certainly a most remarkable experience, and one which for a moment, I must admit, gave a new significance to Armitage's words. I waited by the Blue John Gap for half an hour or more, but there was no return of the sound, so at last I wandered back to the farmhouse, rather mystified by what had occurred. Decidedly I shall explore that cavern when my strength is restored. Of course, Armitage's explanation is too absurd for discussion, and yet that sound was certainly very strange. It still rings in my ears as I write.

April 20.—In the last three days I have made several expeditions to the Blue John Gap, and have even penetrated some short distance, but my bicycle lantern is so small and weak that I dare not trust myself very far. I shall do the thing more systematically. I have heard no sound at all, and could almost believe that I had been the victim of some hallucination suggested, perhaps, by Armitage's conversation. Of course, the whole idea is absurd, and yet I must confess that those bushes at the entrance of the cave do present an appearance as if some heavy creature had forced its way through them. I begin to be keenly interested. I have said nothing to the Miss Allertons, for they are quite superstitious enough already, but I have bought some candles, and mean to investigate for myself.

I observed this morning that among the numerous tufts of sheep's wool which lay among the bushes near the cavern there was one which was smeared with blood. Of course, my reason tells me that if sheep wander into such rocky places they are likely to injure themselves, and yet somehow that splash of crimson gave me a sudden shock, and for a moment I found myself shrinking back in horror from the old Roman arch. A fetid breath seemed to ooze from the black depths into which I peered. Could it indeed be possible that some nameless thing, some dreadful presence, was lurking down yonder? I should have been incapable of such feelings in the days of my strength, but one grows more nervous and fanciful when one's health is shaken.

For the moment I weakened in my resolution, and was ready to leave the secret of the old mine, if one exists, forever unsolved. But tonight my interest has returned and my nerves grown more steady. Tomorrow I trust that I shall have gone more deeply into this matter.

April 22.—Let me try and set down as accurately as I can my extraordinary experience of yesterday. I started in the afternoon, and made my way to the Blue John Gap. I confess that my misgivings returned as I gazed into its depths, and I wished that I had brought a companion to share my exploration. Finally, with a return of resolution, I lit my candle, pushed my way through the briars, and descended into the rocky shaft.

It went down at an acute angle for some fifty feet, the floor being covered with broken stone. Thence there extended a long, straight passage cut in the solid rock. I am no geologist, but the lining of this corridor was certainly of some harder material than limestone, for there were points where I could actually see the tool marks which the old miners had left in their excavation, as fresh as if they had been done yesterday. Down this strange, old-world corridor I stumbled, my feeble flame throwing a dim circle of light around me, which made the shadows beyond the more threatening and obscure. Finally, I came to a spot where the Roman tunnel opened into a water-worn cavern—a huge hall, hung with long white icicles of lime deposit. From this central chamber I could dimly perceive that a number of passages worn by the subterranean streams wound away into the depths of the earth. I was standing there wondering whether I had better return, or whether I dare venture farther into this dangerous labyrinth, when my eyes fell upon something at my feet which strongly arrested my attention.

The greater part of the floor of the cavern was covered with boulders of rock or with hard incrustations of lime, but at this particular point there had been a drip from the distant roof, which had left a patch of soft mud. In the very center of this there was a huge mark—an ill-defined blotch, deep, broad, and irregular, as if a great boulder had fallen upon it. No loose stone lay near, however, nor was there anything to account for the impression. It was far too large to be caused by any possible animal, and besides, there was only the one, and the patch of mud was of such a size that no reasonable stride could have covered it. As I rose from the examination of that singular mark and then looked round into the black shadows which hemmed me in, I must confess that I felt for a moment a most unpleasant sinking of my heart, and that, do what I could, the candle trembled in my outstretched hand.

I soon recovered my nerve, however, when I reflected how absurd it was to associate so huge and shapless a mark with the track of any known animal. Even an elephant could not have produced it. I determined, therefore, that I would not be scared by vague and senseless fears from carrying out my exploration. Before proceeding, I took good note of a curious rock formation in the wall by which I could recognize the entrance of the Roman tunnel. The precaution was very necessary, for the great cave, so far as I could see it, was intersected by passages. Having made sure of my position, and reassured myself by examining my spare candles and my matches, I advanced slowly over the rocky and uneven surface of the cavern.

And now I come to the point where I met with such sudden and desperate disaster. A stream, some twenty feet broad, ran across my path, and I walked for some little distance along the bank to find a spot where I could cross dry-shod. Finally, I came to a place where a single flat boulder lay near the center, which I could reach in a stride. As it chanced, however, the rock had been cut away and made top heavy by the rush of the stream, so that it tilted over as I landed on it and shot me into the ice-cold water. My candle went out, and I found myself floundering about in utter and absolute darkness.

I staggered to my feet again, more amused than alarmed by my adventure. The candle had fallen from my hand, and was lost in the stream, but I had two others in my pocket, so that it was of no importance. I got one of them ready, and drew out my box of matches to light it. Only then did I realize my position. The box had been soaked in my fall into the river. It was impossible to strike the matches.

A cold hand seemed to close round my heart as I realized my position. The darkness was opaque and horrible. It was so utter one put one's hand up to one's face as if to press off something solid. I stood still, and by an effort I steadied myself. I tried to reconstruct in my mind a map of the floor of the cavern as I had last seen it. Alas! The bearings which had impressed themselves upon my mind were high on the wall, and not to be found by touch. Still, I remembered in a general way how the sides were situated, and I hoped that by groping my way along them I should at last come to the opening of the Roman tunnel. Moving very slowly, and continually striking against the rocks, I set out on this desperate quest.

But I very soon realized how impossible it was. In that black, velvety darkness one lost all one's bearings in an instant. Before I had made a dozen paces, I was utterly bewildered as to my whereabouts. The rippling of the stream, which was the one sound audible, showed me where it lay, but the moment that I left its bank I was utterly lost. The idea of finding my way back in absolute darkness through that limestone labyrinth was clearly an impossible one.

I sat down upon a boulder and reflected upon my unfortunate plight. I had not told anyone that I proposed to come to the Blue John mine, and it was unlikely that a search party would come after me. Therefore I must trust to my own resources to get clear of the danger. There was only one hope, and that was that the matches might dry. When I fell into the river, only half of me had got thoroughly wet. My left shoulder had remained above the water. I took the box of matches, therefore, and put it into my left armpit. The moist air of the cavern might possibly be counteracted by the heat of my body, but even so, I knew that I could not hope to get a light for many hours. Meanwhile there was nothing for it but to wait.

By good luck I had slipped several biscuits into my pocket before I left the farmhouse. These I now devoured, and washed them down with a draught from that wretched stream which had been the cause of all my misfortunes. Then I felt about for a comfortable seat among the rocks, and, having discovered a place where I could get a support for my back, I stretched out my legs and settled myself down to wait. I was wretchedly damp and cold, but I tried to cheer myself with the reflection that modern science prescribed open windows and walks in all weather for my disease. Gradually, lulled by the monotonous gurgle of the stream, and by the absolute darkness, I sank into an uneasy slumber.

How long this lasted I cannot say. It may have been for an hour, it may have been for several. Suddenly I sat up on my rock couch, with every nerve thrilling and every sense acutely on the alert. Beyond all doubt I had heard a sound—some sound very distinct from the gurgling of the waters. It had passed, but the reverberation of it still lingered in my ear. Was it a search party? They would most certainly have shouted, and vague as this sound was which had wakened me, it was very distinct from the human voice. I sat palpitating and hardly daring to breathe. There it was again! And again! Now it had become continuous. It was a tread—yes, surely it was the tread of some living creature. But what a tread it was! It gave one the impression of enormous weight carried upon spongelike feet, which gave forth a muffled but ear-filling sound. The darkness was as complete as ever, but the tread was regular and decisive. And it was coming beyond all question in my direction.

My skin grew cold, and my hair stood on end as I listened to that steady and ponderous footfall. There was some creature there, and surely by the speed of its advance, it was one which could see in the dark. I crouched low on my rock and tried to blend myself into it. The steps grew nearer still, then stopped, and presently I was aware of a loud lapping and gurgling. The creature was drinking at the stream. Then again there was silence, broken by a succession of long sniffs and snorts of tremendous volume and energy. Had it caught the scent of me? My own nostrils were filled by a low fetid odor, mephitic and abominable. Then I heard the steps again. They were on my side of the stream now. The stones rattled within a few yards of where I lay. Hardly daring to breathe, I crouched upon my rock. Then the steps drew away. I heard the splash as it returned across the river, and the sound died away into the distance in the direction from which it had come.

For a long time I lay upon the rock, too much horrified to move. I thought of the sound which I had heard coming from the depths of the cave, of Armitage's fears, of the strange impression in the mud, and now came this final and absolute proof that there was indeed some inconceivable monster, something utterly unearthly and dreadful, which lurked in the hollow of the mountain. Of its nature or form I could frame no conception, save that it was both light-footed and gigantic. The combat between my reason, which told me that such things could not be, and my senses, which told me that they were, raged within me as I lay. Finally, I was almost ready to persuade myself that this experience had been part of some evil dream, and that my abnormal condition might have conjured up an hallucination. But there remained one final experience which removed the last possibility of doubt from my mind.

I had taken my matches from my armpit and felt them. They seemed perfectly hard and dry. Stooping down into a crevice of the rocks, I tried one of them. To my delight it took fire at once. I lit the candle, and, with a terrified backward glance into the obscure depths of the cavern, I hurried in the direction of the Roman passage. As I did so I passed the patch of mud on which I had seen the huge imprint. Now I stood astonished before it, for there were three similar imprints upon its surface, enormous in size, irregular in outline, of a depth which indicated the ponderous weight which had left them. Then a great terror surged over me. Stooping and shading my candle with my hand, I ran in a frenzy of fear to the rocky archway, hastened up it, and never stopped until, with weary feet and panting lungs, I rushed up the final slope of stones, broke through the tangle of briars, and flung myself exhausted upon the soft grass under the peaceful light of the stars. It was three in the morning when I reached the farmhouse, and today I am all unstrung and quivering after my terrific adventure. As yet I have told no one. I must move warily in the matter. What would the poor lonely women, or the uneducated yokels here think of it if I were to tell them my experience? Let me go to someone who can understand and advise.

April 25.—I was laid up in bed for two days after my incredible adventure in the cavern. I use the adjective with a very definite meaning, for I have had an experience since which has shocked me almost as much as the other. I have said that I was looking round for someone who could advise me. There is a Dr. Mark Johnson who practices some few miles away, to whom I had a note of recommendation from Professor Saunderson. To him I drove, when I was strong enough to get about, and I recounted to him my whole strange experience. He listened intently, and then carefully examined me, paying special attention to my reflexes and to the pupils of my eyes. When he had finished, he refused to discuss my adventure, saying that it was entirely beyond him, but he gave me the card of a Mr. Picton at Castleton, with the advice that I should instantly go to him and tell him the story exactly as I had done to himself. He was, according to my adviser, the very man who was preeminently suited to help me. I went on to the station, therefore, and made my way to the little town, which is some ten miles away. Mr. Picton appeared to be a man of importance, as his brass plate was displayed upon the door of a considerable building on the outskirts of the town. I was about to ring his bell, when some misgiving came into my mind, and, crossing to a neighboring shop, I asked the man behind the counter if he could tell me anything of Mr. Picton. "Why," said he, "he is the best mad doctor in Derbyshire, and yonder is his asylum." You can imagine that it was not long before I had shaken the dust of Castleton from my feet and returned to the farm, cursing all unimaginative pedants who cannot conceive that there may be things in creation which have never yet chanced to come across their mole's vision. After all, now that I am cooler, I can afford to admit that I have been no more sympathetic to Armitage than Dr. Johnson has been to me.

April 27.—When I was a student I had the reputation of being a man of courage and enterprise. I remember that when there was a ghost-hunt at Coltbridge it was I who sat up in the haunted house. Is it advancing years (after all, I am only thirty-five), or is it this physical malady which has caused degeneration? Certainly my heart quails when I think of that horrible cavern in the hill, and the certainty that it has some monstrous occupant. What shall I do? There is not an hour in the day that I do not debate the question. If I say nothing, then the mystery remains unsolved. If I do say anything, then I have the alternative of mad alarm over the whole country-side, or of absolute incredulity which may end in consigning me to an asylum. On the whole, I think that my best course is to wait, and to prepare for some expedition which shall be more deliberate and better thought out than the last. As a first step I have been to Castleton and obtained a few essentials—a large acetylene lantern for one thing, and a good double-barreled sporting rifle for another. The latter I have hired, but I have bought a dozen heavy-game cartridges, which would bring down a rhinoceros. Now I am ready for my troglodyte friend. Give me better health and a little spate of energy, and I shall try conclusions with him yet. But who and what is he? Ah! There is the question which stands between me and my sleep. How many theories do I form, only to discard each in turn! It is all so utterly unthinkable. And yet the cry, the footmark, the tread in the cavern—no reasoning can get past these. I think of the old-world legends of dragons and of other monsters. Were they, perhaps, not such fairy tales as we have thought? Can it be that there is some fact which underlies them, and am I, of all mortals, the one who is chosen to expose it?

May 3.—For several days I have been laid up by the vagaries of an English spring, and during those days there have been developments, the true and sinister meaning of which no one can appreciate save myself. I may say that we have had cloudy and moonless nights of late, which according to my information were the seasons upon which sheep disappeared. Well, sheep *have* disappeared. Two of Miss Allerton's, one of old Pearson's of the Cat Walk, and one of Mrs. Moulton's. Four in all during three nights. No trace is left of them at all, and the countryside is buzzing with rumors of gypsies and of sheep-stealers.

But there is something more serious than that. Young Armitage has disappeared also. He left his moorland cottage early on Wednesday night and has never been heard of since. He was an unattached man, so there is less sensation than would otherwise be the case. The popular explanation is that he owes money, and has found a situation in some other part of the country, whence he will presently write for his belongings. But I have grave misgivings. Is it not much more likely that the recent tragedy of the sheep has caused him to take some steps which may have ended in his own destruction? He may, for example, have lain in wait for the creature and been carried off by it into the recesses of the mountains. What an inconceivable fate for a civilized Englishman of the twentieth century! And yet I feel that it is possible and even probable. But in that case, how far am I answerable both for his death and for any other mishap which may occur? Surely with the knowledge I already possess it must be my duty to see that something is done, or if necessary to do it myself. It must be the latter, for this morning I went down to the local police station and told my story. The inspector entered it all in a large book and bowed me out with commendable gravity, but I heard a burst of laughter before I had got down his garden path. No doubt he was recounting my adventure to his family.

June 10.—I am writing this, propped up in bed, six weeks after my last entry in this journal. I have gone through a terrible shock both to mind and body, arising from such an experience as has seldom befallen a human being before. But I have attained my end. The danger from the Terror which dwells in the Blue John Gap has passed never to return. Thus much at least I, a broken invalid, have done for the common good. Let me now recount what occurred as clearly as I may.

The night of Friday, May 3rd, was dark and cloudy—the very night for the monster to walk. About eleven o'clock I went from the farmhouse with my lantern and my rifle, having first left a note upon the table of my bedroom in which I said that, if I were missing, search should be made for me in the direction of the gap. I made my way to the mouth of the

Roman shaft, and, having perched myself among the rocks close to the opening, I shut off my lantern and waited patiently with my loaded rifle ready to my hand.

It was a melancholy vigil. All down the winding valley I could see the scattered lights of the farmhouses, and the church clock of Chapel-le-Dale tolling the hours came faintly to my ears. These tokens of my fellow men served only to make my own position seem the more lonely, and to call for a greater effort to overcome the terror which tempted me continually to get back to the farm, and abandon forever this dangerous quest. And yet there lies deep in every man a rooted self-respect which makes it hard for him to turn back from that which he has once undertaken. This feeling of personal pride was my salvation now, and it was that alone which held me fast when every instinct of my nature was dragging me away. I am glad now that I had the strength. In spite of all that it has cost me, my manhood is at least above reproach.

Twelve o'clock struck in the distant church, then one, then two. It was the darkest hour of the night. The clouds were drifting low, and there was not a star in the sky. An owl was hooting somewhere among the rocks, but no other sound, save the gentle sough of the wind, came to my ears. And then suddenly I heard it! From far away down the tunnel came those muffled steps, so soft and yet so ponderous. I heard also the rattle of stones as they gave way under that giant tread. They drew nearer. They were close upon me. I heard the crashing of the bushes round the entrance, and then dimly through the darkness I was conscious of the loom of some enormous shape, some monstrous inchoate creature, passing swiftly and very silently out from the tunnel. I was paralyzed with fear and amazement. Long as I had waited, now that it had actually come I was unprepared for the shock. I lay motionless and breathless, whilst the great dark mass whisked by me and was swallowed up in the night.

But now I nerved myself for its return. No sound came from the sleeping countryside to tell of the horror which was loose. In no way could I judge how far off it was, what it was doing, or when it might be back. But not a second time should my nerve fail me, not a second time should it pass unchallenged. I swore it between my clenched teeth as I laid my cocked rifle across the rock.

And yet it nearly happened. There was no warning of approach now as the creature passed over the grass. Suddenly, like a dark, drifting shadow, the huge bulk loomed up once more before me, making for the entrance of the cave. Again came that paralysis of volition which held my crooked forefinger impotent upon the trigger. But with a desperate effort I shook it off. Even as the brushwood rustled, and the monstrous beast blended with the shadow of the gap, I fired at the retreating form. In the blaze of the gun I caught a glimpse of a great shaggy mass, something with rough and bristling hair of a withered gray color, fading away to white in its lower parts, the huge body supported upon short, thick, curving legs. I had just that glance, and then I heard the rattle of the stones as the creature tore down into its burrow. In an instant, with a triumphant revulsion of feeling, I had cast my fears to the wind, and uncovering my powerful lantern, with my rifle in my hand, I sprang down from my rock and rushed after the monster down the old Roman shaft.

My splendid lamp cast a brilliant flood of vivid light in front of me, very different from the yellow glimmer which had aided me down the same passage only twelve days before. As I ran, I saw the great beast lurching along before me, its huge bulk filling up the whole space from wall to wall. Its hair looked like coarse faded oakum, and hung down in long, dense masses which swayed as it moved. It was like an enormous unclipped sheep in its fleece, but in size it was far larger than the largest elephant, and its breadth seemed to be nearly as great as its height. It fills me with amazement now to think that I should have dared to follow such a horror into the bowels of the earth, but when one's blood is up, and when one's quarry seems to be flying, the old primeval hunting spirit awakes and prudence is cast to the wind. Rifle in hand, I ran at the top of my speed upon the trail of the monster.

I had seen that the creature was swift. Now I was to find out to my cost that it was also very cunning. I had imagined that it was in panic flight, and that I had only to pursue it. The idea that it might turn upon me never entered my excited brain. I have already explained that the passage down which I was racing opened into a great central cave. Into this I rushed, fearful lest I should lose all trace of the beast. But he had turned upon his own traces, and in a moment we were face to face.

That picture, seen in the brilliant white light of the lantern, is etched forever upon my brain. He had reared up on his hind legs as a bear would do, and stood above me, enormous, menacing—such a creature as no nightmare had ever brought to my imagination. I have said that he reared like a bear, and there was something bearlike—if one could conceive a bear which was tenfold the bulk of any bear seen upon earth—in his whole pose and attitude, in his great crooked forelegs with their ivory white claws, in his rugged skin, and in his red, gaping mouth, fringed with monstrous fangs. Only in one point did he differ from the bear, or from any other creature which walks the earth, and even at that supreme moment a shudder of horror passed over me as I observed that the eyes which glistened in the glow of my lantern were huge, projecting bulbs, white and sightless. For a moment his great paws swung over my heard. The next he fell forward upon me, I and my broken lantern crashed to the earth, and I remember no more.

When I came to myself I was back in the farmhouse of the Allertons. Two days had passed since my terrible adventure in the Blue John Gap. It seems that I had lain all night in the cave insensible from concussion of the brain, with my left arm and two ribs badly fractured. In the morning my note had been found, a search party of a dozen farmers assembled, and I had been tracked down and carried back to my bedroom, where I had lain in high delirium ever since. There was, it seems, no sign of the creature, and no bloodstain which would show that my bullet had found him as he passed. Save for my own plight and the marks upon the mud, there was nothing to prove that what I said was true.

Six weeks have now elapsed, and I am able to sit out once more in the sunshine. Just opposite me is the steep hillside, gray with shaly rock, and yonder on its flank is the dark cleft which marks the opening of the Blue John Gap. But it is no longer a source of terror. Never again through that ill-omened tunnel shall any strange shape flit out into the world of men. The educated and the scientific, the Dr. Johnsons and the like, may smile at my narrative, but the poorer folk of the countryside had never a doubt as to its truth. On the day after my recovering consciousness they assembled in their hundreds round the Blue John Gap. As the *Castleton Courier* said:

> It was useless for our correspondent, or for any of the adventurous gentlemen who had come from Matlock, Buxton, and other parts, to offer to descend, to explore the cave to the end, and to finally test the extraordinary nar-

rative of Dr. James Hardcastle. The country people had taken the matter into their own hands, and from an early hour of the morning they had worked hard in stopping up the entrance of the tunnel. There is a sharp slope where the shaft begins, and great boulders, rolled along by many willing hands, were thrust down it until the gap was absolutely sealed. So ends the episode which has caused such excitement throughout the country. Local opinion is fiercely divided upon the subject. On the one hand are those who point to Dr. Hardcastle's impaired health, and to the possibility of cerebral lesions of tubercular origin giving rise to strange hallucinations. Some *idée fixe,* according to these gentlemen, caused the doctor to wander down the tunnel, and a fall among the rocks was sufficient to account for his injuries. On the other hand, a legend of a strange creature in the gap has existed for some months back, and the farmers look upon Dr. Hardcastle's narrative and his personal injuries as a final corroboration. So the matter stands, and so the matter will continue to stand, for no definite solution seems to us to be now possible. It transcends human wit to give any scientific explanation which could cover the alleged facts.

Perhaps before the *Courier* published these words they would have been wise to send their representative to me. I have thought the matter out, as no one else has occasion to do, and it is possible that I might have removed some of the more obvious difficulties of the narrative and brought it one degree nearer to scientific acceptance. Let me then write down the only explanation which seems to me to elucidate what I know to my cost to have been a series of facts. My theory may seem to be wildly improbable, but at least no one can venture to say that it is impossible.

My view is—and it was formed, as is shown by my diary, before my personal adventure—that in this part of England there is a vast subterranean lake or sea, which is fed by the great number of streams which pass down through the limestone. Where there is a large collection of water there must also be some evaporation, mists or rain, and a possibility of vegetation. This in turn suggests that there may be animal life, arising, as the vegetable life would also do, from those seeds and types which had been introduced at an early period of the world's history, when communication with the outer air was more easy. This place had then developed a fauna and flora of its own, including such monsters as the one which I had seen, which may well have been the old cave-bear, enormously enlarged and modified by its new environment. For countless eons the internal and the external creation had kept apart, growing steadily away from each other. Then there had come some rift in the depths of the mountain which had enabled one creature to wander up and, by means of the Roman tunnel, to reach the open air. Like all subterranean life, it had lost the power of sight, but this had no doubt been compensated for by nature in other directions. Certainly it had some means of finding its way about, and of hunting down the sheep upon the hillside. As to its choice of dark nights, it is part of my theory that light was painful to those great white eyeballs, and that it was only a pitch black world which it could tolerate. Perhaps, indeed, it was the glare of my lantern which saved my life at that awful moment when we were face to face. So I read the riddle. I leave these facts behind me, and if you can explain them, do so; or if you choose to doubt them, do so. Neither your belief nor your incredulity can alter them, nor affect one whose task is nearly over.

So ended the strange narrative of Dr. James Hardcastle.

CREATURE OF THE SNOWS
BY WILLIAM SAMBROT

The towering Himalayas, "thrusting miles high on all sides, stretching in awesome grandeur from horizon to horizon, each pinnacle tipped with immense banners of snow plumes, streaming out in the wind, vivid against the darkly blue sky"; a climbing expedition, complete with scientists, a photographer, and Sherpa porters, in search of the fabled Yeti; and an encounter both frightening and poignant in a twenty-thousand-foot, snow-packed amphitheater . . . the stuff of high adventure, and of the best and most famous of the stories about the Abominable Snowman, William Sambrot's "Creature of the Snows."

First published in 1960, in The Saturday Evening Post *(an unlikely market for such a story, or so it might seem until one has read it), "Creature of the Snows" has been widely acclaimed for its realistic portrait of a Himalayan expedition and for its sensitive handling of the Yeti theme. The feeling it evokes is not one of horror but of wonder, rich and pure—the type such films as* Close Encounters of the Third

Kind, 2001, *and* Star Wars *offered their audiences. It is not surprising that almost no other Yeti short stories have been written in the past twenty years; any writer of fantasy/horror who has read this one (and a great many have) seems to feel that there is nothing much he or she can do to top it.*

William Sambrot (born in 1930) is that rara avis, *a professional short story writer—he has yet to publish a novel—whose work appeared most prominently in the fifties and sixties in such quality "slick" magazines as* The Saturday Evening Post, Colliers, Cosmopolitan, *and* Playboy. *Many of his stories deal with classic science fictional and fantasy themes; some of the best of these may be found in his only collection,* Island of Fear and Other Stories, *published in 1963.*

ED MCKALE straightened up under his load of cameras and equipment, squinting against the blasting wind, peering, staring, sweeping the jagged, unending expanse of snow and wind-scoured rock. Looking, searching, as he'd been doing now for two months, cameras at the ready.

Nothing. Nothing but the towering Himalayas, thrusting miles high on all sides, stretching in awesome grandeur from horizon to horizon, each pinnacle tipped with immense banners of snow plumes, streaming out in the wind, vivid against the darkly blue sky. The vista was one of surpassing beauty. Viewing it, Ed automatically thought of light settings, focal length, color filters—then just as automatically rejected the thought. He was here on top of the world to photograph something infinitely more newsworthy, if only he could find it.

The expedition paused, strung out along a ridge of blue

snow, with shadows falling away to the right and left into terrifying abysses, and Ed sucked for air. Twenty thousand feet is really quite high, although many of the peaks beyond rose nearly ten thousand feet above him.

Up ahead, the Sherpa porters (each a marvelous shot—gap-toothed, ebullient grins, seamed faces, leathery brown) bowed under stupendous loads for this altitude, leaning on their coolie crutches, waiting for Dr. Schenk to make up his mind. Schenk, the expedition leader, was arguing with the guides again, his breath spurting little puffs of vapor, waving his arms, pointing down.

Obviously Schenk was calling it quits. He was within his rights, Ed knew; two months was all Schenk had contracted for. Two months of probing snow and ice; scrambling over crevasses, up rotten rock cliffs, wind-ravaged, bleak, stretching endlessly toward Tibet and the never-never lands beyond. Two months of searching for footprints where none should be. Searching for odors, for droppings, anything to disclose the presence of creatures other than themselves. Without success.

Two months of nothing. Big, fat nothing.

The expedition was a bust. The goofiest assignment of this or any other century, as Ed felt it would be from the moment he'd sat across the desk from the big boss in the picture magazine's New York office two months ago, looking at a blurred photograph, while the boss filled him in on the weird details.

The photograph, his boss had told him gravely, had been taken in the Himalayan mountains, at an altitude of twenty-one thousand feet, by a man who had been soaring overhead in a motorless glider.

"A glider," Ed had said noncommittally, staring at the fuzzy, enlarged snapshot of a great expanse of snow and rocky ledges, full of harsh light and shadows, a sort of roughly bowl-shaped plateau apparently, and in the middle of it, a group of indistinct figures, tiny, lost against the immensity of great ice pinnacles. Ed looked closer. Were the figures people? If so, what had happened to their clothes?

"A glider," his boss reiterated firmly. The glider pilot, the boss said, was maneuvering in an updraft, attempting to do the incredible—soar over Mount Everest in a homemade glider. The wide-winged glider had been unable to achieve the flight over Everest, but flitting silently about seeking updrafts, it cleared a jagged pinnacle and there, less than a thousand feet below, the pilot saw movement where none should have been. And dropping lower, startled, he'd seen, the boss said dryly, "Creatures—creatures that looked exactly like a group of naked men and women and kids playing in the snow—at an altitude of twenty thousand five hundred feet." He'd had the presence of mind to take a few hasty snapshots before the group disappeared. Only one of the pictures had developed.

Looking at the snapshot with professional scorn, Ed had said, "These things are indistinct. I think he's selling you a bill of goods."

"No," the boss said, "we checked on the guy. He really did make the glider flight. We've had experts go over that blow-up. The picture's genuine. Those are naked, biped, erect-walking creatures." He flipped the picture irritably. "I can't publish this thing. I want closeups, action shots, the sort of thing our subscribers have come to expect of us."

He'd lighted a cigar slowly. "Bring me back some pictures I can publish, Ed, and you can write your own ticket."

"You're asking me to climb Mount Everest," Ed said carefully, keeping the sarcasm out of his voice, "to search for this plateau here," he tapped the shoddy photograph, "and take pix of—what are they—biped, erect-walking creatures, you say?"

The boss cleared his throat. "Not Mount Everest, Ed. It's Gauri Sankar, one of the peaks near Mount Everest. Roughly, it's only about twenty-three thousand feet or so high."

"That's pretty rough," Ed said.

The boss looked pained. "Actually it's not Gauri Sankar either. Just one of the lesser peaks of the Guari Sankar massif. Well under twenty-three thousand. Certainly nothing to bother a hot-shot ex-paratrooper like you, Ed."

Ed winced, and the boss continued: "This guy—this glider pilot—wasn't able to pinpoint the spot, but he did come up with a pretty fair map of the terrain, for a pretty fair price. We've checked it out with the American Alpine Club; it conforms well with their own charts of the general area. Several expeditions have been in the vicinity but not at this exact spot, they tell me. It's not a piece of cake by any means, but it's far from being another Annapurna or K2 for accessibility."

He sucked at his cigar thoughtfully. "The Alpine Club says we've got only about two months of good weather before the inevitable monsoons hit that area, so time, as they say, is of the essence, Ed. But two months for this kind of thing ought to be plenty. Everything will be first class—we're even including these new gas guns that shoot hypodermic needles or something similar. We'll fly the essentials in to Katmandu and airdrop everything possible along the route up to your base,"—he squinted at a map—"Namche Bazar, a Sherpa village which is twelve thousand feet high."

He smiled amiably at Ed. "That's a couple of weeks march up from the nearest railhead and ought to get you acclimatized nicely. Plenty of experienced porters at Namche, all

Sherpas. We've lined up a couple of expert mountain climbers with Himalayan backgrounds. And expedition leader will be Dr. Schenk, top man in his field."

"What is his field?" Ed asked gloomily.

"Zoology. Whatever these things are in this picture, they're animal, which is his field. Everyone will be sworn to secrecy. You'll be the only one permitted to use a camera, Ed. This could be the biggest thing you'll ever cover, if these things are what I think they are."

"What do you think they are?"

"An unknown species of man—or sub-man," his boss said, and prudently Ed remained silent. Two months would tell the tale.

But two months didn't tell.

Oh, there were plenty of wild rumors by the Nepalese all along the upper route. Hushed stories of the two-legged creature that walked like a man. A monster the Sherpas called Yeti. Legends. Strange encounters; drums sounding from snow-swept heights; wild snatches of song drifting down from peaks that were inaccessible to ordinary men. And one concrete fact: a ban, laid on by the Buddhist monks, against the taking of any life in the high Himalayas. What life? Ed wondered.

Stories, legends—but nothing else.

Two months of it. Starting from the tropical flatlands, up through the lush, exotic rain forest, where sun struggled through immense trees festooned with orchids. Two months, moving up into the arid foothills, where foliage abruptly ceased, and the rocks and wind took over. Up and ever up to where the first heavy snow pack lay. And higher still, following the trail laid out by the glider pilot. (And what impelled a man, Ed wondered, to soar over Mount Everest in a homemade glider?)

Two months during which Ed had come to dislike Dr. Schenk intensely. Tall, saturnine, smelling strongly of form- aldehyde, Schenk classified everything into terms of verte- brate, invertebrate.

So now, standing on this wind-scoured ridge with the shadows falling into the abysses on either side, Ed peered through ice-encrusted goggles, watching Schenk arguing with the guides. He motioned to the ledge above, and obediently the Sherpas moved toward it. Obviously that would be the final camping spot. The two months were over by several days; Schenk was within his rights to call it quits. It was only Ed's assurances that the plateau they were seeking lay just ahead that had kept Schenk from bowing out exactly on the appointed time—that and the burning desire to secure his niche in zoology forever with a new specimen: biped, erect-walking—what?

But the plateau just ahead and the one after that and all the rest beyond had proved just as empty as those behind.

A bust. Whatever the unknown creatures were the glider pilot had photographed, they would remain just that— unknown.

And yet as Ed slogged slowly up toward where the porters were setting up the bright blue and yellow nylon tents, he was nagged by a feeling that the odd-shaped pinnacle ahead looked awfully much like the one in the blurred photograph. With his unfailing memory for pictures, Ed remembered the tall, jagged cone that had cast a black shadow across a snowy plateau, pointing directly toward the little group that was in the center of the picture.

But Schenk wasn't having any more plateaus. He shook his head vehemently, white-daubed lips a grim line on his sun- blistered face. "Last camp, Ed," he said firmly. "We agreed this would be the final plateau. I'm already a week behind schedule. If the monsoons hit us, we could be in serious trouble below. We have to get started back. I know exactly how you feel, but I'm afraid this is it."

Later that night, while the wind moved ceaselessly, sucking at the tent, they burrowed in sleeping bags, talking.

"There must be some basis of fact in those stories," Ed said to Dr. Schenk. "I've given them a lot of thought. Has it occurred to you that every one of the sightings, the few face-to-face meetings of the natives and these, these unknowns, has generally been just around dawn and usually when the native was alone?"

Schenk smiled dubiously. "Whatever this creature may be—and I'm convinced that it's either a species of large bear or one of the great anthropoids—it certainly must keep off the well-traveled routes. There are very few passes through these peaks, of course, and it would be quite simple for them to avoid these locales."

"But we're not on any known trail," Ed said thoughtfully. "I believe our methods have been all wrong, stringing out a bunch of men, looking for trails in the snow. All we've done is announce our presence to anything with ears for miles around. That glider pilot made no sound; he came on them without warning."

Ed looked intently at Schenk. "I'd like to try that peak up ahead and the plateau beyond." When Schenk uttered a protesting cry, Ed said, "Wait—this time I'll go alone with just one Sherpa guide. We could leave several hours before daybreak. No equipment, other than oxygen, food for one meal—and my cameras, of course. Maintain a strict silence. We could be back before noon. Will you wait long enough for this one last try?" Schenk hesitated. "Only a few hours more," Ed urged.

Schenk stared at him; then he nodded slowly. "Agreed. But

aren't you forgetting the most important item of all?" When
Ed looked blank, Schenk smiled. "The gas gun. If you should
run across one, we'll need more proof than just your word for
it."

There was very little wind, no moon, but cold, the cold
approaching that of outer space, as Ed and one Sherpa porter
started away from the sleeping camp, up the shattered floor of
an ice river that swept down from the jagged peak ahead.

They moved up, hearing only the squeak of equipment, the
peculiar gritty sound of crampons biting into packed snow, an
occasional hollow crash of falling ice blocks. To the east a
faint line of gray was already visible; daylight was hours
away, but at this tremendous height sunrise came early. They
moved slowly, breathing through woolen masks, the thin air
cutting cruelly into their lungs, moving up, up.

They stopped once for hot chocolate from a thermos, and
Ed slapped the Sherpa's shoulder, grinning, pointing ahead
to where the jagged peak glowed pink and gold in the first
slanting rays of the sun. The Sherpa looked at the peak and
quickly shifted his glance to the sky. He gave a long, careful
look at the gathering clouds in the east, then muttered
something, shaking his head, pointing back, back down to
where the camp was hidden in the inky shadows of enormous
boulders.

When Ed resumed the climb, the Sherpa removed the long
nylon line which had joined them. The route was compara-
tively level, on a huge sweeping expanse of snow-covered
glacier that flowed about at the base of the peak. The Sherpa,
no longer in the lead, began dropping behind as Ed pressed
eagerly forward.

The sun was up, and with it the wind began keening again,
bitterly sharp, bringing with it a scent of coming snow. In the
east, beyond the jagged peak just ahead, the immense es-

carpment of the Himalayas was lost in approaching cloud. Ed hurried as best he could; it would snow, and soon. He'd have to make better time.

But above the sky was blue, infinitely blue, and behind, the sun was well up, although the camp was still lost in night below. The peak thrust up ahead, near, with what appeared to be a natural pass skirting its flank. Ed made for it. As he circled an upthrust ridge of reddish rotten rock, he glanced ahead. The plateau spread out before him, gently sloping, a natural amphitheater full of deep smooth snow, with peaks surrounding it and the central peak thrusting a long, black shadow directly across the center. He paused, glancing back. The Sherpa had stopped well below him, his face a dark blur, looking up, gesticulating frantically, pointing to the clouds. Ed motioned, then moved around, leaning against the rock, peering ahead.

That great shadow against the snow was certainly similar to the one in the photo, only, of course, the shadow pointed west now, when later it would point northwest as the sun swung to the south. And when it did, most certainly it was the precise—. He sucked in a sharp, lung-piercing breath.

He stared, squinting against the rising wind that seemed to blow from earth's outermost reaches. Three figures stirred slightly and suddenly leaped into focus, almost perfectly camouflaged against the snow and wind-blasted rock. Three figures not more than a hundred feet below him. Two small, one larger.

He leaned forward, his heart thudding terribly at this twenty-thousand-foot height. A tremor of excitement shook him. My God, it was true. They existed. He was looking at what was undeniably a female and two smaller—what? Apes?

They were covered with downy hair, nearly white, resembling nothing so much as tight-fitting leotards. The female was exactly like any woman on earth except for the hair. No larger than most women, with arms slightly longer, more muscular. Thighs heavier, legs out of proportion to the trunk, shorter. Breasts full and firm.

Not apes.

Hardly breathing, Ed squinted, staring, motionless. Not apes. Not standing so erectly. Not with those broad, high brows. Not with the undeniable intelligence of the two young capering about their mother. Not—and seeing this, Ed trembled against the freezing rock—not with the sudden affectionate sweep of the female as she lifted the smaller and pressed it to her breast, smoothing back hair from its face with a motion common to every human mother on earth. A wonderfully tender gesture.

What were they? Less than human? Perhaps. He couldn't be certain, but he thought he heard a faint gurgle of laughter from the female, fondling the small one, and the sound stirred him strangely. Dr. Schenk had assured him that no animal was capable of genuine laughter; only man.

But they laughed, those three, and hearing it, watching the mother tickling the youngest one, watching its delighted squirming, Ed knew that in that marvelous little grouping below, perfectly lighted, perfectly staged, he was privileged to observe one of earth's most guarded secrets.

He should get started shooting his pictures; afterward, he should stun the group into unconsciousness with the gas gun and then send the Sherpa back down for Dr. Schenk and the others. Clouds were massing, immensities of blue black. Already the first few flakes of snow, huge, wet, drifted against his face.

But for a long moment more he remained motionless, oddly unwilling to do anything to destroy the harmony, the aching purity of the scene below, so vividly etched in brilliant light and shadow. The female, child slung casually on one hip, stood erect, hand shading her eyes, and Ed grinned. Artless, but perfectly posed. She was looking carefully about and above, scanning the great outcroppings of rock, obviously searching for something. Then she paused.

She was staring directly at him.

Ed froze, even though he knew he was perfectly concealed by the deep shadows of the high cliff behind him. She was still looking directly at him, and then, slowly, her hand came up.

She waved.

He shivered uncontrollably in the biting wind, trying to remain motionless. The two young ones suddenly began to jump up and down and show every evidence of joy. And suddenly Ed knew.

He turned slowly, very slowly, and with the sensation of a freezing knife plunging deeply into his chest he saw the male less than five yards away.

It was huge, by far twice the size of the female below. (And crazily Ed thought of Schenk's little lecture, given what seemed like eons ago, six weeks before, in the incredible tropical grove far below where rhododendrons grew in wild profusion and enormous butterflies flitted above: "In primitive man," Schenk had said, "as in the great apes today, the male was far larger than the female.")

The gas gun was hopelessly out of reach, securely strapped to his shoulder pack. Ed stared, knowing there was absolutely nothing he could do to protect himself before this creature, fully eight feet tall, with arms as big as Ed's own thighs and eyes (my God—*blue* eyes!) boring into his. There was a light of savage intelligence there—and something else.

The creature (man?) made no move against him, and Ed stared at it, breathing rapidly, shallowly and with difficulty, noting with his photographer's eyes the immense chest span, the easy rise and fall of his breathing, the large, square, white teeth, the somber cast of his face. There was long sandy fur on the shoulders, chest and back, shortening to off-white over the rest of the magnificent torso. Ears rather small and close to the head. Short, thick neck, rising up from the broad shoulders to the back of the head in a straight line. Toes long and definitely prehensile.

They looked silently at one another across the abyss of time and mystery. Man and—what? How long, Ed wondered, had it stood there observing him? Why hadn't it attacked? Had it been waiting for Ed to make a single threatening gesture such as pointing a gun or camera? Seeing the calm awareness in those long, slanting blue eyes, Ed sped a silent prayer of thanks upwards; most certainly if he had made a move for camera or gun, that move would have been his last.

They looked at one another through a curtain of falling snow, and suddenly there was a perfect, instantaneous understanding between them. Ed made an awkward, half-frozen little bow, moving backward. The great creature stood motionless, merely watching, and then Ed did a strange thing: he held out his hands, palm out, gave a wry grin and ducked quickly around the outcropping of rock and began a plunging, sliding return, down the way he'd come. In spite of the harsh, snow-laden wind, bitterly cold, he was perspiring.

Ed glanced back once. Nothing. Only the thickening veil of swift glowing snow blanking out the pinnacle, erasing every trace, every proof that anyone, anything, had stood there moments before. Only the snow, only the rocks, only the unending, wind-filled silence of the top of the world.

Nothing else.

The Sherpa was struggling up to him from below, terribly anxious to get started back; the storm was rising. Without a word they hooked up and began the groping, stumbling descent back to the last·camp. They found the camp already broken, Sherpas already moving out. Schenk paused only long enough to give Ed a questioning look.

What could Ed say? Schenk was a scientist, demanding material proof. If not a corpse, at the very least a photograph. The only photographs Ed had were etched in his mind, not on film. And even if he could persuade Schenk to wait, when the storm cleared, the giant, forewarned, would be gone. Some farther peak, some remoter plateau would echo to his young ones' laughter.

Feeling not a bit bad about it, Ed gave Schenk a barely perceptible negative nod. Instantly Schenk shrugged, turned and went plunging down into the thickening snow, back into the world of littler men. Ed trailed behind.

On the arduous trek back through that first great storm, through the snowline, through the rain forest, hot and humid, Ed thought of the giant, back up there where the air was thin and pure.

Who, what were he and his race? Castaways on this planet, forever marooned, yearning for a distant, never-to-be-reached home?

Or did they date in unbroken descent from the Pleistocene, man's first beginning, when all the races of not-quite-man were giants, unable or unwilling to take the fork in the road that led to smaller, cleverer man; forced to retreat higher and higher, to more and more remote areas, until finally there was only one corner of earth left to them—the high Himalayas?

Or were he and his kind earth's last reserves; not-yet-men, waiting for the opening of still another chapter in earth's unending mystery story?

Whatever the giant was, his secret was safe with him, Ed thought. For who would believe it even if he chose to tell?

WAZIAH

BY JOE R. LANSDALE

Among the many beliefs of North American tribes—in particular, those tribes of the northern United States and southwestern Canada—is that the creature known as Bigfoot not only exists but has on occasion mated with Indian women. One of the Denna Indians of British Columbia, in the heart of Sasquatch country, has even gone so far as to refer to Sasquatch as "big nice man catch little Indian woman for make love to all they want." It is the argument of biologists that one species cannot mate and produce offspring with another, but who is to say that this is an absolute truth? Who is to say that some Sasquatch are not at least partly human?

The Sioux are another of the tribes, once if no longer, which entertained this belief. In the days a century ago, when the Sioux controlled much of the Black Hills region, there were tales of maidens being carried off by "Waziah," the giant beast, the "Great God of the North," to become its mate and bear its children. Legends, based on native superstition? Or facts, based on the presence in the wild Dakotas of a Bigfoot-type creature? Joe Lansdale's atmospheric and suspenseful

71

glimpse into that bygone era provides one possible answer—and one possible encounter with an angry and fearful "Waziah."

A native Texan, Joe R. Lansdale is a prolific writer of fantasy/horror, detective, and Western fiction whose future appears bright. To date his short stories have appeared in Mike Shayne Mystery Magazine *(some of these featuring a detective named Slater), in fantasy and men's publications, and in the most recent chrestomathy in this series,* Mummy! *Several of his novels will be published this year and next, including* Act of Love, *a Western, and* Let There Be Blood! *a tale of psychological suspense. He and his wife Karen live in Nacogdoches, Texas.*

THE SNOW blew furiously, wound down through the peaks and canyons like a thick swathe of cold, wet gauze, wrapping the Black Hills tight in a Canadian-born blizzard. It was the first winter blow of 1874, and from the looks of things, a real icer.

Roland McArthur trudged through the knee-deep snow, stopped for a moment to get his bearings. He was leading his horse, Mick, and tied behind Mick was his pack mule, Clancy. He had given up riding old Mick an hour or so back. The blizzard had grown too thick and McArthur could see better down low than on horseback, so he had put on his snowshoes.

He was looking for a line shack. The same where he camped yearly on his fur-trapping run. He had come to the area none too soon: the blizzard had overtaken him without forewarning. One moment the sky was blue, the next nearly black, then it was full of churning snow.

What worried McArthur most was that the shack might

not still be standing. It had been pretty ragged his last time passing, and unless some enterprising stop-over had lent work to it, it might well be a crumble of logs and stone now.

Whoever had built it in the first place had given up ownership, and it had not known extended habitation since. It was primarily an overnight stop for passing trappers, scouts, and mountain men. McArthur fit all those categories.

McArthur held tight to Mick's reins, cradled his Sharps rifle in his arms, and bent his head against the snow. He had tied his bandanna over his hat and beneath his chin. It kept his hat in place and lent a bit of warmth to his ears until the snow saturated the bandanna with wet and cold.

A short growl out of the blinding whiteness of the storm brought McArthur up short. He unslung his Sharps from his shoulder and held it at ready. The sound had not been unlike that of a grizzly. McArthur sniffed. He had lived in the mountains so long that his senses of smell and hearing were like those of an Indian. And there came to his nostrils, even through the wild blow of the snow, a thick cloying odor the likes of which he had never smelled. It was strong for only a moment, then gradually died on the wind.

McArthur cradled the rifle in his arms and moved forward again. Suddenly, a dark hulking thing wrapped in white loomed up before him. The shack. McArthur felt a tingle of relief in his belly, and lifting his legs high, he made short work of the distance between him and the cabin.

McArthur could smell smoke and meat cooking. Someone was inside. All the better. Company was a thing he needed. It would make the approaching night go faster.

"Hello, the shack," McArthur yelled in customary mountain greeting. The wind grabbed his voice and carried it away.

He slung his rifle over his shoulder and knocked on the

thick plank door. No one answered, so he pounded. Still no one answered.

McArthur left the door and walked around to the side of the shack where, he remembered, a few of the logs were spaced well apart and uncaulked.

He discovered that someone had worked on the cabin since he had last seen it, yet there were still wide spaces here and there. As McArthur leaned forward to look inside he saw a flickering orange light. Then suddenly there was a scrabbling sound on the other side of the wall and a long, black thing was poking out of the chink and into his face.

McArthur threw up his arm and stumbled back. A rifle blast sent him flailing backwards into the snow.

Whiteness everywhere for a moment, then a journey down into a cold, black sea . . .

McArthur awoke and saw no angels. He saw first the flicker of fire and thought, "Uh-oh, the other place."

But no. He was comfortable, except for a slight headache, and he hardly felt the hellfires of eternal damnation.

McArthur blinked, brought his eyes into focus. Above him was a roof of log beams and split-log shingles. The roof seemed to tremble beneath the fury of the blizzard.

He sat up and looked toward the rock fireplace. That was where the glow was coming from—a warm, well-made fire. A grizzled old man sat by the fireplace on a hunk of log and looked at him—as ugly a geezer as McArthur had seen. The face was wrinkled like a sun-shriveled grape and dark as overdried leather. The man's eyes were black and so were most of the teeth showing through the salt-and-pepper beard. The old man had a Sharps rifle cradled in his arms and he was smiling, saying something that McArthur, still slightly addled, could not quite catch.

McArthur shook his head. That made it hurt. He touched

his hand to his forehead and found a bandage there. Moaning, he lay back, realizing now that he was lying on a bundle of pelts.

The old man came to stand over him.

"You ain't hit bad, sonny. Threw your arm up just as I shot, hit my barrel, knocked off my aim. Just grazed your scalp a bit. Did a halfway bandage job on it. Sorry about that. I thought you was the thing."

"Thing?"

"Yeah, damn Wooly-Bugger."

McArthur had heard tales of the Wooly-Bugger. It was supposed to be some sort of huge beast that walked upright like a man, could imitate animals and birds, and had a stink that . . . McArthur remembered the strange odor he had smelled just before reaching the cabin.

"My horse . . . and mule?" McArthur asked.

"Ran off. Me, I'm on foot. Horse died a couple of days back. Hell, them critters ain't gone far. Not in this mess. And it's gettin' dark now. They'll be a wanderin' back . . . if the Wooly-Bugger don't get 'em."

McArthur sat up. "You mean grizzly?"

"Naw, I mean Wooly-Bugger. This ain't no grizz. It's been after us in the cabin all day long."

"Us?"

"Dauncy Injun gal and her papoose."

McArthur turned. Behind him, on a rickety bed of furs and pine boughs, an Indian girl lay, holding a bundle wrapped in fur to her breast. A cradle board lay next to her.

"Crow?" McArthur asked.

"She don't speak nothin' but a bit of Sioux. She ain't no kind of Injun I know. Least not right off. Flathead, maybe. She's a strange one. Can't look you right in the eye. Don't reckon her dough's done in the middle."

"You buy her someplace?"

"Naw. Ain't my woman. *Found* her here. I got here just before the blizzard hit, and then after that we had the Wooly-Bugger to mess with. He gets madder each time he comes back, and that damn, dauncy gal just sits there mumblin' to herself."

"It attacks the cabin?"

"Came prowlin' around right after I got here, finally started scratchin' at the door, and not like no damn puppy dog neither. Thought the door was gonna come off the hinges. I put a round through the top of the door and it moved on, but it didn't act like it was hurt none. Course that damn gal screechin' at the top of her lungs didn't do nothin' for my aim neither. It came back a couple of times after, sniffed around the place lookin' for a way in."

"You saw it?"

"Not good. It peeped in that hole over there, same where I took a shot at you, and what I saw of it weren't like nothin' I'd ever seen before. Those eyes . . . like somethin' from hell, fella. Which reminds me. I don't rightly know your name."

"McArthur."

"McArthur, mine's Crawford. I call that gal Snowflake on account of I can't get nothin' out of her 'cept a few words of Sioux and ain't none of them words her name."

"Maybe she is Sioux."

"Maybe, but if so, she don't speak her own language none too good."

To McArthur she looked barely fifteen. She clutched the bundled baby to her chest tightly. Her eyes were like those of a frightened doe. McArthur thought her very beautiful.

He smiled at her, made a wavy sign with his hand; the sign of the snake, the symbol of the Sioux. It was his way of asking if she were Sioux.

For a moment she made no move. Then: "Heyah," she said

softly. The Sioux word for no. Suddenly she looked away, seemingly no longer aware of McArthur or Crawford. She rocked back and forth from the waist, mumbling an incoherent melody.

"See?" Crawford said. "She ain't no Sioux, and she's shy some smarts, just like I told you. All I could get out of her is that she's from a tribe far away, and that she was stolen . . . Injuns, I guess. Said she learned Sioux from an older woman, a captive like her. Knows sign language pretty good. Anyway, she escaped and was running away. That's how she got here."

McArthur nodded.

"She don't have much to do with me, 'cept eatin' my food," Crawford said. "She takes care of that readily enough. Only person I ever saw that would eat my cookin' without chokin'. But hell, that ain't no compliment. I ain't cooked for no Injun before. They'll eat anything. I once saw some Digger Injuns eat grub worms out from under a rotten log."

"This Wooly-Bugger as you call it," McArthur said, his tone skeptical. "Think it's gone?"

"Hell, I don't know . . . you don't believe it's no Wooly-Bugger, do you?"

"I just reckon it's a bear."

Crawford smiled, went over to the fireplace and picked a pot of coffee from the edge of the fire. "Cup?"

McArthur nodded.

"I been in these mountains nigh on twenty years," Crawford said. "There's all sorts of things in here, things you wouldn't understand, less'n you seen them with your own eyes."

Crawford poured a cup and brought it to McArthur.

"There's Wooly-Bugggers all right," Crawford continued. "Until now I've only seen sign of 'em. Them things is all through the Rockies, used to be thick with them, the Injuns say. They stretch all the way from here to Northern Californy. Injuns there call them Omah, and up farther north, Sasquatch. Supposed to be different types of 'em, but they all boil down to one thing, Wooly-Buggers.

"Them out toward Californy, if the Injuns can be believed, are a tamer variety. These here . . . well. Remember hearin' about them pilgrims from out East last year? That Monahan party?"

"Something about them," McArthur admitted. "Got killed by a bunch of grizzlies."

Crawford poured himself a cup of coffee and sipped. "You ain't never heard of no grizz pullin' a man's head off, have you? I don't mean claw it off, or bite it off. *I mean pull it off*, like it was a cork in a bottle. That's what happened to that Monahan man, leader of the bunch. His head was pulled off and thrown about thirty feet from where the rest of them lay. Them Wooly-Buggers scattered pilgrims all over the place."

McArthur finished off is coffee, sat the cup down . . . then suddenly he stood. It was the smell. The odor that had assaulted him outside earlier.

"Yeah," Crawford said, putting down his cup, picking up his Sharps. "I smell it too, boy. Your rifle and Colt's over there against the wall. I dried 'em out and reloaded 'em for you."

McArthur moved for the Sharps, and as he reached to take it up, the caulking between the logs just above the rifle burst apart and a huge, hairy hand groped for him.

McArthur stumbled back as the claws reached out, flicking snow from their razor-sharp tips.

From behind him came the roar of Crawford's Sharps. A gout of blood leaped up from the waving arm of the beast, and suddenly the arm retreated into the night. Its disappearance was followed by a loud noise that was somewhere between a grizzly's growl and a puma's scream.

Then silence.

But only for a moment. Then came a sound like a hog rooting, then more like a grizzly grunting, and then there was a growl that shook the rafters of the cabin.

"Sonofabitch won't say quit," Crawford said.

By this time McArthur had gotten hold of his Sharps and had pushed the Colt into his belt. He looked at the Indian girl. She was hunkered over her baby, her eyes deep, dark pools of fear.

"Get away from the wall," McArthur warned the girl in Sioux.

"Waziah," the girl said, "Waziah." McArthur recognized it as the Sioux word for Great God of the North.

And as if in response to her words, the wall shook with a powerful blow. A log creaked, sagged. Dirt and bark and mud caulking tumbled in, and then came the huge, hairy arms, heaving aside the logs, letting in the freezing outside air. Through the big rent in the wall McArthur could glimpse the beast. A behemoth nearly eight feet tall with eyes glowing like two falling stars.

The girl bent forward, almost out of its range. But one of the hands caught her long, black hair and jerked her back, causing the baby to fall from her arms and onto the bough bed.

McArthur fired at a spot between the glowing eyes. The beast tossed its head back in pain, roared. Its Bowie knife–sized teeth glinted in the glow of the firelight.

And then, fast as a panther, it was gone, and with it, right through the gap in the wall, the Indian girl Crawford called Snowflake.

But for a moment McArthur and Crawford were aware of only one thing, the whining baby on the bed. The furs had fallen away to reveal it.

It was only part human.

"It . . . it's a *thing,*" Crawford said.

"Can't be . . . just can't be," McArthur said.

"Well, there that sucker is."

"How could a woman . . . and a beast that size . . . mate?"

"Must be a lot like the grizz. That old Wooly is built like a mountain, but I reckon he must be hung like a rabbit."

"My God," McArthur said after a time, "that's what the beast wanted. Its mate and child."

"Well, maybe we ought to put it out there where he can find it real easy like. If I'd known that's what he was after, I'd have given him Snowflake and her ugly little youngster long time back."

"Are you crazy? This . . . this baby is part human."

"Part Injun," Crawford said. "Well, now wait a minute. I think I see what you mean. Why, we could make us a bundle off this little sucker. Put him in one of them Wild West shows like they got goin' now. 'Come see the Beast of the Black Hills, taken at great risk of our lives . . .' "

"That's not what I meant at all. I mean it's part human, and that part is our concern. For that matter, I wouldn't turn a wild animal over to that thing."

"You ain't hintin' what I think you're hintin'?"

"I'm not hinting et all. I'm going after Snowflake."

"Yeah, well, write when you get time."

"And I'm taking this papoose with me, Crawford. I think it's got a better chance against the snow than me leaving it here with you."

"That's ugly talk, McArthur."

"Saying my opinion." McArthur picked up the screaming beast-child, looked at it closely. Its shape and face were human, but its body was covered with a thick gray fur. The eyes that looked up at him with a pleading expression were the eyes of Snowflake.

Bundling the baby up tight, so that it had only enough exposure to breathe, McArthur attached it to the cradle board.

"You're goin' out there?" Crawford said suddenly.

McArthur grunted that he was.

"Well, get the hell on out there then. You don't see me holdin' you back. I ain't goin' after that thing."

"Suit youslf." McArthur fastened the baby to his back by slipping his arms through the cradle board straps.

"Ain't that cute," Crawford said.

McArthur fastened on his snowshoes and picked up his rifle. Without a word he stepped through the hole in the cabin wall and out into the night.

The blizzard had stopped. There was a fair wind a-humming, but little snow came with it, just chill. The stars were out.

"You're gonna get your head popped off," Crawford yelled after McArthur.

McArthur began to trudge across the snow. The sign of the creature was obvious. Great tracks, looking more like the prints of snowshoes than of men, wound off toward the tall trees; thick, blue black shadows in the moonlight.

The little creature on McArthur's back whined softly, then was silent. McArthur found himself wondering if the child was male or female. The whole thing had happened so fast he had not had time to speculate on anything. He could only guess that these beasts, being some sort of near-humans, stole their mates from Indian tribes, or perhaps some of the more superstitious bands offered the women in tribute to the creatures, thinking them some sort of gods. What had Snowflake said? "Waziah." Great God of the North.

It was certainly true that the Sioux often dressed up in the skins of animals, the bear for instance, and danced in a manner that led most to believe they were offering tribute to the strength of the beast. Could it be that their dances were not to the bear at all, that the outfits they wore were in fact representative of the Wooly-Buggers, as Crawford called them? Could it be the dances were more than a tribute to the creature's strength? Perhaps it was all part of a ritual to appease the beasts and keep them away? The offering of women could well be another part of the ritual, something no white man's eyes had seen.

"Wait the hell up!"

McArthur stopped in his tracks and turned. Crawford was puffing his way across the snow, his snowshoes throwing up little clouds of white in the moonlight.

"I ain't stayin' in that rickety cabin. Not with that thing out here. I'd just as soon have me some company out under the stars when it pulls my head off and spits down my windpipe."

McArthur nodded, turned back to following the tracks. They had not gone far when they found McArthur's mule, Clancy. Its head had been twisted around at an odd angle. The supplies that had been trapped to its back were tossed about and partially covered by snow.

Not far from where Clancy lay, they found what was left of Mick. The animal's head was gone and generous portions of meat had been ripped from its rump.

"Had him a snack," Crawford said.

McArthur clenched the Sharps, turned back to following the tracks. Crawford came close behind.

The forest grew thick about them, and had the great beast not gone before them, slapping down brush and uprooting trees, clearing a path for itself, it would have been hard going indeed. Now, in fact, the path was easy to follow. Too easy, thought McArthur, but by that time they had come to the end of the trail. Thick trees lay in front of them and on either side.

"You thinkin' what I'm thinkin'?" Crawford said.

"I'm thinking it laid a mighty easy trail to follow, and now it's gone into the woods and is doubling back."

"Figures we can't move through the trees as well as it can."

"Probably figures right. Big as it is, it still moves like a ghost."

"Nearby, I reckon. I think maybe we ought to do a fast melt before . . ."

But it was too late. Suddenly a small spruce crashed down on McArthur's left, whipped across and knocked Crawford off his feet. And there was the beast.

It didn't have Snowflake with it, just its naked fury. It stood eight feet tall. Saliva dripped from its knifelike teeth and its eyes were fiery points of hate. Its odor was overwhelming. A small spot of red glistened on the beast's forehead where McArthur had shot it earlier. It looked no worse than his own wounded forehead.

McArthur jerked up his Sharps and fired. He thought he had at least hit the creature's right shoulder, but it stepped forward anyway, took hold of McArthur by the head and started to lift.

Crawford rolled to his feet, lifted his rifle and fired at the back of the thing's head. "Take that!" he yelled. The shot was on target, but the thick fur, flesh, and bone stopped the 550-grain bullet as if it were a gnat. It was a shot that would have dropped a grizzly or a bull buffalo dead in its tracks.

But it only got the creature's attention. It wheeled, dropped McArthur and went for Crawford. Crawford dove for the thicket, squirmed his way into the brush.

The creature stepped forward, and grasping a pair of small pines in the crook of either arm, uprooted them and tossed them aside.

Crawford scrambled back farther into the brush, crawling on hands and knees, dragging the Sharps after him.

McArthur stumbled to his feet and attempted to pull his pistol from his belt. His Sharps lay somewhere in the snow. He had the Colt worked loose when the creature turned back to him.

McArthur fired twice. The bullets could have been fleas for all the creature noticed them. Turning to run, McArthur found that he could not get through the thick trees. The cradle board held him.

The beast reached for him, took hold of the cradle board and ripped it free of McArthur's back. McArthur kept moving forward, into the trees. The creature held the cradle board high above its head, and raising its angry face to the heavens, bellowed like a bull buffalo, loud enough to shake down the moon.

Turning, holding the child gently beneath one arm, the beast swatted aside trees and brush, made a new path for itself, disappeared into the gloom.

McArthur recovered his rifle and reloaded. He replaced the bullets in his revolver, looked down the jagged trail of broken trees and trampled brush, watched the darkness where he had last seen the beast.

"A mite bad-tempered, ain't he?" Crawford said, edging out of the trees.

McArthur ignored him, started in the direction the creature had gone.

"Hey," Crawford said. "Give it up."

McArthur kept moving forward, traveling at a half-trot now. Cursing, Crawford began to follow.

They had not gone far when they found Snowflake. She stumbled out of the trees and into McArthur's arms. Immediately she began to scream and fight, but after a moment she realized it was McArthur and not the creature.

In Sioux McArthur asked her what had happened. She quickly explained in broken Sioux that the beast had reached her into the uppermost branches of a small pine, and then, tearing all the lower branches off, had deserted her, probably intending to come back for her later. Snowflake had managed to jump into a snowbank. The next thing she knew she was stumbling into McArthur's arms. But the one thing that concerned her most was her child.

Grimly McArthur told her, gestured to where the creature had disappeared. In the next instant Snowflake was running, and McArthur and Crawford ran with her.

The creature was easy to follow for a while. It had made no effort to hide its trail. Its massive footprints were everywhere, as were uprooted and knocked-aside trees. But soon they came to a clearing where the trees ended and the bare rocks tumbled off and down into what seemed like blue black infinity.

"I don't like the looks of this place none," Crawford said. "That blessed thing is smart. Woods behind us, canyon in front of us, narrow rock path left and right. . . . Naw, I don't like it at all. Could be another trap."

McArthur had bent down close to the ground to look for a sign. Even in the moonlight he could see none.

"Could have gone either way," McArthur said. "I think we should spread out. You go left, we'll go right. You game?"

Crawford shook his head, but said, "Ah, why the hell not. I ain't been actin' much smarter than a pig's ass up till now, so why not get et like one?"

McArthur took Snowflake's arm and they went right. Crawford went left, moving along the edge of the canyon rim.

The sky was clouding up again, covering the moon so that it looked like a filmed-over eye. McArthur looked to his left, looked out into the darkness of the canyon, thought of the forever-fall down and shivered.

After a while of moving at a fast trot, McArthur stopped to examine for a sign again. There was none that he could see. He decided that the creature had most likely gone the other direction.

Crawford couldn't believe his luck. He found the cradle board complete with baby before he had gone a hundred yards. It hung from a low limb where the creature had wrapped one of the straps about it. The furs had come undone around the little creature's face and Crawford could see its features distinctly. It looked much more human to him at a second glance.

Unfastening the cradle board, Crawford whispered, "You're gonna make me rich, little critter."

Crawford tied one of the straps back together and swung it over his left shoulder, leaving his gun arm free. "Tough luck, McArthur. I'm headin' for the Wild West show."

As Crawford moved off he saw huge footprints in the snow. The creature was circling back, moving toward where McArthur and Snowflake were.

Crawford considered the situation for a moment, then said

aloud, "I didn't want to go chasin' after no damn Injun in the first place."

Turning, Crawford started away from the tracks.

McArthur and Snowflake were about to turn back down the trail when they heard a voice saying repeatedly, "Take that, take that, take that, take that . . ." It was Crawford's voice, and it sounded as if he had gone plumb loco.

"Come," McArthur said. *"Hoppo!"*

"Take that, take that, take that, take that," the voice continued.

McArthur moved toward the sound, Snowflake trailing close behind. A ridge of snow lay before them; at its crest were two stubby pines. The voice seemed to be coming from there, or just over the rise.

Upwards McArthur went, over the snow-covered rocks. Snowflake came on close behind him.

And suddenly the snow between the two scrubby pines burst upwards and expanded . . . and proved to not be snow at all, but the creature.

McArthur understood too late. The voice had been the creature's. It had merely imitated Crawford's words back when it first ambushed them, imitated them in the way it imitated other animals. Then, crouching down against the snow, blending in, it had waited.

The beast raised its arms high above its head, a great stone in its hands. The stone flew as if launched from a catapult. McArthur stepped nimbly aside, but the stone hit Snowflake in the chest, carried her back and down the ridge. She hit on her back, and still clutching the stone, she began to roll. Head over heels she went, right over the edge of the cliff and out into the maw of the canyon, down into pitch blackness.

She screamed once.

The creature screamed as if in anguish.

"Bastard," McArthur yelled, and he brought up the Sharps. He avoided aiming for the head. He had learned his lesson there. The rifle went off and the shot hit the creature in the throat.

The beast gurgled, stumbled back, but regained its footing. It looked more furious than hurt. Flashing its huge teeth in the weak moonlight, it came charging down the rise.

McArthur grabbed the Sharps by the barrel and flung it. It bounced off the creature's chest like a twig, didn't slow the beast at all.

The creature swung its razor-sharp claws.

McArthur tried to step back, but the snowshoes sent him off balance. He couldn't quite get away from the claws. They ripped across his chest, sending waves of agony through his body. The snow in front of him was suddenly sprinkled with red.

McArthur dropped to one knee.

The beast raised its huge arm for another swipe, when abruptly thunder filled the air and the beast threw back its head and screamed.

Crawford, the baby still slung on the cradle board across his left shoulder, stood at the top of the rise, his Sharps pointed down. His shot had hit the creature in the small of the back and penetrated deeply, but not deep enough.

The beast turned, and as before was attracted to its immediate tormenter. It began climbing the rise at a run.

Crawford drew his revolver, and as the beast climbed upwards, stumbling a bit now, he took steady aim and fired a shot directly into the creature's left eye. The animal's head jerked back.

"Come and get it, Wooly-Bugger," Crawford snarled. In

rapid succession he emptied his revolver into the beast. But still it came.

Crawford dropped the cradle board off his arm, tossed aside his revolver and drew his Bowie. The creature grabbed at him, but Crawford avoided the arms, jumped straight into the creature. He grasped the thick fur at the creature's chest with one hand, locked his legs around its waist. With the other hand he drove the Bowie into the beast repeatedly. It was like trying to stick a needle through a half-dozen bear hides lumped together.

The beast clutched Crawford to its chest, began to squeeze. Crawford's hands were now pinned and he could no longer strike. His brain filled with the awful odor of the creature and he began to fall away into darkness.

McArthur, seeing through a haze, drew his revolver and half-stumbled, half-ran up the rise. When he was less than six feet away he began to fire into the creature, hitting in and around the wound Crawford had made in the small of the thing's back.

The creature staggered, dropped Crawford. Crawford rolled halfway down the rise and stopped rolling. He didn't move.

The beast turned slowly to face McArthur and his empty revolver. Blood covered its face, dripped off its fur. Even in the cloudy moonlight, McArthur could see that one eye was gone.

The creature roared, staggered.

McArthur pushed two shells into the revolver, but before he could fire the beast stumbled back and fell, landing directly on top of the cradle board, driving it deep into the snow.

McArthur went down to Crawford. The man was breathing but it sounded like wind whistling through a hollow rock.

McArthur knew as well as Crawford that ribs had punctured a lung.

Crawford grinned with his black, now bloodstained teeth. "Should of went ahead and run off," he said. "Could of made a lot of money . . . Wild West Show. But . . . but you're a mountain man, same . . . same as me."

And then the life went out of Crawford's eyes.

High up there in the Black Hills McArthur left them to the wind, the sky, the sun, the snow—where their bones would mingle with those of all the other creatures of the wild Dakotas.

BARNEY'S BIGFOOT MUSEUM
BY RICHARD LAYMON

*Those sections of the Pacific Northwest and British Columbia where
there have been large numbers of Bigfoot sightings attract equally large
numbers of Bigfoot hunters every year. These adventurous individuals
are either scientifically minded, intent on studying rather than harming
the creatures, or mercenary-minded and bent on capturing or killing a
Sasquatch for profit. Nearly all such hunters come away disappointed,
without having seen so much as a single Bigfoot track; but every now
and then, one or a small group of them will get lucky. Or unlucky, as in
the case of a certain foursome led by a man named Hodgson.*

*The native residents of these areas also fall into two categories: those
who keep to themselves and ignore all the flap, and those who, like the
hunters, are caught up in the Sasquatch mystique and take an active role
in it. Barney, the owner of "Barney's Bigfoot Museum," is a member of
the latter camp, and when he meets Hodgson, and hears the strange and
fearful tale the hunter has to tell, his excitement knows no bounds. As*

91

you'll discover when you reach the conclusion, with its dandy and chilling little twist, of Richard Laymon's mordant experiment in terror.

Richard Laymon was born in Chicago in 1947, educated at three universities in California and Oregon (B.A. and M.A. in English Literature), and has held such positions as librarian, English teacher, editor of two short-lived mystery magazines, creator and publisher of a periodical for pipe smokers called Smokers' Blend, *and full-time writer. His first professional sale was a short to* Ellery Queen's Mystery Magazine; *other of his stories have appeared in* Alfred Hitchcock's Mystery Magazine *and* Cavalier, *among other periodicals. His first two novels were published last year—*Your Secret Admirer, *a suspense novel for young adults, and a grisly tale of horror,* The Cellar, *which is definitely not for young readers (adults, however found it much to* their *liking; it was a paperback bestseller). A second horror novel,* The Woods Are Dark, *is due for publication at about the same time as this chrestomathy.*

ALL DAY long, people stopped by. Not just for a beer or a meal, or to stock up on minnows or bug spray, or to have a look at my Bigfoot Museum. That's not why. I'll tell you why.

It was the gray, lonely weather out there, the kind that makes you ache for a brightly lighted diner, a cup of chili, a familiar tune on the jukebox. You can get all that at my place. Mine's the first spot after almost fifty miles of forest so heavy and bleak you think you'll never see another human face. I call it Barney's Bigfoot Museum 'n Diner.

My wife was working the lunch counter, late that afternoon, when this fellow came in. He climbed out of a Dodge pickup with a Pathfinder camper on the back, and came up the porch steps. At the door he stopped and glanced around like he thought someone might be sneaking up on his back. Then he came in.

He looked lean and hard, and banged up. The sleeve of his flannel shirt was torn. His face and neck were threaded with scratches.

Turning away from the counter, he limped toward the museum entrance. He had my curiosity up, so I followed him through the door. He must've heard me. With a small sound, he spun around and grabbed under his shirt. I glimpsed black steel—the butt-plate of an automatic—before he dropped his hand and the shirttails fell shut.

"Damn," he said.

"You all right?"

He didn't answer. He just turned away, and gazed up at the Winchester. It hung on the wall above a display case, its barrel bent toward the ceiling.

"Bigfoot did that?" he asked.

"So I'm told."

"Where'd you get it?"

"Bought it off a fellow."

He lowered his eyes to the display case and looked for a while at the plaster casts of giant footprints.

"Buy these, too?"

"Some. I made two of them, myself, from prints I found near Clamouth."

"Authentic?"

"Far as I know."

He limped to the next display case and peered through the glass at half a dozen photos.

"Ever seen one?" he asked.

"A Bigfoot?"

"Yeah."

"No. Not yet. I keep hoping, though. There've been several

sightings in the area. And I've seen the footprints, like I said. I go out, when I get the chance."

He stepped over to the corner and peered at the plaster bust.

"That's lifesize," I told him. "A sculptor over in Kalama claims he saw one, back in '78."

"Pay much for this?"

"It wasn't cheap."

"You got took."

"Oh?" I'd been suspicious, at the time, but finally agreed to pay the artist's exorbitant price. Whether or not he'd actually seen the beast, the simian features conformed with other eye-witness accounts and blurred photos. "What makes you think he's wrong?" I asked.

The man turned to me. He rubbed a scabbed-over scratch above his eye, as if it might be itchy.

"My God," I gasped. "You've seen one, haven't you!"

A grim smile creased his face. "More than that."

"Tell me—tell me *all* about it! I mean, what I'm doing, I'm writing a book. It'll be *the* book on Sasquatch. I've been working on it for five years, collecting artifacts and stories. . . . My museum, it draws everyone who—"

He held up a hand for me to stop. He smiled as if amused by my eager babbling. "I'll tell you about it."

"Great. Just great. Wait and I'll get my recorder. That okay, if I record you?"

"Help yourself." He glanced out the window at the gloomy sky. "Make it quick."

"Right."

I hurried to my office, and lugged my heavy reel-to-reel tape recorder back to the museum room. The man was still alone. I shut the door to keep intruders out, plugged in the machine. I put on a fresh spool of tape and ran it through.

"One thing before I start," he said.

I glanced up, ready for bad news.

"I want something in return. Do you have a car?"

I nodded.

"What kind?"

"A '79 Bushmaster, four-wheel drive."

"Do you have the pink slip?"

"In my office."

"I'll leave you my Dodge and Pathfinder. You sign your Bushmaster over to me."

"I don't—"

"It'll be worth it, believe me. So far, you've paid out a lot of money for junk. Nothing but junk." He gazed at me with weary, red eyes. "I'll let you in on something that'll put your museum on the map."

I hesitated.

"Wait till I'm done, then decide."

I couldn't see any objection to that. "I guess . . ."

"Start the machine."

I turned on the recorder, and the man began to speak. He talked swiftly, staring at the floor, often turning for a quick glance out the window.

"My name is Thomas Hodgson. I'm thirty-two. I come from Enumclaw. For the past two weeks, I've been hunting Bigfoot in the woods about thirty miles north of here.

"I had three friends with me—Charles Raider, Bob Chambers, and Armando Ruiz—all from Enumclaw. It was Chambers's idea. He'd run into some tracks back in early June. He figured we'd all be millionaires if we could capture Bigfoot. Or kill it. Either way. I don't suppose we really figured we'd find the thing, though. Just an excuse to spend our vacation running wild. We'd all been together in the Marines—that's where we met—in Vietnam. We all came to

Enumclaw in '72, and started a sporting goods . . . forget all that. The thing is, we went out looking for Bigfoot, and we sure as hell found it.

"Ruiz saw tracks on the twelfth day out. He was picking up firewood and sucking on a brew. *Cerveza,* he called it. You never saw Ruiz, he didn't have a *cerveza* in his fist.

"We spent the next day and a half following the tracks. We finally lost them at a stream about twenty miles from our base camp. They just ended at the stream. Couldn't pick them up again, so we decided to stick around and see what developed.

"We camped near the stream that night. Ruiz had the first watch, then Chambers. At about two in the morning, I heard a gunshot. Chambers started yelling his head off. 'Hey, I bagged one! I bagged one!'

"I grabbed my rifle and got outside just as he came running into camp. Raider and Ruiz popped out of the other tent. They hit Chambers with their flashlight beams. Christ, what a . . . He stood there with his feet planted and lifted this . . . *thing* by its arms. It hung there, like it was dead. Blood kept pumping out, though. You could hear it pattering on the ground.

"Chambers lowered the thing.

"Ruiz shined his flashlight in its face, and we all saw it wasn't human. It was covered with bristly fur, and the shape wasn't right: the arms too long, the rump more like a bear than a man. But its face was bare and pale, and it somehow made you think of a little kid.

" 'It came along for a drink at the stream,' Chambers muttered. 'I figured, you know, it's Bigfoot.'

" 'Kind of small, don't you think?' Raider sounded bitter.

" 'I think it is a Sasquatch,' I said. 'A young one. What else could it be? Have you ever seen anything like it?' None argued. 'We've got a hell of an opportunity here. We came in after Bigfoot and by God, we got one! You're looking at the one and only specimen, guys. We'll be famous. And rich! We can sell this thing, or tour with it, or parlay it into a whopping book contract. The possibilities are staggering!'

"After that, Chambers made a half-hearted plea to dig a grave with his trenching tool and bury the thing. Nobody bought it. While Ruiz and Raider were still dazed with the specter of riches, I tried another pitch on them.

" 'We'd be better off, though, with a full-grown version. If it is a baby Bigfoot, its parents have got to be nearby.' They all looked at me as if they'd been thinking the same thing, and not liking the idea much. But I went on, 'We'll put out the kid as bait. When papa or mama come along, *wham!*'

" 'No way,' Chambers said. 'Count me out.'

" 'What've you got against more money?' I asked him.

" 'There's ways and there's ways, Hodgson. I just killed this thing. That's enough for me. More than enough.'

" 'How about you?' I asked the others.

"Ruiz shook his head. 'I don't know, man.'

" 'I say we get while the gettin's good,' Raider said. 'A bird in the hand, you know?'

"Ruiz nodded. 'We killed the kid, man. If its folks come looking . . .' He shook his head, fear in his eyes.

"I argued for staying, but the others wouldn't give in. Finally, we tied up the carcass, slipped it under a tent pole, and started out. Raider led the way, with Chambers and me on the pole, and Ruiz bringing up the rear. None of us talked. I guess we were listening, half-expecting to hear footsteps or a roar or something. None of that happened. The woods were silent except for the usual night sounds: owls and frogs, that sort of thing.

"Then Raider shrieked and left his feet. He went straight up, flapping his arms and kicking. I couldn't see anything but him. He just hung there, squirming and yelling, for a second. Then he fell. He landed right at my feet, and he didn't have a head any more.

"Yeah, his head was still up there about twelve feet above the ground. In the hands of this *thing*. This huge, dark *thing!* Bigfoot. It had to be. It threw Raider's head to the ground and stomped on it—crushed it.

"We'd dropped the pole, by this time. While the creature was busy mashing Raider's head into the ground, I shouldered my rifle and fired. The thing flinched and staggered back. Then it left. It just ran off.

"The three of us stood around for a while, looking at what was left of Raider and staring off into the dark woods. Ruiz kept shaking his head and muttering, 'Holy Jesus.'

" 'It's gonna get us all,' Chambers was yelling.

" 'It had its chance,' I told him. 'Probably going off someplace to die in peace.'

" 'It'll be back,' Chambers said. 'It'll keep coming back.'

" 'Since when are you psychic?' I asked him. But Chambers ignored me.

" 'It wants the kid,' Ruiz said. 'I say we leave the kid.'

" 'I'm not leaving it,' I told them.

" 'That's your problem,' Chambers said. He gestured to Ruiz, and they started away together.

"That's how I found them, an hour later. Together—their arms and legs all broken and intertwined like a terrible, bloody knot.

"I kept moving. I hardly expected to survive the night, but I kept trudging along, the creature on my back, its tied hands pulling at my neck like a kid riding piggyback.

"Dawn came and I kept moving. The sun beat through the trees, and the body stank, and flies swarmed all around us, but I kept moving. Finally, I reached base camp where my

Pathfinder was parked. I threw the carcass in back, then drove out of the woods.

"That was this afternoon. A couple of hours ago."

"You mean . . . ?"

He nodded, anticipating my question. "Yeah. The thing's in my camper."

"My God! Can I . . . can I *see* it?"

"Just sign over your Bushmaster. I'll give you the papers on my Pathfinder. Fair trade."

I hesitated. "Something wrong with it?"

A grim smile twisted his face. "Not a thing. I feel a bit uneasy with it, that's all."

"You don't think Sasquatch could follow a truck!"

"Of course not. I'd just feel better in a different one."

"I'll be right back."

With a nod, he turned toward the window and stared out at the dark forest.

I left him. I ran for my office, ignoring the curious looks of my wife and half-a-dozen customers at the lunch counter.

In the office, I searched madly through my desk. My hands trembled as I flipped through the papers, searching for the pink title slip. Finally, I found it. As I shoved the drawer shut, I heard a burst of glass out front. Then a loud gunshot.

I ran for the museum room ahead of the customers, and shoved open the door.

Hodgson was gone.

The room reeked of a foul, musty stench that made me think of mold and dead things.

Gagging, I raced to the broken window. I looked out, but saw only the dark road and the timber on the other side of it.

I climbed out. I ran through the windy night. To the side of the diner. To the parking lot. To Hodgson's battered Pathfinder.

Its rear door lay on the gravel.

Stepping over it, I peered into the camper and saw a dark shape on the floor. I scurried inside. On hands and knees, I picked up the thing by the hair.

Voices! Rushing footsteps!

Before the curious arrived, it was safely concealed in a cupboard until I could move it later.

It's the pride of my Bigfoot Museum, but I show it to no one, not even my wife. I stuffed and mounted it myself. I keep it inside a locked case, in the corner below the twisted metal door of the Pathfinder.

Perhaps, when my Bigfoot epic is complete, I'll reveal it to the world.

Perhaps not. It's so much more precious, as my secret exhibit.

Often, late at night, I lock myself in the darkness of my museum and open the case. I hold Hodgson's head on my lap as I listen to the tape of his voice. Sometimes, I half-expect to feel his lips move with the words.

But they never do.

SURVIVAL EXERCISE
BY TALMAGE POWELL

Swamps, particularly such vast and mostly uncharted swamps as the Florida Everglades, provide a natural habitat for all sorts of large and small creatures. Isn't it likely, then, that one such creature might be a cousin, or at least a distant relative, of the Sasquatch and the Yeti of northern climes? Indeed, there have been many accounts of similar-looking beings in the bayous of Louisiana and in the Everglades itself. There is even an old Seminole Indian legend of the Stuestaw Enawchee, "gigantic beings from some nether world that had inhabited the Rivers of Grass from the time of creation," who had come out of the swamps to war on the first Seminoles a thousand generations before the appearance of the white man.

When, as part of a routine military "Survival Exercise," three tough U.S. Marines are first set down in a remote section of the 'Glades, they do not believe in, or fear, the Stuestaw Enawchee or any swamp creature. But what happens to them in that primitive and alien environment is enough to make a believer of any man—and in the case of one, Master

Sergeant James C. Kelly, to add a whole new dimension to the exercise of survival. For even as creatures go, the one which he encounters is extraordinary . . .

Talmage Powell is a native Southerner, born in 1920, who sold his first story to the pulp market in 1943 and who is now in his fifth decade as a professional writer. He has published more than five hundred short stories and sixteen novels, and also has ten visual media credits. His books, testimony to his versatility, include a fine suspense tale, The Smasher *(1959); a series of five novels about a realistically and sympathetically drawn Tampa private detective named Ed Rivers (*The Killer Is Mine, Start Screaming Murder, The Girl's Number Doesn't Answer, Corpus Delectable, *and* With a Madman Behind Me*); an acclaimed offbeat Western,* The Cage *(1969); and a tale of the supernatural,* The Thing in B-3 *(1969), for young readers. When he isn't traveling throughout the United States and elsewhere, he makes his home in North Carolina.*

To: CAPT. L. G. McCabe, Intelligence Officer
5th Bn., 22nd Marines, Parris Island, S.C.
Sir:

In the event that I can't appear in person for debriefing re Survival Exercise to which I, Master Sergeant James C. Kelly, and Privates Rodney Gordon and Sidney Finklestein were assigned, I offer the following informal report.

This may be the only means of making known the events that began at Point E. I feel that my chances are good of returning to Point E, if only temporarily. If I must abandon the location or fail to survive, the report will be there, awaiting the helicopter scheduled to pick up the Survival Exercise team.

As you know, it was to be a routine exercise to provide experience in living off the land, as would a small unit isolated in enemy territory.

Enemy territory is hardly the phrase to describe the locale in which the team composed of Gordon, Finklestein, and I found ourselves. We stepped from the normal into a delirium in which survival became a mockery—and if you find this report beyond belief I would remind you, sir, that I have no reason for deceit and am testifying on my honor as a United States Marine.

Ferried in by helicopter, the team was in top form, even by Marine standards. Young, tough, battle-ready, Finklestein and Gordon regarded the week-long exerxise as an adventuresome break in base camp routine. They fully expected to be cracking an icy beer eight days from now and telling their buddies what it was like, going into a tropical wilderness without supplies, equipped only with trench knives at their waists and matches in their pockets.

In my own case, I had been on one previous Survival Exercise, in Alaska, and I felt the coming week would be something of a camp out. After all, Florida was my native state. Even though I had never set foot in the deep interior of the Everglades, I had fished the murmuring bayous and hunted the pine forests before they were overcome by condominiums, retirement cities, expressways, Disney Worlds, and Big Mac wrappers. As a rural boy I had rubbed shoulders with Seminoles. Later, during my two years at Florida State, a Seminole had been one of my closest friends. I knew the Indian legends and lore, the basics for living bare-handedly off the lush land. You would think, Captain McCabe, that I was going into a classroom with the quiz answers up my sleeve.

But as the helicopter whirred us deeper into the 'Glades, I

was reminded that it wasn't all going to be crabcakes and beer.

Beyond the horizon the familiar planet had vanished. The uninhabited reaches overwhelmed our senses as we stared down through the Plexiglas bubble. We looked out over the limitless sweep of a watery jungle unlike any other on earth, a sun-broiled morass that could swallow the state of Rhode Island almost four times over. It was a world of molten sun reflections from shallow water, of razor-sharp sawgrass and small, low islands—hummocks—scattered wherever vegetation had reared up and rotted for a million years. It was stands of cypress older than the Crusades, burdened with heavy gray curtains of Spanish moss, providing life for the enormous, parasitic, obscenely hued wild orchids strung along the tall trunks. It was a seething incubator where mists and vapors slithered and the nights crashed and roared in the eternal struggle for survival. It was alligator, and poisonous vipers, and puma on the prowl, and stalk-legged birds, and shifting clouds of insects unclassified by the taxonomist, and deer, muskrat, fang-toothed cousins of the piranha, and creatures born to twitch in fear and die.

The chopper hovered. The pilot, a husky, weathered, gray-templed veteran, gave the team a badgering squint. "Welcome to a week in hell's furnace, you gyrenes. I'll go have a beer."

He had chosen and zeroed Point Exercise, a finger-shaped hummock about a mile in length. A relative clearing, grown in waist-high grass on its eastern end, beckoned as a landing pad.

The pilot carefully rechecked readings on the electronic dials before him and clicked a switch, programming the coordinates into the mini-computer for a return to this precise spot one week from today.

He brought the chopper down feather-light, and Gordon, Finklestein, and I spilled out—three men in fatigues hunched in the flicking shadow of the idling overhead rotor.

The pilot grinned and yelled a parting, "Have fun." And the helicopter was quickly up and away, leaving a small, empty moment.

"Home sweet home," Finklestein said, looking around. He was twenty years old, wiry and agile.

"Bring on the girls," Gordon added. A rawboned, slightly gawky, sandy-haired farm boy from Iowa, he listened to his words die in a muggy silence accented by the soft insect hum.

I'd spotted a probable campsite while the chopper had hovered, a shadowed glen about three hundred yards west of where we stood. "Let's see what the Everglades Hilton has to offer."

We strung out and walked, the grass slashing our calves. I was at point, senior in rank, age, experience—and size. I have not always been comfortable about my size. I stand six feet, seven inches, weigh in at two-forty. Gordon and Finklestein were by no means shorties, but I towered above them, and at the moment they seemed a bit grateful for my shadow.

A dozen yards, and the cloying heat swathed us in oily sweat. It was only a foretaste. Knives, matches, brains, and hands—tools for survival. Two concessions only had been made. In my hip pocket was the notebook in which I would keep a daily log—and which is now receiving this report. And Finklestein carried a portable short-wave transmitter, rigged with shoulder straps. It was insurance against the most desperate emergency.

Still, I thought of what we'd look like a week from today when we stepped aboard the helicopter. Baked out. Cheeks and noses peeling. Lumpy from insect bites. But I hadn't the slightest doubt we'd be wearing the cocksure grin of Marines at the end of maneuvers.

The glade looked even better than it had from the air. It was sheltered by twisted pines and cabbage palms, carpeted with a soft sponge of pine needles. Two stunted trees would anchor the southern corners of a tchiki, the open-sided shelter favored by the Seminoles of old.

By sunset, we were pioneering in style. Our campfire was a friendly flicker in a muggy twilight, our bodies were tired, and the details of a busy day ran together in our minds. Or at least in mine. We'd cut pole framing and fronds for the tchiki roof. Plaited cordage from slender vines. Split bamboo for fish spears and crab traps. Gordon had turned up a fifty-pound turtle and we had him staked out alive as larder of future fresh meat. Finklestein had trapped an enormous king snake. I'd robbed a quail's nest and climbed a cabbage palm to cut out the bud. Now we were belching pleasant echoes of a dinner of roast snake, baked eggs, and crisp, juicy palm fruit.

Under a bright moon we talked in the desultory way of men whose friendship needs little conversation. Gordon volunteered for first watch. I left him and Finklestein talking and sacked out under the tchiki. Another too-short bunk; the soles of my combat boots stuck out from the shadow of the thatch roof.

I lay there for a little while, liquidly tired, listening to sounds already ancient before man dressed out his first skin. Skirlings . . . rustlings . . . basso frogs (frog legs for breakfast?) . . . snarlings . . . thrashings . . . screams, sometimes cut short . . .

I'm not sure just what awakened me. Maybe it was the impact of the club as it crushed Gordon's skull, or Finklestein's movements as he stirred from sleep during the final second of his life when the crude club rose and fell once more.

The first thing I consciously heard was an absolute silence. The writing violence of the 'Glades had come to a total halt, and the silence, so sudden, was a ringing in my ears.

And while the silence deafened, the darkness became a gagging odor like something out of a slimy pit that had formed when the earth was young. It was the steam from the excretion of dinosaurs, the musk of a female creature long dead, the fetid effluvia of some unspeakable thing.

My first impression of the source of the smell was of two hairy, columnar legs standing beside the open-sided tchiki. As I reared up, spun, drew the trench knife, enormous hands grabbed the front roof and ripped it away.

I rolled through the open side, bounced to my feet away from the monstrous thing. I glimpsed Gordon and Finklestein sprawled in the open glade, their heads shattered. The thing had dropped its tree limb club to smash the tchiki and get to me. Its shadow engulfed me. I had an impression of a hairy black humanoid shape, about nine feet tall. Then I was enveloped by massive arms, and the smell of the thing shot down my throat, through my guts.

Maybe I screamed in a very un-Marinelike way. I'm not sure. I had the nightmarish certainty that I was going to be crushed and carried to some time-forgotten lair as dinner for a couple of hungry cubs.

The creature mewled, gibbered, and resisted my thrashings by crushing me against its sickening mass. I felt the tip of my knife bite into a yielding surface, and the thing barked in querulous anger and pain. For a second the embrace was uncertain, and I managed to break away.

I plunged through a thicket and ran. Heard my feet splash water and felt the slash of sawgrass. I looked over my shoulder at the shifting of shadows on the hummock, trying to separate the gigantic creature from the background blackness. It spotted me and called out, a bark-bark-barking note, high in pitch. The weird sound struck me as a pronouncement, a promise. I was the invader. I had hurt something that ruled here, and I must pay a price for that.

As I churned on through the sawgrass, my Marine training took hold of me again and my thoughts began to order themselves. Objective: survive the night; don't get lost; return to the campsite and the short-wave transmitter. Obstacle: I could hear the slashing of sawgrass as the thing narrowed the distance in long strides. I had no hope of outrunning it. And no chance if I faced it squarely, even as large and strong as I was by everyday measurements.

The shallow water thinned out and was gone. Moist black sand became firmer under my pounding feet. Dense jungle shadows closed about me. The next hummock was a couple of hundred yards south of the campsite.

I veered in that direction, ducked behind a giant banyan tree and stood sucking for breath. The night was silent for a moment. The thing, I knew, had reached the edge of the hummock, its night vision searching for me. It bark-barked a note of angry frustration, as if demanding that I stop this foolishness and give myself up to it.

I heard the thud of heavy footsteps and knew the banyan was poor cover. I broke away, going deeper into the hummock, burrowing through a dry thicket. Never mind the sounds, the dry rattlings that revealed the direction of my flight; I had matches in my hand now.

Scratch. Pouf. Wink of fire. I dropped one after another in the brush as I ran. If the first one didn't catch, I prayed the second or third would.

I burst out of the underbrush into a small clearing, changed directions, dropped belly flat, and wriggled into a maze of twisted pine trees. As I looked back, tongues of fire were lapping in the thicket. More than one of the matches had caught and touched off the dry grass.

There was a hesitant crackling, then a soft roar as more of the tinder-dry brush flamed. I saw the humanoid silhouette towering at the further edge of the thicket. It barked again, looking this way and that, still searching for me. Then it reeled back as the flames swept toward it.

I wormed down to the water's edge. This time, I didn't run. I stayed low, on all fours below the level of the sawgrass. Several yards out, I took my bearings. The Big Dipper, the North Star—I wanted to keep Polaris directly behind me and move due south. A subsequent trip due north, when I had the chance, would return me to the campsite and short-wave transmitter.

Half an hour later I crawled onto another hummock, sprawling, taking painful breaths. Looking back, I could see the dark image of the monster towering above the sawgrass. Quarter of a mile behind me now. Slogging back and forth uncertainly, mewling and whining in the same angry frustration as before.

I lay, hands knotted, silently begging the creature to turn east, west, north—any direction but south. The fire had made it lose sight of me and it seemed to be searching haphazardly. I was beginning to hope that the odds now were several dozen compass points in my favor.

Then I saw it come to a standstill. Its processes were working, crystallizing. As if with sudden decision, it began to move toward the hummock where I lay. I backed off, the sick emptiness working again in my belly. I wondered if the thing could smell me as I smelled it, and if my own odor was equally repulsive.

Always south . . . keeping the invisible, tenuous lifeline of direction between me and the transmitter. Every furlong, every hellish mile increased the risk of losing my fix on the campsite and transmitter forever. From a distance each hummock looked like all the others. How many hummocks?

Ten thousand? If I did lose direction, the transmitter would become the proverbial needle in a haystack.

The night became a nightmare of fatigue, sawgrass and water, lattices of iron-hard mangrove in impenetrable tangles. Forever due south, Polaris winking behind me whenever I could see the sky.

Finally I collapsed under a great live oak, too exhausted to get up, too frightened to feel safe where I was. I lay there, my cheek against rotting humus that a week ago had been avid green vegetation, listening. Waiting for the echoes of giant footsteps.

But they didn't come, and I realized that my ears were trying to tell me something. Yes . . . once more the swamp shimmered with its normal predawn sounds; it no longer crouched in silence because the thing was there. The creature must have lost my trail . . .

My spry old grandmother was at my bedside, her face filled with concern in its soft cloud of fine gray hair. I was ten years old and my temperature had been a hundred and three, and my grandmother was smiling and touching my forehead with a cool cloth. "Hi there, Mr. James C. Kelly! I do declare, the delirious boy who had a franzy is back with us, the nasty old fever all gone. What are we having for breakfast, Jimmy the Rugged?" . . .

Then my senses struggled up out of the dream, and there was merciless sun-glare, dappled through gnarled pines and shaggy wild palms. There was timeless emptiness and the hiss of insects. I wasn't ten; and the "franzy" had been for real. A hint of the creature's smell from the moment of close contact still clung to me, nauseatingly.

I sat up, took hold of a knotty sapling, and pulled to my feet. The sun was still low in the east, but the morning was already a shroud of heat.

Working against muscle stiffness, I walked across the narrow island, keeping the sun on my right. I looked north—and a small, bright jolt went through me. I was anything but lost. In the distance a thin feather of pale gray smoke high in the sky marked the location of the hummock I had set on fire. I had picked up a spin-off dividend. The masses of green stuff on the hummock would smolder and smoke for perhaps days—a beacon two hundred yards south of Point E, the campsite.

I wanted food, a bath. My own stink was overlaid by the creature's effluvium. My belly rumbled emptily. I imagined dining on roast portions from Gordon's fifty-pound turtle tethered at the campsite while I transmitted an endless Mayday on the radio. But the thought was a crutch; it didn't ease my heavy sorrow. I was alive, on a day that Gordon and Finklestein would not see. They would be my first objective at Point E.

I laid the mutilated bodies side by side, expressed a prayer over them, and, burial being out of the question, covered them with a makeshift shield of palm fronds. Then I crossed the clearing to where the radio was—

A tearing sensation went through me. And I squatted slowly and fingered the wreckage of the short-wave transmitter. A heavy foot had come down on it in passing, crushing it under what must have been at least five hundred pounds of weight.

I could only hunker there, suspended in the prehistoric immensity of this place. I felt eyes watching me, felt the swamp humming a baleful promise all around me. Bamboo clicked softly, like the rattle of clods on my coffin.

Drawing a breath, I fought down the spooky feeling. "The hell with you!" I muttered at the swamp, and pushed to my feet. I wasn't dead yet. This was still a Survival Exercise.

My first task was to kill and roast the turtle—rations for a trip north. Somewhere in that direction lay the only mark of civilization I had a hope of reaching, the old Tamiami Trail which crosses the 'Glades from Naples on the Gulf to Miami on the Atlantic.

By midday I figured I'd made five or six miles. My surroundings didn't show it. From any vantage point the 'Glades were the same, an expanding universe of sawgrass and water dotted with hummocks like minor galaxies without number.

In the late afternoon I finally stopped to rest. I stripped off and bathed in a waist-deep lagoon off the perimeter of a hummock. Scrubbed myself with sand. But some of the smell of the monster lingered, whether in my pores or in my imagination. I no longer knew which.

I thought of a legend an old Seminole had once told me. It was the story of Stuestaw Enawchee. Literally translated, the words come out to mean "too much body." In the old legendary application, the Stuestaw Enawchee were the gigantic beings from some netherworld that had inhabited the Rivers of Grass since the time of creation. They had come out of the great swamp to war on the first Seminoles a thousand generations before the white man appeared. The People, so went the legend, had a shaman who was sent down from heaven with a magic herb with which he anointed his body as he went into the swamp to confront the creatures. The herb killed off so many of the Stuestaw Enawchee that they began to fear the People and retreated into the great swamp, and the People were able to live in peace.

Trekking on northward, I thought about the Stuestaw Enawchee. From what I had seen I was certain that this legend was, like many others, grounded in fact. Troy and Ur were legends until archeologists went after them with their picks and shovels. The African legends of a man-thing were legends no more after Leakey turned up his first fossilized find. In the present case, Captain McCabe, it is imperative that you not dismiss the Stuestaw Enawchee—the SE—as a figment of a Marine's heat-blasted mind. At the dawn of man, there must have been many such descendants of something that came crawling out of primordial slime, isolated and indigenous to this tropical wilderness a mapmaker would ultimately label the Everglades. The aboriginal ancestors of the Seminoles had discovered a poison, a magic herb, a bait that would kill off the SEs, beat them back, until it *seemed* that the hideous beings had vanished forever,

But forever is a long, long time . . .

As the gray fur of twilight spread over the reaches, I slogged onto a hummock and was content to sprawl belly flat for a while. I guessed that I'd covered about fifteen miles. Not much of a hike for a six-foot-seven-inch Marine? Sir, I hope you never have to try it through sawgrass.

I half-dozed, not letting myself think of where I was. After a little, I roused myself, ate a piece of roast turtle, and then curled in for the night in a tiny alcove inside a clump of wild palms. It was not much of a bivouac, but I slept anyway.

And then, when the night was old and strained in a hush, a mist came seeping out of a cauldron from a time when dinosaurs were dying . . . a body dew . . . a musk . . . a nauseating essence coiling over my flesh . . .

My eyes snapped open. I admit to choking back a scream. My heart felt as if it would burst through my chest. The palms rustled as the SE parted the fronds. The slow steps thudded, heavy beats measuring off the remnants of my life. The great hairy head blocked off the light of a dying moon.

I twisted around and got out through a break between the palms. Into the water once more. Running, fighting aside the sawgrass.

Behind me the SE barked churlishly.

I floundered onto a hummock. Wrong direction, headed south away from the old trail. But I had no choice. The thing was herding me back toward the depths of the 'Glades.

I could hear the splashing of the huge feet. Nocturnal creatures . . . quiescent by day, but by night imbued with powers of which I had no knowledge. I felt the sick certainty that the thing had antennae, a sense unknown to human beings—a guidance system like the sonar of a bat, the instinct of a Capistrano swallow, the built-in controls of an SAM missile. A tool evolved a thousand millenia ago to compensate for the bulk that made it hard for an SE to slip up undetected on its prey. No need to crouch and spring when the creature could dog its quarry to exhaustion.

Why had I been given a day's reprieve? Because the SE's unique function was impaired by solar radiation, the way sunspots interfere with our own sub-light-level transmissions? Because the thing saw better at night in the infrared range? It didn't matter now; I was already scrambling onto another hummock, hearing the creature coming through sawgrass and underbrush, forcing me southward.

I turned right and went off the end of the hummock. Calmer now. Again staying low, taking the cover of the sawgrass.

I eeled my way across to the next island as dawn came, hot and angry red out of the east. Tearing through a wall of vines, I squished up onto firmer ground. A clearing spread before me. My footsteps wavered. In the middle of the glen was a low mound about ten feet long. And in the gray light I realized it was not a natural mound at all. I jarred to a halt, staring. The SE lay before me, stretched on its back as if asleep. How had it circled and got here? Why didn't it move?

By then I had the knife in my hand. Then the scent came, that permeating muskiness, seeping through the dawn . . .

from *behind* me. I heard crashings in the underbrush in the direction from which I'd come.

In a crouch I circled the clearing, eased into the shallow water, took cover in the sawgrass. So there were two of them. A living SE with the single thought of pursuit in its primeval brain. And one dead thing in the clearing. Not like any animal, either of them. Nor like any human. A gigantic blending of the two.

Looking back through the spiny green, I saw the living SE arrive at the side of the dead one. The living one stopped, and for a brief moment I seemed to be forgotten as it knelt beside the dead creature, took one of the enormous dead hands and pressed it to a broad, hairy cheek. The living one's head lifted and the shrill bark-bark became a lament of pain and heartbreak.

I understood, then. The living SE was a female, and her mate had fallen ill and died.

I was held by the depths of the SE's—Essie's—grief as she hunkered beside her mate. I wondered if this had been part of her purpose, to bring me here for a sharing of her bereavement and suffering. If so, it was a ritual beyond my comprehension.

I faded back quietly, working my way through the sawgrass and canebreaks as the sun rose higher. I knew when she returned to my trail. Through the brightening heat came her high-pitched mewling, the note of loneliness and despair that had so often told me her position. The cries became less strident as the sun neared its zenith. Finally, there was only the insect hum and the sound of my own exhausted breathing.

At midday I looked out through a screen of brush on the island where I'd finally come to roost. I saw no sign of Essie, but I knew she was out there, waiting for nightfall again.

I took a bearing. Far to the southeast a thin sliver of smoke hung in the brazen sky, marking the approximate location of Point E. If I survived, I would meet the helicopter there as scheduled. If not, I would leave this report beside the bodies of my two comrades.

Meanwhile, my body machinery demanded attention. I dug out some coontie root with the knife and munched the starchy provender of the old-time Seminoles. It was flat, tasteless, but filling and nourishing. Then I rolled into the water, clothed, to cool off. A mess of a Marine, face hamburgered from insect bites, each hair a painful quill in the tenderness of my sun-burned scalp . . .

Afterward I crawled into the palmetto shadows and slept.

Now, Captain McCabe, I have regained enough strength to move out again. My destination is Point E, and I would like to complete this report insofar as possible in case I am not there to file a verbal report when the helicopter returns for the pickup of the survival team.

If I'm missing, when you view the bodies of good men such as Gordon and Finklestein you must give all due thought to my explanation. There are things unknown in the recesses of the 'Glades, Captain McCabe. You must accept that.

Just as I am accepting the clarity of certain factors.

I know why Essie didn't club me to death in the first attack on the campsite. She had seen that I was the biggest of the three strange SE-oid creatures that had invaded her domain. She had a reason to spare the largest.

I know the meaning of her mewlings and whimperings, her high-pitched barking notes of entreaty.

I can begin to understand, to imagine, how the big, dead male must have felt when he in vigorous life smelled that primeval odor, the exudation of musk, that perfume of hers.

Now he is dead, and the laws of her nature can't be set aside, any more than we could stop a female deer from exuding her mating scent when she is in heat.

Essie is a passion-heavy female in full season, on the prowl for a mate.

I can't help feeling for her innocence, her helplessness in her hormonal situation. But even though I feel compassion for her, I have my knife out and ready. If I am denied sanctuary at Point E, one of us will die.

She is out there now in the lengthening shadows, mewling and whimpering and bark-barking her impatience. She is out there, sir, singing her hellish song of love . . .

PART II

SEA CREATURES

THE CONVENIENT MONSTER

BY LESLIE CHARTERIS

Loch Ness, the home of Nessie, is probably the most famous lake in the world. Twenty-four miles long and one mile wide, it lies in the Great Glen, the major geological fault slanting across Scotland, and is the largest body of fresh water in the British Isles. It is also a placid lake, calm as a millpond—until Nessie appears on a dark night, that is, and begins to churn the water to foam, her shallow humps moving in rapid undulations, her great neck and head lifted toward the black sky . . .

An encounter between Nessie and that rogue of rogues, Simon Templar, better known as the Saint, may seem a bit unlikely at first thought. But Templar has found himself in strange circumstances before (some of his other adventures involve mad scientists, dream worlds, wild inventions, and zombies) and a joust with a sea serpent seems somehow fitting, if not downright inevitable. Still, Nessie is not the Saint's only problem when he ventures to Loch Ness; there is also a little matter of

121

murder and mayhem to be dealt with. "The Convenient Monster" is an unusual blend of the detective and the fantasy / horror story, written with style, wit, and a fine sense of background. One might even describe it as, um, saintly.

Leslie Charteris has been chronicling the adventures of the Saint for more than half a century; to date there have been close to fifty books in the Templar saga, not to mention hundreds of films, radio plays, and television shows both here and in England. (There was also a Saint Mystery Magazine, *edited by Charteris and published in both countries from 1953 to 1967.) At no time during those fifty years of Templar's existence has he been out of print or out of the public eye—quite an achievement for any person, fictional or real.*

Born Leslie Charles Bowyer Yin in Singapore in 1907, Charteris (he changed his name legally in 1926) was educated in England and began to contribute to British magazines in the late 1920s. (The first Saint short stories appeared in The Thriller *in 1930.) He later moved to the United States, became a naturalized American citizen in 1946 and traveled extensively. He also wrote screenplays, radio plays, and the comic strip* Secret Agent X-9, *in addition to the Templar adventures. In recent years he returned to England and currently makes his home in Surrey.*

"OF COURSE," said Inspector Robert Mackenzie, of the Inverness-shire Constabulary, with a burr as broad as his boots seeming to add an extra R to the word, "I know ye're only in Scotland as an ordinary visitor, and no' expectin' to be mixed up in any criminal business."

"That's right," said the Saint cheerfully.

He was so used to this sort of thing that the monotony sometimes became irritating, but Inspector Mackenzie made the conventional gambit with such courteous geniality that it almost sounded like an official welcome. He was a large and homely man with large red hands and small twinkling gray eyes and sandy hair carefully plastered over the bare patch above his forehead, and so very obviously and traditionally a policeman that Simon Templar actually felt a kind of nostalgic affection for him. Short of a call from Chief Inspector Claud Eustace Teal in person, nothing could have brought back more sharply what the Saint often thought of as the good days; and he took it as a compliment that even after so many years, and even as far away as Scotland itself, he was not lost to the telescopic eye of Scotland Yard.

"And I suppose," Mackenzie continued, "ye couldna even be bothered with a wee bit of a local mystery."

"What's your problem?" Simon asked. "Has somebody stolen the haggis you were fattening for the annual police banquet?"

The inspector ignored this with the same stony dignity with which he would have greeted the hoary question about what a Scotsman wore under his kilt.

"It might be involvin' the Loch Ness Monster," he said with the utmost gravity.

"All right," said the Saint good-humoredly. "I started this. I suppose I had it coming. But you're the first policeman who ever tried to pull my leg. Didn't they tell you that I'm the guy who's supposed to do the pulling?"

"I'm no' makin' a joke," Mackenzie persisted aggrievedly, and the Saint stared at him.

It was in the spring of 1933 that a remarkable succession of sober and reputable witnesses began to testify that they had seen in Loch Ness a monstrous creature whose existence had been a legend of region since ancient times, but which few persons in this century had claimed to have seen for themselves. The descriptions varied in detail, as human observations are prone to do, but they seemed generally to agree that the beast was roughly thirty feet long and could swim at about the same number of miles per hour; it was a dark gray in color, with a small horselike head on a long tapering neck, which it turned from side to side with the quick movements of an alert hen. There were divergencies as to whether it had one or more humps in its back, and whether it churned the water with flippers or a powerful tail; but all agreed that it could not be classified with anything known to modern natural history.

The reports culminated in December with a photograph showing a strange reptilian shape thrashing in the water, taken by a senior employee of the British Aluminum Company, which had a plant nearby. A number of experts certified the negative to be unretouched and unfaked, and the headline writers took it from there.

Within a fortnight a London newspaper had a correspondent on the scene with a highly publicized big-game authority in tow; some footprints were found and casts made of them—which before the New Year was three days old had been pronounced by the chief zoologists of the British Museum to have all been made by the right hind foot of a hippopotamus, and a stuffed hippopotamus at that. In the nationwide guffaw which followed the exposure of this hoax, the whole matter exploded into a theme for cartoonists and comedians, and that aura of hilarious incredulity still colored the Saint's vague recollections of the subject.

It took a little while for him to convince himself that the inspector's straight face was not part of an elaborate exercise in Highland humor.

"What has the monster done that's illegal?" Simon inquired at length, with a gravity to match Mackenzie's own.

"A few weeks ago, it's thocht to h' eaten a sheep. And last night if may ha' killed a dog."

"Where was this?"

"The sheep belonged to Fergus Clanraith, who has a farm by the loch beyond Foyers, and the dog belongs to his neighbors, a couple named Bastion from doon in England who settled here last summer. 'Tis only aboot twenty miles away, if ye could spairr the time with me."

The Saint sighed. In certain interludes, he thought that everything had already happened to him that could befall a man even with his exceptional gift for stumbling into fantastic situations and being offered bizarre assignments, but apparently there was always some still more preposterous imbroglio waiting to entangle him.

"Okay," he said resignedly. "I've been slugged with practically every other improbability you could raise an eyebrow at, so why should I draw the line at dog-slaying monsters. Lay on, Macduff."

"The name is Mackenzie," said the inspector seriously.

Simon paid his hotel bill and took his own car, for he had been intending to continue his pleasantly aimless wandering that day anyhow, and it would not make much difference to him where he stopped along the way. He followed Mackenzie's somewhat venerable chariot out of Inverness on the road that takes the east bank of the Ness River, and in a few minutes the slaty grimness of the town had been gratefully forgotten in the green and gold loveliness of the countryside.

The road ran at a fairly straight tangent to the curves of the river and the Caledonian Canal, giving only infrequent glimpses of the seven locks built to lift shipping to the level of the lake, until at Dores he had his first view of Loch Ness at its full breadth.

The Great Glen of Scotland transects the country diagonally from northeast to southwest, as if a giant had tried to break off the upper end of the land between the deep natural notches formed by Loch Linnhe and the Beauly Firth. On the map which Simon had seen, the chain of lochs stretched in an almost crow-flight line that had made him look twice to be sure that there was not in fact a clear channel across from the Eastern to the Western Sea. Loch Ness itself, a tremendous trough twenty-four miles long but only averaging about a mile in width, suggested nothing more than an enlargement of the canal system which gave access to it at both ends.

But not many vessels seemed to avail themselves of the passage, for there was no boat in sight on the lake that afternoon. With the water as calm as a millpond and the fields and trees rising from its shores to a blue sky dappled with soft wooly clouds, it was as pretty as a picture postcard and utterly unconvincing to think of as a place which might be haunted by some outlandish horror from the mists of antiquity.

For a drive of twenty minutes, at the sedate pace set by Mackenzie the highway paralleled the edge of the loch a little way up its steep stony banks. The opposite shore widened slightly into the tranquil beauty of Urquhart Bay with its ancient castle standing out gray and stately on the far point, and then returned to the original almost uniform breadth. Then, within fortunately brief sight of the unpicturesque aluminum works, it bore away to the south through the small stark village of Foyers and went winding up the glen of one of the tumbling streams that feed the lake.

Several minutes further on, Mackenzie turned off into a narrow side road that twisted around and over a hill and swung down again, until suddenly the loch was spread out squarely before them once more and the lane curled past the first of two houses that could be seen standing solitarily apart from each other but each within a bowshot of the loch. Both of them stood out with equal harshness against the gentle curves and colors of the landscape with the same dark graceless austerity as the last village or the last town or any other buildings Simon had seen in Scotland, a country whose unbounded natural beauty seemed to have inspired no corresponding artistry in its architects, but rather to have goaded them into competition to offset it with the most contrasting ugliness into which bricks and stone and tile could be assembled. This was a paradox to which he had failed to fit a plausible theory for so long that he had finally given up trying.

Beside the first house a man in a stained shirt and corduroy trousers tucked into muddy canvas leggings was digging in a vegetable garden. He looked up as Mackenzie brought his rattletrap to a stop, and walked slowly over to the hedge. He was short but powerfully built, and his hair flamed like a stormy sunset.

Mackenzie climbed out and beckoned to the Saint. As Simon reached them, the red-haired man was saying: "Aye, I've been over and seen what's left o' the dog. It's more than they found of my sheep, I can tell ye."

"But could it ha' been the same thing that did it?" asked the inspector.

"That' no' for me to say, Mackenzie. I'm no' a detective. But remember, it wasna me who said the monster took my sheep. It was the Bastions who thocht o' that, it might be to head me off from askin' if *they* hadn't been the last to see it—pairhaps on their Sunday dinner table. There's nae such trick I wouldna put beyond the Sassenach."

Mackenzie introduced them: "This is Mr. Clanraith, whom I was tellin' ye aboot. Fergus, I'd like ye to meet Mr. Templar, who may be helpin' me to investigate."

Clanraith gave Simon a muscular and horny grip across the untrimmed hedge, appraising him shrewdly from under shaggy ginger brows.

"Ye dinna look like a policeman, Mr. Templar."

"I try not to," said the Saint expressionlessly. "Did you mean by what you were just saying that you don't believe in the monster at all?"

"I didna say that."

"Then apart from anything else, you think there might actually be such a thing."

"There might."

"Living where you do, I should think you'd have as good a chance as anyone of seeing it yourself—if it does exist."

The farmer peered at Simon suspiciously.

"Wad ye be a reporrter, Mr. Templar, pairhaps?"

"No, I'm not," Simon assured him; but the other remained wary.

"When a man tells o' seein' monsters, his best friends are apt to wonder if he may ha' taken a wee drop too much. If I had seen anything, ever, I wadna be talkin' aboot it to every stranger, to be made a laughin'-stock of."

"But ye'll admit," Mackenzie put in, "it's no' exactly norrmal for a dog to be chewed up an' killed the way this one was."

"I wull say this," Clanraith conceded guardedly. "It's strange that nobody hairrd the dog bark, or e'en whimper."

Through the Saint's mind flickered an eerie vision of something amorphous and loathsome oozing soundlessly out of night-blackened water, flowing with obscene stealth towards a hound that slept unwarned by any of its senses.

"Do you mean it mightn't've had a chance to let out even a yip?"

"I'm no' sayin'," Clanraith maintained cautiously. "But it was a guid watchdog, if naught else."

A girl had stepped out of the house and come closer while they talked. She had Fergus Clanraith's fiery hair and greenish eyes, but her skin was pink and white where his was weather-beaten and her lips were full where his were tight. She was a half-a-head taller than he, and her figure was slim where it should be.

Now she said: "That's right. He even barked whenever he heard me coming, although he saw me every day."

Her voice was low and well-modulated, with only an attractive trace of her father's accent.

"Then if it was a pairrson wha' killed him, Annie, 'twad only mean it was a body he was still more used to."

"But you can't really believe that any human being would do a thing like that to a dog that knew them—least of all to their own dog!"

"That's the trouble wi' lettin' a lass be brocht up an' schooled on the wrong side o' the Tweed," Clanraith said darkly. "She forgets what the English ha' done to honest Scotsmen no' so lang syne."

The girl's eyes had kept returning to the Saint with candid interest, and it was to him that she explained, smiling: "Father still wishes he could fight for Bonnie Prince Charlie. He's glad to let me do part-time secretarial work for Mr. Bastion because I can live at home and keep house as well, but he still feels I'm guilty of fraternizing with the enemy."

"We'd best be gettin' on and talk to them ourselves," Mackenzie said. "And then we'll see if Mr. Templar has any more questions to ask."

There was something in Annie Clanraith's glance which seemed to say that she hoped that he would, and the Saint was inclined to be of the same sentiment. He had certainly not expected to find anyone so decorative in the cast of characters, and he began to feel a tentative quickening of optimism about this interruption in his travels. He could see her in his rearview mirror, still standing by the hedge and following with her gaze after her father had turned back to his digging.

About three hundred yards and a few bends farther on, Mackenzie veered between a pair of stone gateposts and chugged to a standstill on the circular driveway in front of the second house. Simon stopped behind him and then strolled after him to the front door, which was opened almost at once by a tall thin man in a pullover and baggy gray flannel slacks.

"Good afternoon, sir," said the detective courteously. "I'm Inspector Mackenzie from Inverness. Are ye Mr. Bastion?"

"Yes."

Bastion had a bony face with a long aquiline nose, lank black hair flecked with gray, and a broad toothbrush moustache that gave him an indeterminately military appearance. His black eyes flickered to the Saint inquiringly.

"This is Mr. Templar, who may be assistin' me," Mackenzie said. "The constable who was here this morning told me all aboot what ye showed him, on the telephone, but could we ha' a wee look for ourselves?"

"Oh, yes, certainly. Will you come this way?"

The way was around the house, across an uninspired formal garden at the back which looked overdue for the attention of a gardener, and through a small orchard beyond which a stretch of rough grass sloped quickly down to the water. As the meadow fell away, a pebbly beach came into view, and Simon saw that this was one of the rare breaches in the steep average angle of the loch's sides. On either side of the little beach the ground swelled up again to form a shallow bowl that gave an easy natural access to the lake. The path that they traced led to a short rustic pier with a shabby skiff tied to it, and on the ground to one side of the pier was something covered with potato sacking.

"I haven't touched anything, as the constable asked me," Bastion said. "Except to cover him up."

He bent down and carefully lifted off the burlap.

They looked down in silence at what was uncovered.

"The puir beastie," Mackenzie said at last.

It had been a large dog of confused parentage in which the Alsatian may have predominated. What had happened to it was no nicer to look at than it is to catalogue. Its head and hindquarters were partly mashed to a red pulp; and plainly traceable across its chest was a row of slotlike gashes, each about an inch long and close together, from which blood had run and clotted in the short fur. Mackenzie squatted and stretched the skin with gentle fingers to see the slits more clearly. The Saint also felt the chest: it had an unnatural contour where the line of punctures crossed it, and his probing touch found only sponginess where there should have been a hard cage of ribs.

His eyes met Mackenzie's across the pitifully mangled form.

"That would be quite a row of teeth," he remarked.

"Aye," said the inspector grimly. "But what lives here that has a mouth like that?"

They straightened up and surveyed the immediate surroundings. The ground here, only a stride or two from the beach, which in turn was less than a yard wide, was so moist that it was soggy, and pockets of muddy liquid stood in the deeper indentations with which it was plentifully rumpled.

The carpet of coarse grass made individual impressions difficult to identify, but three or four shoe-heel prints could be positively distinguished.

"I'm afraid I made a lot of those tracks," Bastion said. "I know you're not supposed to go near anything, but all I could think of at the time was seeing if *he* was still alive and if I could do anything for him. The constable tramped around a bit too, when he was here." He pointed past the body. "But neither of us had anything to do with those marks there."

Close to the beach was a place where the turf looked as if it had been raked by something with three gigantic claws. One talon had caught in the roots of a tuft of grass and torn it up bodily: the clump lay on the pebbles at the water's edge. Aside from that, the claws had left three parallel grooves, about four inches apart and each about half-an-inch wide. They dug into the ground at their upper ends to a depth of more than two inches, and dragged back towards the lake for a length of about ten inches as they tapered up.

Simon and Mackenzie stood on the pebbles to study the marks, Simon spanning them experimentally with his fingers while the detective took exact measurements with a tape and entered them in his notebook.

"Anything wi' a foot big enough to carry claws like that," Mackenzie said, "I'd no' wish to ha' comin' after me."

"Well, they call it a monster, don't they?" said the Saint dryly. "It wouldn't impress anyone if it made tracks like a mouse."

Mackenzie unbent his knees stiffly, shooting the Saint a distrustful glance, and turned to Bastion.

"When did ye find all this, sir?" he asked.

"I suppose it was about six o'clock," Bastion said. "I woke up before dawn and couldn't get to sleep again, so I decided to try a little early fishing. I got up as soon as it was light—"

"Ye didna hear any noise before that?"

"No."

"It couldna ha' been the dog barkin' that woke ye?"

"Not that I'm aware of. And my wife is a very light sleeper, and she didn't hear anything. But I was rather surprised when I didn't see the dog outside. He doesn't sleep in the house, but he's always waiting on the doorstep in the morning. However, I came on down here—and that's how I found him."

"And you didn't see anything else?" Simon asked. "In the lake, I mean."

"No. I didn't see the monster. And when I looked for it, there wasn't a ripple on the water. Of course, the dog may have been killed some time before, though his body was still warm."

"Mr. Bastion," Mackenzie said, "do *ye* believe it was the monster that killed him?"

Bastion looked at him and at the Saint.

"I'm not a superstitious man," he replied. "But if it wasn't a monster of some kind, what else could it have been?"

The inspector closed his notebook with a snap that seemed to be echoed by his clamping lips. It was evident that he felt that the situation was wandering far outside his professional province. He scowled at the Saint as though he expected Simon to do something about it.

"It might be interesting," Simon said thoughtfully, "if we get a vet to do a postmortem."

"What for?" Bastion demanded brusquely.

"Let's face it," said the Saint. "Those claw marks *could* be fakes. And the dog *could* have been mashed up with some sort of club—even a club with spikes set in it to leave wounds that'd look as if they were made by teeth. But by all accounts, no one could have got near enough to the dog to do that without him barking. *Unless the dog was doped first.* So before we

go overboard on this monster theory, I'd like to rule everything else out. An autopsy would do that."

Bastion rubbed his scrubby moustache.

"I see your point. Yes, that might be a good idea."

He helped them to shift the dog on to the sack which had
previously covered it, and Simon and Mackenzie carried it
between them back to the driveway and laid it in the boot of
the detective's car.

"D'ye think we could ha' a wurrd wi' Mrs. Bastion, sir?"
Mackenzie asked, wiping his hands on a clean rag and passing
it to the Saint.

"I suppose so," Bastion assented dubiously. "Although
she's pretty upset about this, as you can imagine. It was really
her dog more than mine. But come in, and I'll see if she'll talk
to you for a minute."

But Mrs. Bastion herself settled that by meeting them in
the hall, and she made it obvious that she had been watching
them from a window.

"What are they doing with Golly, Noel?" she greeted her
husband wildly. "Why are they taking him away?"

"They want to have him examined by a doctor, dear."

Bastion went on to explain why, until she interrupted him
again:

"Then don't let them bring him back. It's bad enough to
have seen him the way he is, without having to look at him
dissected." She turned to Simon and Mackenzie. "You must
understand how I feel. Golly was like a son to me. His name
was really Goliath—I called him that because he was so big
and fierce, but actually he was a pushover when you got on
the right side of him."

Words came from her in a driving torrent that suggested
the corollary of a powerhouse. She was a big-boned, strong-
featured woman who made no attempt to minimize any of

her probable forty-five years. Her blonde hair was unwaved and pulled back into a tight bun, and her blue eyes were set in a nest of wrinkles that would have been called characterful on an outdoor man. Her lipstick, which needed renewing, had a slapdash air of being her one impatient concession to feminine artifice. But Bastion put a soothing arm around her as solicitously as if she had been a dimpled bride.

"I'm sure these officers will have him buried for us, Eleanor," he said. "But while they're here I think they wanted to ask you something."

"Only to confairrm what Mr. Bastion told us, ma'am," said Mackenzie. "That ye didna hear an disturrbance last night."

"Absolutely not. And if Golly had made a sound, I should have heard him. I always do. Why are you trying so hard to get around the facts? It's as plain as a pikestaff that the monster did it."

"Some monsters have two legs," Simon remarked.

"And I suppose you're taught not to believe in any other kind. Even with the evidence under your very eyes."

"I mind a time when some other footprints were found, ma'am," Mackenzie put in deferentially, "which turned oot to be a fraud."

"I know exactly what you're referring to. And that stupid hoax made a lot of idiots disbelieve the authentic photograph which was taken just before it, and refuse to accept an even better picture that was taken by a thoroughly reputable London surgeon about four months later. I know what I'm talking about. As a matter of fact, the reason we took this house was mainly because I'm hoping to discover the monster."

Two pairs of eyebrows shot up and lowered almost in unison, but it was the Saint who spoke for Mackenzie as well as himself.

"How would you do that, Mrs. Bastion?" he inquired with some circumspection. "If the monster has been well-known around here for a few centuries, at least to everyone who believes in him—"

"It still hasn't been scientifically and officially established. I'd like to have the credit for doing that, beyond any shadow of doubt, and naming it *Monstrum eleanoris*."

"Probably you gentlemen don't know it," Bastion elucidated, with a kind of quaintly protective pride, "but Mrs. Bastion is a rather distinguished naturalist. She's hunted every kind of big game there is, and even holds a couple of world's records."

"But I never had a trophy as important as this would be," his better half took over again. "I expect you think I'm a little cracked—that there couldn't really be any animal of any size in the world that hasn't been discovered by this time. Tell them the facts of life, Noel."

Bastion cleared his throat like a schoolboy preparing to recite, and said with much the same awkward air: "The gorilla was only discovered in 1847, the giant panda in 1869, and the okapi wasn't discovered till 1901. Of course explorers brought back rumors of them, but people thought they were just native fairy tales. And you yourselves probably remember reading about the first coelacanth being caught. That was only in 1938."

"So why shouldn't there still be something else left that I could be the first to prove?" Eleanor Bastion concluded for him. "The obvious thing to go after, I suppose, was the Abominable Snowman; but Mr. Bastion can't stand high altitudes. So I'm making do with the Loch Ness Monster."

Inspector Mackenzie, who had for some time been looking progressively more confused and impatient in spite of his politely valiant efforts to conceal the fact, finally managed to interrupt the antiphonal barrage of what he could only be expected to regard as delirious irrelevancies.

"All that I'm consairned wi', ma'am," he said heavily, "is tryin' to detairrmine whether there's a human felon to be apprehended. If it should turn oot to be a monster, as ye're thinkin', it wadna be in my jurisdeection. However, in that case, pairhaps Mr. Templar, who is no' a police officer, could be o' more help to ye."

"Templar," Bastion repeated slowly. "I feel as if I ought to recognize that name, now, but I was rather preoccupied with something else when I first heard it."

"Do you have a halo on you somewhere?" quizzed Mrs. Bastion, the huntress, in a tone which somehow suggested the aiming of a gun.

"Sometimes."

"Well, by Jove!" Bastion said. "I should've guessed it, of course, if I'd been thinking about it. You didn't sound like a policeman."

Mackenzie winced faintly, but both the Bastions were too openly absorbed in reappraising the Saint to notice it.

Simon Templar should have been hardened to that kind of scrutiny, but as the years went on it was beginning to cause him a mixture of embarrassment and petty irritation. He wished that new acquaintances could dispense with the reactions and stay with their original problems.

He said, rather roughly: "It's just my bad luck that Mackenzie caught me as I was leaving Inverness. I was on my way to Loch Lomond, like any innocent tourist, to find out how bonnie the banks actually are. He talked me into taking the low road instead of the high road, and stopping here to stick my nose into your problem."

"But that's perfectly wonderful!" Mrs. Bastion announced like a bugle. "Noel, ask him to stay the night. I mean, for the weekend. Or for the rest of the week, if he can spare the time."

"Why—er—yes," Bastion concurred obediently. "Yes, of course. We'd be delighted. The Saint ought to have some good ideas about catching a monster."

Simon regarded him coolly, aware of the invisible glow of slightly malicious expectation emanating from Mackenzie, and made a reckless instant decision.

"Thank you," he said. "I'd love it. I'll bring in my things, and Mac can be on his way."

He sauntered out without further palaver, happily conscious that only Mrs. Bastion had not been moderately rocked by his casual acceptance.

They all ask for it, he thought. Cops and civilians alike, as soon as they hear the name. Well, let's oblige them. And see how they like whatever comes of it.

Mackenzie followed him outside, with a certain ponderous dubiety which indicated that some of the joke had already evaporated.

"Ye'll ha' no authorrity in this, ye underrstand," he emphasized, "except the rights o' any private investigator—which are no' the same in Scotland as in America, to judge by some o' the books I've read."

"I shall try very hard not to gang agley," Simon assured him. "Just phone me the result of the P.M. as soon as you possibly can. And while you're waiting for it, you might look up the law about shooting monsters. See if one has to take out a special license, or anything like that."

He watched the detective drive away, and went back in with his two-suiter. He felt better already, with no official eyes and ears absorbing his most trivial responses. And it would be highly misleading to say that he found the bare facts of the case, as they had been presented to him, utterly banal and boring.

Noel Bastion showed him to a small but comfortable room upstairs, with a window that faced towards the home of Fergus Clanraith but which also afforded a sidelong glimpse of the loch. Mrs. Bastion was already busy there, making up the bed.

"You can't get any servants in a place like this," she explained. "I'm lucky to have a woman who bicycles up from Fort Augustus once a week to do the heavy cleaning. They all want to stay in the towns where they can have what they think of as a bit of life."

Simon looked at Bastion innocuously and remarked: "You're lucky to find a secretary right on the spot like the one I met up the road."

"Oh, you mean Annie Clanraith." Bastion scrubbed a knuckle on his upper lip. "Yes. She was working in Liverpool, but she came home at Christmas to spend the holidays with her father. I had to get some typing done in a hurry, and she helped me out. It was Clanraith who talked her into staying. I couldn't pay her as much as she'd been earning in Liverpool, but he pointed out that she'd end up with just as much in her pocket if she didn't have to pay for board and lodging, which he'd give her if she kept house. He's a widower, so it's not a bad deal for him."

"Noel's a writer," Mrs. Bastion said. "His big book isn't finished yet, but he works on it all the time."

"It's a life of Wellington," said the writer. "It's never been done, as I think it should be, by a professional soldier."

"Mackenzie didn't tell me anything about your background," said the Saint. "What should he have called you—colonel?"

"Only major. But that was in the Regular Army."

Simon did not miss the faintly defensive tone of the addendum. But the silent calculation he made was that the pension of a retired British Army major, unless augmented by some more commercial form of authorship than an unfinished biography of distinctly limited appeal, would not finance enough big-game safaris to earn an ambitious huntress a great reputation.

"There," said Mrs. Bastion finally. "Now, if you'd like to settle in and make yourself at home, I'll have some tea ready in five minutes."

The Saint had embarked on his Scottish trip with an open mind and an attitude of benevolent optimism, but if anyone had prophesied that it would lead to him sipping tea in the drawing room of two practically total strangers, with his valise unpacked in their guest bedroom, and solemnly chatting about a monster as if it were as real as a monkey, he would probably have been mildly derisive. His hostess, however, was obsessed with the topic.

"Listen to this," she said, fetching a well-worn volume from a bookcase. "It's a quotation from the biography of St. Columba, written about the middle of the seventh century. It tells about his visit to Inverness some hundred years before, and it says *he was obliged to cross the water of Nesa; and when he had come to the bank he sees some of the inhabitants bringing an unfortunate fellow whom, as those who were bringing him related, a little while before some aquatic monster seized and savagely bit while he was swimming. . . . The blessed man orders one of his companions to swim out and bring him from over the water a coble . . . Lugne Mocumin without delay takes off his clothes except his tunic and casts himself into the water. But the monster comes up and moves towards the man as he swam. . . . The blessed man, seeing it, commanded the ferocious monster saying, 'Go thou no further nor touch the man; go back at once.' Then on hearing his word of the saint the monster was terrified and fled away again more quickly than if it had been dragged off by ropes.*"

"I must try to remember that formula," Simon murmured, "and hope the monster can't tell one saint from another."

" 'Monster' is really a rather stupid name for it," Mrs. Bastion said. "It encourages people to be illogical about it. Actually, in the old days the local people called it *an Niseag,* which is simply the name 'Ness' in Gaelic with a feminine diminutive ending. You could literally translate it as 'Nessie.' "

"That does sound a lot cuter," Simon agreed. "If you forget how it plays with dogs."

Eleanor Bastion's weathered face went pale, but the muscles under the skin did not flinch.

"I haven't forgotten Golly. But I was trying to keep my mind off him."

"Assuming this beastie does exist," said the Saint, "how did it get here?"

"Why did it have to 'get' here at all? I find it easier to believe that it always was here. The loch is seven hundred and fifty feet deep, which is twice the mean depth of the North Sea. *An Niseag* is a creature that obviously prefers the depths and only comes to the surface occasionally. I think its original home was always at the bottom of the loch, and it was trapped there when some prehistoric geological upheaval cut off the loch from the sea."

"And it's lived there ever since—for how many million years?"

"Not the original ones—I suppose we must assume at least a couple. But their descendants. Like many primitive creatures, it probably lives to a tremendous age."

"What do you think it is?"

"Most likely something of the plesiosaurus family. The descriptions sound more like that than anything—large body, long neck, paddlelike legs. Some people claim to have seen stumpy projections on its head, rather like the horns of a snail, which aren't part of the usual reconstruction of a plesiosaurus. But after all, we've never seen much of a plesiosaurus except its skeleton. You wouldn't know exactly what a snail looked like if you'd only seen its shell."

"But if Nessie has been here all this time, why wasn't she reported much longer ago?"

"She was. You heard that story about St. Columba. And if you think only modern observations are worth paying attention to, several reliable sightings were recorded from 1871 onwards."

"But there was no motor road along the loch until 1933," Bastion managed to contribute at last, "and a trip like you made today would have been quite an expedition. So there weren't many witnesses about until fairly recently, of the type that scientists would take seriously."

Simon lighted a cigarette. The picture was clear enough. Like the flying saucers, it depended on what you wanted to believe—and whom.

Except that here there was not only fantasy to be thought of. There could be felony.

"What would you have to do to make it an official discovery?"

"We have movie and still cameras with the most powerful telephoto lenses you can buy," said the woman. "I spend eight hours a day simply watching the lake, just like anyone might put in at a regular job, but I vary the times of day systematically. Noel sometimes puts in a few hours as well. We have a view for several miles in both directions, and by the law of averages *an Niseag* must come up eventually in the area we're

covering. Whenever that happens, our lenses will get closeup
pictures that'll show every detail beyond any possibility of
argument. It's simply a matter of patience, and when I came
here I made up my mind that I'd spend ten years on it if
necessary."

"And now," said the Saint, "I guess you're more convinced
than ever that you're on the right track and the scent is hot."

Mrs. Bastion looked him in the eyes with terrifying
equanimity.

"Now," she said, "I'm going to watch with a Weatherby
Magnum as well as the cameras. *An Niseag* can't be much
bigger than an elephant, and it isn't any more bulletproof. I
used to think it'd be a crime to kill the last survivor of a
species, but since I saw what it did to poor Golly, I'd like to
have it as a trophy as well as a picture."

There was much more of this conversation, but nothing
that would not seem repetitious in verbatim quotation. Mrs.
Bastion had accumulated numerous other books on the subject, from any of which she was prepared to read excerpts in
support of her convictions.

It was hardly eight-thirty, however, after a supper of cold
meat and salad, when she announced that she was going to
bed.

"I want to get up at two o'clock and be out at the loch well
before daylight—the same time when that thing must have
been there this morning."

"Okay," said the Saint. "Knock on my door, and I'll go
with you."

He remained to accept a nightcap of Peter Dawson, which
seemed to taste especially rich and smooth in the land where
they made it. Probably this was his imagination, but it gave
him a pleasant feeling of drinking the wine of the country on
its own home ground.

"If you're going to be kind enough to look after her, I may sleep a bit later," Bastion said. "I must get some work done on my book tonight, while there's a little peace and quiet. Not that Eleanor can't take care of herself better than most women, but I wouldn't like her being out there alone after what's happened."

"You're thoroughly sold on this monster yourself, are you?"

The other stared into his glass.

"It's the sort of thing that all my instincts and experience would take with a grain of salt. But you've seen for yourself that it isn't easy to argue with Eleanor. And I must admit that she makes a terrific case for it. But until this morning I was keeping an open mind."

"And now it isn't so open?"

"Quite frankly, I'm pretty shaken. I feel it's got to be settled now, one way or the other. Perhaps you'll have some luck tomorrow."

It did in fact turn out to be a vigil that gave Simon goose pimples, but they were caused almost entirely by the predawn chill of the air. Daylight came slowly, through a gray and leaky-looking overcast. The lake remained unruffled, guarding its secrets under a pale pearly glaze.

"I wonder what we did wrong," Mrs. Bastion said at last, when the daylight was as broad as the clouds evidently intended to let it become. "The thing should have come back to where it made its last kill. Perhaps if we hadn't been so sentimental we should have left Golly right where he was and built a *machan* over him where we could have stood watch in turns."

Simon was not so disappointed. Indeed, if a monster had actually appeared almost on schedule under their expectant eyes, he would have been inclined to sense the hand of a Hollywood B-picture producer rather than the finger of fate.

"As you said yesterday, it's a matter of patience," he observed philosophically. "But the odds are that the rest of your eight hours, now, will be just routine. So if you're not nervous I'll ramble around a while."

His rambling had brought him no nearer to the house than the orchard when the sight of a coppery rosy head on top of a shapely free-swinging figure made his pulse fluctuate enjoyably with a reminder of the remotely possible promise of romantic compensation that had started to warm his interest the day before.

Annie Clanraith's smile was so eager and happy to see him that he might have been an old and close friend who had been away for a long time.

"Inspector Mackenzie told my father he'd left you here. I'm so glad you stayed!"

"I'm glad you're glad," said the Saint, and against her ingenuous sincerity it was impossible to make the reply sound even vestigially skeptical. "But what made it so important?"

"Just having someone new and alive to talk to. You haven't stayed long enough to find out how bored you can be here."

"But you've got a job that must be a little more attractive than going back to an office in Liverpool."

"Oh, it's not bad. And it helps to make father comfortable. And it's nice to live in such beautiful scenery, I expect you'll say. But I read books and I look at the TV, and I can't stop having my silly dreams."

"A gal like you," he said teasingly, "should have her hands full, fighting off other dreamers."

"All I get my hands full of is pages and pages of military strategy, about a man who only managed to beat Napoleon. But at least Napoleon had Josephine. The only thing Wellington gave his name to was an old boot."

Simon clucked sympathetically.

"He may have had moments with his boots off, you know. Or has your father taught you to believe nothing good of anyone who was ever born south of the Tweed?"

"You must have thought it was terrible, the way he talked about Mr. Bastion. And he's so nice, isn't he? It's too bad he's married!"

"Maybe his wife doesn't think so."

"I mean, I'm a normal girl and I'm not old-fashioned, and the one thing I do miss here is a man to fight off. In fact, I'm beginning to feel that if one did come along I wouldn't even struggle."

"You sound as if that Scottish song was written about you," said the Saint, and he sang softly:

> *"Ilka lassie has her laddie,*
> *Ne'er a ane ha' I;*
> *But all the lads they smile at me,*
> *Comin' through the rye."*

She laughed.

"Well, at least you smiled at me, and that makes today look a little better."

"Where were you going?"

"To work. I just walked over across the fields—it's much shorter than by the lane."

Now that she mentioned it, he could see a glimpse of the Clanraith house between the trees. He turned and walked with her through the untidy little garden towards the Bastions' entrance.

"I'm sorry that stops me offering to take you on a picnic."

"I don't have any luck, do I? There's a dance in Fort Augustus tomorrow night, and I haven't been dancing for months, but I don't know a soul who'd take me."

"I'd like to do something about that," he said. "But it rather depends on what develops around here. Don't give up hope yet, though."

As they entered the hall, Bastion came out of a back room and said: "Ah, good morning, Annie. There are some pages I was revising last night on my desk. I'll be with you in a moment."

She went on into the room he had just come from, and he turned to the Saint.

"I suppose you didn't see anything."

"If we had, you'd've heard plenty of gunfire and hollering."

"Did you leave Eleanor down there?"

"Yes. But I don't think she's in any danger in broad daylight. Did Mackenzie call?"

"Not yet. I expect you're anxious to hear from him. The telephone's in the drawing room—why don't you settle down there? You might like to browse through some of Eleanor's collection of books about the monster."

Simon accepted the suggestion, and soon found himself so absorbed that only his empty stomach was conscious of the time when Bastion came in and told him that lunch was ready. Mrs. Bastion had already returned and was dishing up an agreeably aromatic lamb stew which she apologized for having only warmed up.

"You were right, it was just routine," she said. "A lot of waiting for nothing. But one of these days it won't be for nothing."

"I was thinking about it myself, dear," Bastion said, "and it seems to me that there's one bad weakness in your eight-hour-a-day system. There are enough odds against you already in only being able to see about a quarter of the loch, which leaves the monster another three-quarters where it could just as easily pop up. But on top of that, watching only eight hours out of the twenty-four only gives us a one-third chance of being there even if it does pop up within range of our observation post. That doesn't add to the odds against us, it multiplies them."

"I know; but what can we do about it?"

"Since Mr. Templar pointed out that anyone should really be safe enough with a high-powered rifle in their hands and everyone else within call, I thought that three of us could divide up the watches and cover the whole day from before dawn till after dusk, as long as one could possibly see anything. That is, if Mr. Templar would help out. I know he can't stay here indefinitely, but—"

"If it'll make anybody feel better, I'd be glad to take a turn that way," Simon said indifferently.

It might have been more polite to sound more enthusiastic, but he could not make himself believe that the monster would actually be caught by any such system. He was impatient for Mackenzie's report, which he thought was the essential detail.

The call came about two o'clock, and it was climactically negative.

"The doctor canna find a trrace o' drugs or poison in the puir animal."

Simon took a deep breath.

"What did he think of its injuries?"

"He said he'd ne'er seen the like o' them. He dinna ken anything in the wurruld wi' such crrushin' power in its jaws as yon monster must have. If 'twas no' for the teeth marrks, he wad ha' thocht it was done wi' a club. But the autopsy mak's that impossible.';

"So I take it you figure that rules you officially out," said the Saint bluntly. "But give me a number where I can call you if the picture changes again."

He wrote it down on a pad beside the telephone before he turned and relayed the report.

"That settles it," said Mrs. Bastion. "It can't be anything else but *an Niseag*. And we've got all the more reason to try Noel's idea of keeping watch all day."

"I had a good sleep this morning, so I'll start right away," Bastion volunteered. "You're entitled to a siesta."

"I'll take over after that," she said. "I want to be out there again at twilight. I know I'm monopolizing the most promising times, but this matters more to me than to anyone else."

Simon helped her with the dishes after they had had coffee, and then she excused herself.

"I'll be fresher later if I do take a little nap. Why don't you do the same? It was awfully good of you to get up in the middle of the night with me."

"It sounds as if I won't be needed again until later tomorrow morning," said the Saint. "But I'll be reading and brooding. I'm almost as interested in *an Niseag* now as you are."

He went back to the book he had left in the drawing room as the house settled into stillness. Annie Clanraith had already departed, before lunch, taking a sheaf of papers with her to type at home.

Presently he put the volume down on his thighs and lay passively thinking, stretched out on the couch. It was his uniquely personal method of tackling profound problems, to let himself relax into a state of blank receptiveness in which half-subconscious impressions could grow and flow together in delicately fluid adjustments that could presently mold a conclusion almost as concrete as knowledge. For some time he gazed sightlessly at the ceiling, and then he continued to meditate with his eyes closed.

He was awakened by Noel Bastion entering the room, humming tunelessly. The biographer of Wellington was instantly apologetic.

"I'm sorry, Templar—I thought you'd be in your room."

"That's all right." Simon glanced at his watch, and was mildly surprised to discover how sleepy he must have been. "I was doing some thinking, and the strain must have been too much for me."

"Eleanor relieved me an hour ago. I hadn't seen anything, I'm afraid."

"I didn't hear you come in."

"I'm pretty quiet on my feet. Must be a habit I got from commando training. Eleanor often says that if she could stalk like me she'd have a lot more trophies." Bastion went to the bookcase, took down a book, and thumbed through it for some reference. "I've been trying to do some work, but it isn't easy to concentrate."

Simon stood up and stretched himself.

"I guess you'll have to get used to working under difficulties if you're going to be a part-time monster hunter for ten years—isn't that how long Eleanor said she was ready to spend at it?"

"I'm hoping it'll be a good deal less than that."

"I was reading in this book *More Than a Legend* that in 1934, when the excitement about the monster was at its height, a chap named Sir Edward Mountain hired a bunch of men and organized a systematic watch like you were suggesting, but spacing them all around the lake. It went on for a month or two, and they got a few pictures of distant splashings, but nothing that was scientifically accepted."

Bastion put his volume back on the shelf. "You're still skeptical, aren't you?"

"What I've been wondering," said the Saint, "is why this savage behemoth with the big sharp teeth and the nutcracker jaws chomped up a dog but didn't swallow even a little nibble of it."

"Perhaps it isn't carnivorous. An angry elephant will mash

a man to pulp, but it won't eat him. And that dog could be very irritating, barking at everything—"

"According to what I heard, there wasn't any barking. And I'm sure the sheep it's supposed to have taken didn't bark. But the sheep disappeared entirely, didn't it?"

"That's what Clanraith says. But for all we know, the sheep may have been stolen."

"But that could have given somebody the idea of building up the monster legend from there."

Bastion shook his head.

"But the dog *did* bark at everyone," he insisted stubbornly.

"Except the people he knew," said the Saint, no less persistently. "Every dog is vulnerable to a few people. You yourself, for instance, if you'd wanted to, could have come along, and if he felt lazy he'd've opened one eye and then shut it again and gone back to sleep. Now, are you absolutely sure that nobody else was on those terms with him? Could a postman or a milkman have made friends with him? Or anyone else at all?"

The other man massaged his moustache.

"I don't know. . . . Well, perhaps Fergus Clanraith might."

Simon blinked.

"But it sounded to me as if he didn't exactly love the dog."

"Perhaps he didn't. But it must have known him pretty well. Eleanor likes to go hiking across country, and the dog always used to go with her. She's always crossing Clanraith's property and stopping to talk to him, she tells me. She gets on very well with him."

"What, that old curmudgeon?"

"I know, he's full of that Scottish Nationalist nonsense. But Eleanor is half-Scots herself, and that makes her almost human in his estimation. I believe they talk for hours about salmon fishing and grouse shooting."

"I wondered if he had an appealing side hidden away

somewhere," said the Saint thoughtfully, "or if Annie got it all from her mother."

Bastion's deep-set sooty eyes flickered over his appraisingly. "She's rather an attractive filly, isn't she?"

"I have a feeling that to a certain type of man, in certain circumstances, and perhaps at a certain age, her appeal might be quite dangerous."

Noel Bastion had an odd expression of balancing some answer on the tip of his tongue, weighing it for advisability, changing his mind a couple of times about it, and finally swallowing it. He then tried to recover from the pause by making a business of consulting the clock on the mantelpiece.

"Will you excuse me? Eleanor asked me to bring her a thermos of tea about now. She hates to miss that, even for *an Niseag.*"

"Sure."

Simon followed him into the kitchen, where a kettle was already simmering on the black coal stove. He watched while his host carefully scalded a teapot and measured leaves into it from a canister.

"You know, major," he said, "I'm not a detective by nature, even of the private variety."

"I know. In fact, I think you used to be just the opposite."

"That's true, too, I do get into situations, though, where I have to do a bit of deducing, and sometimes I startle everyone by coming up with a brilliant hunch. But as a general rule, I'd rather prevent a crime than solve one. As it says in your kind of textbooks, a little preventive action can save a lot of counterattacks."

The major had poured boiling water into the pot with a steady hand, and was opening a vacuum flask while he waited for the brew.

"You're a bit late to prevent this one, aren't you—if it *was* a crime."

"Not necessarily. Not if the death of Golly was only a steppingstone—something to build on the story of a missing sheep, and pave the way for the monster's next victim to be a person. If a person were killed in a similar way now, the monster explanation would get a lot more believers than if it had just happened out of the blue."

Bastion put sugar and milk into the flask, without measuring, with the unhesitating positiveness of practice, and took the lid off the teapot to sniff and stir it.

"But, good heavens, Templar, who could treat a dog like that, except a sadistic maniac?"

Simon lighted a cigarette. He was very certain now, and the certainty made him very calm.

"A professional killer," he said. "There are quite a lot of them around who don't have police records. People whose temperament and habits have developed a great callousness about death. But they're not sadists. They're normally kind to animals and even to human beings, when it's normally useful to be. But fundamentally they see them as expendable, and when the time comes they can sacrifice them quite impersonally."

"I know Clanraith's a farmer, and he raises animals only to have them butchered," Bastion said slowly. "But it's hard to imagine him doing what you're talking about, much as I dislike him."

"Then you think we should discard him as a red herring?"

Bastion filled the thermos from the teapot, and capped it.

"I'm hanged if I know. I'd want to think some more about it. But first I've got to take this to Eleanor."

"I'll go with you," said the Saint.

He followed the other out of the back door. Outside, the dusk was deepening with a mistiness that was beginning to do more than the failing light to reduce visibility. From the garden, one could see into the orchard but not beyond it.

"It's equally hard for the ordinary man," Simon continued relentlessly, "to imagine anyone who's lived with another person as man and wife, making love and sharing the closest moments, suddenly turning around and killing the other one. But the prison cemeteries are full of 'em. And there are plenty more on the outside who didn't get caught—or who are still planning it. At least half the time, the marriage has been getting a big dull, and someone more attractive has come along. And then, for some idiotic reason, often connected with money, murder begins to seem cleverer than divorce."

Bastion slackened his steps, half-turning to peer at Simon from under heavily contracted brows, then spoke slowly.

"I'm not utterly dense, Templar, and I don't like what you seem to be hinting at."

"I don't expect you to, chum. But I'm trying to stop a murder. Let me make a confession. When you and Eleanor have been out or in bed at various times, I've done quite a lot of prying. Which may be a breach of hospitality, but it's less trouble than search warrants. You remember those scratches in the ground near the dead dog which I said could've been made with something that wasn't claws? Well, I found a gaff among somebody's fishing tackle that could've made them, and the point had fresh shiny scratches and even some mud smeared on it which can be analyzed. I haven't been in the attic and found an embalmed shark's head with several teeth missing, but I'll bet Mackenzie could find one. And I haven't yet found the club with the teeth set in it, because I haven't yet been allowed down by the lake alone; but I think it's there somewhere, probably stuffed under a bush, and just waiting to be hauled out when the right head is turned the wrong way.

Major Bastion had come to a complete halt by that time.

"You unmitigated bounder," he said shakily. "Are you going to have the impertinence to suggest that I'm trying to murder my wife, to come into her money and run off with the farmer's daughter? Let me tell you that I'm the one who has the private income, and—"

"You poor feeble egotist," Simon retorted harshly. "I didn't suspect that for one second after she made herself rather cutely available to me, a guest in your house. She obviously wasn't stupid, and no girl who wasn't would have gambled a solid understanding with you against a transient flirtation. But didn't you ever read *Lady Chatterley's Lover?* Or the Kinsey Report? And hasn't it dawned on you that a forceful woman like Eleanor, just because she isn't a glamour girl, couldn't be bored to frenzy with a husband who only cares about the campaigns of Wellington?"

Noel Bastion opened his mouth, and his fists clenched, but whatever was intended to come from either never materialized. For at that moment came the scream.

Shrill with unearthly terror and agony, it split the darkening haze with an eldritch intensity that seemed to turn every hair on the Saint's nape into an individual icicle. And it did not stop, but ululated again and again in weird cadences of hysteria.

For an immeasurable span they were both petrified; and then Bastion turned and began to run wildly across the meadow, towards the sound.

"*Eleanor!*" he yelled, insanely, in a voice almost as piercing as the screams.

He ran so frantically that the Saint had to call on all his reserves to make up for Bastion's split-second start. But he did close the gap as Bastion stumbled and almost fell over something that lay squarely across their path. Simon had seen it an instant sooner, and swerved, mechanically identifying the steely glint that had caught his eye as a reflection from a long gun barrel.

And then, looking ahead and upwards, he saw through the blue fogginess something for which he would never completely believe his eyes, yet which would haunt him for the rest of his life. Something gray black and scaly-slimy, an immense amorphous mass from which a reptilian neck and head with strange protuberances reared and swayed far up over him. And in the hideous dripping jaws something of human shape, from which the screams came, that writhed and flailed ineffectually with a peculiar-looking club. . . .

With a sort of incoherent sob, Bastion scooped up the rifle at his feet and fired it. The horrendous mass convulsed; and into Simon's eardrums, still buzzing from the heavy blast, came a sickening crunch that cut off the last shriek in the middle of a note.

The towering neck corkscrewed with frightful power, and the thing that had been human was flung dreadfully towards them. It fell with a kind of soggy limpness almost at their feet, as whatever had spat it out lurched backwards and was blotted out by the vaporous dimness with the sound of a gigantic splash while Bastion was still firing again at the place where it had been. . . .

As Bastion finally dropped the gun and sank slowly to his knees beside the body of his wife, Simon also looked down and saw that her hand was still spasmodically locked around the thinner end of the crude bludgeon in which had been set a row of shark's teeth. Now that he saw it better, he saw that it was no homemade affair, but probably a souvenir of some expedition to the South Pacific. But you couldn't be right all the time, about every last detail. Just as a few seconds ago, and until he saw Bastion with his head bowed like that over the woman who had plotted to murder him, he had never expected to be restrained in his comment by the irrational compassion that finally moved him.

"By God," he thought, "now I know I'm aging."

But aloud he said: "She worked awfully hard to sell everyone on the monster. If you like, we can leave it that way. Luckily I'm a witness to what happened just now. But I don't have to say anything about—this."

He released the club gently from the grip of the dead fingers, and carried it away with him as he went to telephone Mackenzie.

A TROPICAL HORROR
BY WILLIAM HOPE HODGSON

Mariners have told tales for centuries of terrible creatures inhabiting the waters of the seven seas. Seventeenth and eighteenth century marine maps are festooned with sea serpents of every type and description, especially to signify "danger areas" theretofore unexplored. As Coleridge's Ancient Mariner says, 'Yea, slimy things did crawl with legs/Upon the slimy sea . . ."

The story that follows is an account of one ship's meeting with a monster of the deep, a "hideous creature [that] lies heaped in writhing, slimy coils," with "a vast slobbering mouth a fathom across." And a fearful account it is, told in graphic detail—a tale of pure riveting horror that is definitely not for the squeamish; what this creature does to the men of the barque Glen Doon, *homeward bound from Melbourne to London, is the terror of a thousand nightmares . . .*

William Hope Hodgson (1875–1918) was one of the finest craftsmen of the turn-of-the-century horror story. In his too-brief career he published several novels and dozens of poems and short stories ("A Tropical Horror" is one of the least known and most effective of these),

158

a large percentage involve the sea, where he had spent eight of his early years. His first novel was The Boats of the 'Glen Carrig' *(1907); a year later, his most acclaimed book,* The House on the Border-land, *appeared. Other works of note are* The Ghost Pirates, The Night Land, *and* Carnacki, The Ghost Finder—*the last-named a collection of superior stories about an investigator of psychic phenomena. Hodgson's life and contribution to the literature of the macabre were cut short by an exploding mortar shell in the waning days of World War I.*

WE ARE a hundred and thirty days out from Melbourne, and for three weeks we have lain in this sweltering calm.

It is midnight, and our watch on deck until four A.M. I go out and sit on the hatch. A minute later, Joky, our youngest 'prentice, joins me for a chatter. Many are the hours we have sat thus and talked in the night watches; though, to be sure, it is Joky who does the talking. I am content to smoke and listen, giving an occasional grunt at seasons to show that I am attentive.

Joky has been silent for some time, his head bent in medi-tation. Suddenly he looks up, evidently with the intention of making some remark. As he does so, I see his face stiffen with a nameless horror. He crouches back, his eyes staring past me at some unseen fear. Then his mouth opens. He gives forth a strangulated cry and topples backward off the hatch, striking his head against the deck. Fearing I know not what, I turn to look.

Great heavens! Rising above the bulwarks, seen plainly in the bright moonlight, is a vast slobbering mouth a fathom across. From the huge dripping lips hang great tentacles. As I look the Thing comes further over the rail. It is rising, rising, higher and higher. There are no eyes visible; only that fearful slobbering mouth set on the tremendous trunklike neck; which, even as I watch, is curling inboard with the stealthy celerity of an enormous eel. Over it comes in vast heaving folds. Will it never end? The ship gives a slow, sullen roll to starboard as she feels the weight. Then the tail, a broad, flat-shaped mass, slips over the teak rail and falls with a loud slump onto the deck.

For a few seconds the hideous creature lies heaped in writing, slimy coils. Then, with quick, darting movements, the monstrous head travels along the deck. Close by the mainmast stand the harness casks, and alongside of these a freshly opened cask of salt beef with the top loosely replaced. The smell of the meat seems to attract the monster, and I can hear it sniffing with a vast indrawing breath. Then those lips open, displaying four huge fangs; there is a quick forward motion of the head, a sudden crashing, crunching sound, and beef and barrel have disappeared. The noise brings one of the ordinary seamen out of the fo'cas'le. Coming into the night, he can see nothing for a moment. Then, as he gets further aft, he *sees,* and with horrified cries rushes forward. Too late! From the mouth of the Thing there flashes forth a long, broad blade of glistening white, set with fierce teeth. I avert my eyes, but cannot shut out the sickening "Glut! Glut!" that follows.

The man on the "lookout," attracted by the disturbance, has witnessed the tragedy, and flies for refuge into the fo'cas'le, flinging to the heavy iron door after him.

The carpenter and sailmaker come running out from the half-deck in their drawers. Seeing the awful Thing, they rush aft to the cabin with shouts of fear. The second mate, after one glance over the break of the poop, runs down the companionway with the helmsman after him. I can hear them barring the scuttle, and abruptly I realize that I am on the main deck alone.

So far I have forgotten my own danger. The past few minutes seem like a portion of an awful dream. Now, however, I comprehend my position and, shaking off the horror that has held me, turn to seek safety. As I do so my eyes fall upon Joky, lying huddled and senseless with fright where he has fallen. I cannot leave him there. Close by stands the empty half-deck—a little steel-built house with iron doors. The lee one is hooked open. Once inside I am safe.

Up to the present the Thing has seemed to be unconscious of my presence. Now, however, the huge barrel-like head sways in my direction; then comes a muffled bellow, and the great tongue flickers in and out as the brute turns and swirls aft to meet me. I know there is not a moment to lose, and, picking up the helpless lad, I make a run for the open door. It is only distant a few yards, but that awful shape is coming down the deck to me in great wreathing coils. I reach the house and tumble in with my burden; then out on deck again to unhook and close the door. Even as I do so something white curls round the end of the house. With a bound I am inside and the door is shut and bolted. Through the thick glass of the ports I see the Thing sweep round the house, in vain search for me.

Joky has not moved yet; so, kneeling down I loosen his shirt collar and sprinkle some water from the breaker over his face. While I am doing this I hear Morgan shout something; then comes a great shriek of terror, and again that sickening "Glut! Glut!"

Joky stirs uneasily, rubs his eyes, and sits up suddenly.

"Was that Morgan shouting—?" He breaks off with a cry. "Where are we? I have had such awful dreams!"

At this instant there is a sound of running footsteps on the deck and I hear Morgan's voice at the door.

"Tom, open—!"

He stops abruptly and gives an awful cry of despair. Then I hear him rush forward. Through the porthole, I see him spring into the fore rigging and scramble madly aloft. Something steals up after him. It shows white in the moonlight. It wraps itself around his right ankle. Morgan stops dead, plucks out his sheath-knife, and hacks fiercely at the fiendish thing. It lets go, and in a second he is over the top and running for dear life up the t'gallant rigging.

A time of quietness follows, and presently I see that the day is breaking. Not a sound can be heard save the heavy gasping breathing of the Thing. As the sun rises higher the creature stretches itself out along the deck and seems to enjoy the warmth. Still no sound, either from the men forward or the officers aft. I can only suppose that they are afraid of attracting its attention. Yet, a little later, I hear the report of a pistol away aft, and looking out I see the serpent raise its huge head as though listening. As it does so I get a good view of the fore part, and in the daylight see what the night has hidden.

There, right about the mouth, is a pair of little pig-eyes, that seem to twinkle with a diabolical intelligence. It is swaying its head slowly from side to side; then, without warning, it turns quickly and looks right in through the port. I dodge out of sight; but not soon enough. It has seen me, and brings its great mouth up against the glass.

I hold my breath. My God! If it breaks the glass! I cower, horrified. From the direction of the port there comes a loud, harsh, scraping sound. I shiver. Then I remember that there are little iron doors to shut over the ports in bad weather. Without a moment's waste of time I rise to my feet and slam to the door over the port. Then I go round to the others and do the same. We are now in darkness, and I tell Joky in a whisper to light the lamp, which, after some fumbling, he does.

About an hour before midnight I fall asleep. I am awakened suddenly some hours later by a scream of agony and the rattle of a water-dipper. There is a slight scuffling sound; then that soul-revolting "Glut! Glut!"

I guess what has happened. One of the men forrad has slipped out of the fo'cas'le to try and get a little water Evidently he has trusted to the darkness to hide his movements. Poor beggar! He has paid for his attempt with his life!

After this I cannot sleep, though the rest of the night passes quietly enough. Towards morning I doze a bit, but wake every few minutes with a start. Joky is sleeping peacefully; indeed, he seems worn out with the terrible strain of the past twenty-four hours. About 8 A.M. I call him, and we make a light breakfast off the dry ship's biscuit and water. Of the latter happily we have a good supply. Joky seems more himself, and starts to talk a little—possibly somewhat louder than is safe; for, as he chatters on, wondering how it will end, there comes a tremendous blow against the side of the house, making it ring again. After this Joky is very silent. As we sit there I cannot but wonder what all the rest are doing, and how the poor beggars forrad are faring, cooped up without water, as the tragedy of the night has proved.

Towards noon, I hear a loud bang, followed by a terrific bellowing. Then comes a great smashing of woodwork, and the cries of men in pain. Vainly I ask myself what has happened. I begin to reason. By the sound of the report it was evidently something much heavier than a rifle or pistol, and judging from the mad roaring of the Thing, the shot must have done some execution. On thinking it over further, I become convinced that, by some means, those aft have got hold of the small signal cannon we carry, and though I know that some have been hurt, perhaps killed, yet a feeling of exultation seizes me as I listen to the roars of the Thing, and realize that it is badly wounded, perhaps mortally. After a while, however, the bellowing dies away, and only an occasional roar, denoting more of anger than aught else, is heard.

Presently I become aware, by the ship's canting over to starboard, that the creature has gone over to that side, and a great hope springs up within me that possibly it has had enough of us and is going over the rail into the sea. For a time all is silent and my hope grows stronger. I lean across and nudge Joky, who is sleeping with his head on the table. He starts up sharply with a loud cry.

"Hush!" I whisper hoarsely. "I'm not certain, but I do believe it's gone."

Joky's face brightens wonderfully, and he questions me eagerly. We wait another hour or so, with hope ever rising. Our confidence is returning fast. Not a sound can we hear, not even the breathing of the beast. I get out some biscuits, and Joky, after rummaging in the locker, produces a small piece of pork and a bottle of ship's vinegar. We fall to with a relish. After our long abstinence from food the meal acts on us like wine, and what must Joky do but insist on opening the door, to make sure the Thing has gone. This I will not allow, telling him that at least it will be safer to open the iron port-covers first and have a look out. Joky argues, but I am immovable. He becomes excited. I believe the youngster is light-headed. Then, as I turn to unscrew one of the after-covers, Joky makes a dash at the door. Before he can undo the bolts I have him, and after a short struggle lead him back to the table. Even as I endeavor to quieten him there comes at the starboard door—the door that Joky has tried to open—a sharp, loud sniff, sniff, followed immediately by a thunderous grunting howl and a foul stench of putrid breath sweeps in under the door. A great trembling takes me, and were it not for the carpenter's tool chest I should fall. Joky turns very white and is violently sick, after which he is seized by a hopeless fit of sobbing.

Hour after hour passes, and, weary to death, I lie down on the chest upon which I have been sitting, and try to rest.

It must be about half-past two in the morning, after a somewhat longer doze, that I am suddenly awakened by a most tremendous uproar away forrad—men's voices shrieking, cursing, praying; but in spite of the terror expressed, so weak and feeble; while in the midst, and at times broken off short with that hellishly suggestive "Glut! Glut!" is the unearthly bellowing of the Thing. Fear incarnate seizes me, and I can only fall on my knees and pray. Too well I know what is happening.

Joky has slept through it all, and I am thankful.

Presently, under the door there steals a narrow riband of light, and I know that the day has broken on the second morning of our imprisonment. I let Joky sleep on. I will let him have peace while he may. Time passes, but I take little notice. The Thing is quiet, probably sleeping. About midday I eat a little biscuit and drink some of the water. Joky still sleeps. It is best so.

A sound breaks the stillness. The ship gives a slight heave, and I know that once more the Thing is awake. Round the deck it moves, causing the ship to roll perceptibly. Once it goes forrad—I fancy to again explore the fo'cas'le. Evidently it finds nothing, for it returns almost immediately. It pauses a moment at the house, then goes on further aft. Up aloft, somewhere in the fore-rigging, there rings out a peal of wild laughter, though sounding very faint and far away. The Horror stops suddenly. I listen intently, but hear nothing save a sharp creaking beyond the after end of the house, as though a strain had come upon the main rigging.

A minute later I hear a cry aloft, followed almost instantly by a loud crash on deck that seems to shake the ship. I wait in anxious fear. What is happening? The minutes pass slowly. Then comes another frightened shout. It ceases suddenly. The suspense has become terrible, and I am no longer able to bear it. Very cautiously I open one of the after port-covers, and peep out to see a fearful sight. There, with its tail upon the deck and its vast body curled round the mainmast, is the monster, its head above the topsail yard, and its great claw-armed tentacle waving in the air. It is the first proper sight that I have had of the Thing. Good heavens! It must weigh a hundred tons! Knowing that I shall have time, I open the port itself, then crane my head out and look up. There on the extreme end of the lower topsail yard I see one of the able seamen. Even down here I note the staring horror of his face. At this moment he sees me and gives a weak, hoarse cry for help. I can do nothing for him. As I look the great tongue shoots out and licks him off the yard, much as might a dog a fly off the window pane.

Higher still, but happily out of reach, are two more of the men. As far as I can judge they are lashed to the mast above the royal yard. The Thing attempts to reach them, but after a futile effort it ceases, and starts to slide down, coil on coil, to the deck. While doing this I notice a great gaping wound on its body some twenty feet above the tail.

I drop my gaze from aloft and look aft. The cabin door is torn from its hinges, and the bulkhead—which, unlike the half-deck, is of teak wood—is partly broken down. With a shudder I realize the cause of those cries after the cannon shot. Turning I screw my head round and try to see the foremast, but cannot. The sun, I notice, is low, and the night is near. Then I draw in my head and fasten up both port and cover.

How will it end? Oh! How will it end?

After a while Joky wakes up. He is very restless, yet though he has eaten nothing during the day I cannot get him to touch anything.

Night draws on. We are too weary—too dispirited to talk. I lie down, but not to sleep. . . . Time passes.

A ventilator rattles violently somewhere on the main deck, and there sounds constantly that slurring, gritty noise. Later I hear a cat's agonized howl, and then again all is quiet. Some time after comes a great splash alongside. Then, for some hours all is silent as the grave. Occasionally I sit up on the chest and listen, yet never a whisper of noise comes to me. There is an absolute silence, even the monotonous creak of the gear has died away entirely, and at last a real hope is springing up within me. That splash, this silence—surely I am justified in hoping. I do not wake Joky this time. I will prove first for myself that all is safe. Still I wait. I will run no unnecessary risks. After a time I creep to the after-port and listen; but there is no sound. I put up my hand and feel at the screw, then again I hesitate, yet not for long. Noiselessly I begin to unscrew the fastening of the heavy shield. It swings loose on its hinge, and I pull it back and peer out. My heart is beating madly. Everything seems strangely dark outside. Perhaps the moon has gone behind a cloud. Suddenly a beam of moonlight enters through the port, and goes as quickly. I stare out. Something moves. Again the light streams in, and now I seem to be looking into a great cavern, at the bottom of which quivers and curls something palely white.

My heart seems to stand still! It is the Horror! I start back and seize the iron port-flap to slam it to. As I do so, something strikes the glass like a steam ran, shatters it to atoms, and flicks past me into the berth. I scream and spring away. The port is quite filled with it. The lamp shows it dimly. It is curling and twisting here and there. It is as thick as a tree, and covered with a smooth slimy skin. At the end is a great claw, like a lobster's, only a thousand times larger. I cower down into the farthest corner. . . . It has broken the tool chest to pieces with one click of those frightful mandibles. Joky has crawled under a bunk. The Thing sweeps round in my direction. I feel a drop of sweat trickle slowly down my face—it tastes salty. Nearer comes that awful death. . . . Crash! I roll over backwards. It has crushed the water breaker against which I leaned, and I am rolling in the water across the floor. The claw drives up, then down, with a quick uncertain movement, striking the deck a dull, heavy blow, a foot from my head. Joky gives a little gasp of horror. Slowly the Thing rises and starts feeling its way round the berth. It plunges into a bunk and pulls out a bolster, nips it in half and drops it, then moves on. It is feeling along the deck. As it does so it comes across a half of the bolster. It seems to toy with it, then picks it up and takes it out through the port . . .

A wave of putrid air fills the berth. There is a grating sound, and something enters the port again—something white and tapering and set with teeth. Hither and thither it curls, rasping over the bunks, ceiling, and deck, with a noise like that of a great saw at work. Twice it flickers above my head, and I close my eyes. Then off it goes again. It sounds now on the opposite side of the berth and nearer to Joky. Suddenly the harsh, raspy noise becomes muffled, as though the teeth were passing across some soft substance. Joky gives a horrid little scream, that breaks off into a bubbling, whistling sound. I open my eyes. The tip of the vast tongue is curled tightly round something that drips, then is quickly withdrawn, allowing the moonbeams to steal again into the berth. I rise to my feet. Looking round, I note in a mechanical sort of way the wrecked state of the berth—the shattered chests, dismantled bunks, and something else—

"Joky!" I cry, and tingle all over.

There is that awful Thing again at the port. I glance round for a weapon. I will revenge Joky. Ah! There, right under the lamp, where the wreck of the carpenter's chest strews the floor, lies a small hatchet. I spring forward and seize it. It is small, but so keen—so keen! I feel its razor edge lovingly. Then I am back at the port. I stand to one side and raise my weapon. The great tongue is feeling its way to those fearsome remains. It reaches them. As it does so, with a scream of "Joky! Joky!" I strike savagely again and again and again, gasping as I strike; once more, and the monstrous mass falls to the deck, writhing like a hideous eel. A vast, warm flood rushes in through the porthole. There is a sound of breaking steel and an enormous bellowing. A singing comes in my ears and grows louder—louder. Then the berth grows indistinct and suddenly dark.

Extract from the log of the steamship *Hispaniola*.

June 24.–Lat.___ N. Long.___ W. 11 A.M.–Sighted four-masted barque about four points on the port bow, flying signal of distress. Ran down to her and sent a boat aboard. She proved to be the *Glen Doon*, homeward bound from Melbourne to London. Found things in a terrible state. Decks covered with blood and slime. Steel deck-house stove in. Broke open door, and discovered youth of about nineteen in last stage of inanition, also part remains of boy about fourteen years of age. There was a great quantity of blood in the place, and a huge curled-up mass of whitish flesh, weighing about half a ton, one end of which appeared to have been hacked through with a sharp in-strument. Found forecastle door open and hanging from one hinge. Doorway bulged, as though something had been forced through. Went inside. Terrible state of affairs, blood everywhere, broken chests, smashed bunks, but no men nor remains. Went aft again and found youth show-ing signs of recovery. When he came round, gave the name of Thompson. Said they had been attacked by a huge serpent—thought it must have been sea serpent. He was too weak to say much, but told us there were some men up the mainmast. Sent a hand aloft, who reported them lashed to the royal mast, and quite dead. Went aft to the cabin. Here we found the bulkhead smashed to pieces, and the cabin door lying on the deck near the after-hatch. Found body of captain down lazarette, but no officers. Noticed amongst the wreckage part of the carriage of a small cannon. Came aboard again.

Have sent the second mate with six men to work her into port. Thompson is with us. He has written out his version of the affair. We certainly consider that the state of the ship, as we have found her, bears out in every respect his story. (Signed)

William Norton (Master).
Tom Briggs (1st Mate).

DANIEL WEBSTER AND THE SEA SERPENT
BY STEPHEN VINCENT BENÉT

Not all sea creatures, of course, are the slobbering monsters of "A Tropical Horror." Most are probably benign, in fact—and some may even be downright benevolent. Not to mention intelligent, attractive, lovesick, and self-sacrificing. You don't think so? Ah, then you're in for a revelation when you encounter, as Daniel Webster and his friends do, the creature who rises out of the briny deep off the coast of New England—

"Neighbors, that was a sight! Shaking the hook from its jaw, it rose, the sea serpent of the Scriptures, exact and to specifications as laid down in the Good Book, with its hairy face and its furlong on furlong of body, wallowing and thrashing in the troubled sea. As it rose, it gave a long low melancholy hoot, like a kind of forsaken steamboat . . ."

Her name is Samanthy, it develops, and quite a "lady" she is. You're bound to find her as engaging as Dan'l does in this good-humored and

171

often rollicking story—a nice change of pace from the horrors we've seen so far.

Stephen Vincent Benét (1898–1943) is a writer who, like the author of the preceding selection, died young but who contributed a large body of important literary work during his short lifetime. He was twice recipient of the Pulitzer Prize for poetry—in 1929 with his narrative poem about the Civil War, John Brown's Body; *and in 1944 with an unfinished and posthumously published narrative poem,* Western Star. *Another of his humorous Daniel Webster stories, "The Devil and Daniel Webster," was adapted by Benét into the libretto for a folk opera, which was later made into the film* All That Money Can Buy *(1941). His other books include the novels* Young People's Pride *and* Spanish Bayonet, *and the volumes of poetry* Five Men and Pompey *and* Heavens and Earth.

IT HAPPENED, one summer's day, that Dan'l Webster and some of his friends were out fishing. That was in the high days of his power and his fame, when the question wasn't if he was going to be President but when he was going to be President, and everybody at Kingston depot stood up when Dan'l Webster arrived to take the cars. But in spite of being Secretary of State and the biggest man in New England, he was just the same Dan'l Webster. He bought his Jamaica personal and in the jug at Colonel Sever's store in Kingston, right under a sign saying ENGLISH AND WEST INDIA GOODS, and he never was too busy to do a hand's turn for a friend. And, as for his big farm at Marshfield, that was just the apple of his eye. He buried his favorite horses with their shoes on, standing up in a private graveyard, and wrote Latin epitaphs for them, and he often was heard to say that his big Hungarian bull, St. Stephen, had more sense in his rear off-hoof than most politicians. But, if there was one thing he loved better than Marshfield itself, it was the sea and the waters around it, for he was a fisherman born.

This time, he was salt-water fishing in the *Comet,* well out of sight of land. It was a good day for fishing, not too hazy, but not too clear, and Dan'l Webster enjoyed it, as he enjoyed everything in life, except maybe listening to the speeches of Henry Clay. He'd stolen a half-dozen days to come up to Marshfield, and well he needed the rest, for we'd nearly gone to war with England the year before, and now he was trying to fix up a real copper-riveted treaty that would iron out all the old differences that still kept the two countries unfriendly. And that was a job, even for Dan'l Webster. But as soon as he stepped aboard the *Comet,* he was carefree and heartwhole. He had his real friends around him and he wouldn't allow a word of politics talked on the boat—though that rule got broken this time, and for a good reason, as you'll see. And when he struck his first cod, and felt the fish take the hook, a kind of big slow smile went over his features, and he said, "Gentlemen, this is solid comfort." That was the kind of man he was.

I don't know how many there were of them aboard—half a dozen or so—just enough for good company. We'll say there were George Blake and Rufus Choate and young Peter Harvey and a boy named Jim Billings. And, of course, there was Seth Peterson, Dan'l's boat captain, in his red flannel shirt, New England as cod and beach plums, and Dan'l Webster's fast friend. Dan'l happened to be Secretary of State, and Seth Peterson happened to be a boat captain, but that didn't make any difference between them. And, once the *Comet* left dock, Seth Peterson ran the show, as it's right that a captain should.

Well, they'd fished all morning and knocked off for a bite of lunch, and some had had segars and snoozes afterward, and some hadn't, but in any case, it was around midafternoon, and everybody was kind of comfortable and contented. They still fished, and they fished well, but they knew in an hour or so they'd be heading back for home with a fine catch on board. So maybe there was more conversation than Seth Peterson would have approved of earlier, and maybe some jokes were passed and some stories told. I don't know, but you know how it is when men get together at the end of a good day. All the same, they were still paying attention to their business—and I guess it was George Blake that noticed it first.

"Dan'l," he said, breathing hard, "I've got something on my line that pulls like a Morgan horse."

"Well, yank him in!" sang out Dan'l, and then his face changed as his own line began to stiffen and twang. "George," he said, "I beat you! I got something on my line that pulls like a pair of steers!"

"Give 'em more line, Mr. Webster!" yells Seth Peterson, and Dan'l did. But at that, the line ran out so fast it smoked when it hit the water, and any hands but Dan'l Webster's would have been cut to the bone. Nor you couldn't see where it went to, except Something deep in the waters must be pulling it out as a cat pulls yarn from a ball. The veins in Dan'l Webster's arm stood out like cords. He played the fish and played the fish; he fought it with every trick he knew. And still the little waves danced and the other men gaped at the fight—and still he couldn't bring the Something to time.

"By the big elm at Marshfield!" he said at last, with his dark face glowing and a fisherman's pride in his eyes. "Have I hooked on to a frigate with all sails set? I've payed out a mile of my own particular line, and she still pulls like ten wild horses. Gentlemen, what's this?"

And even as he said it, the tough line broke in two with a crack like a musket shot, and out of the deep of ocean, a mile away, the creature rose, majestic. Neighbors, that was a sight! Shaking the hook from its jaw, it rose, the sea serpent of the Scriptures, exact and to specifications as laid down in the Good Book, with its hairy face and its furlong on furlong of body, wallowing and thrashing in the troubled sea. As it rose, it gave a long low melancholy hoot, like a kind of forsaken steamboat; and when it gave out that hoot, young Jim Billings, the boy, fainted dead away on the deck. But nobody even noticed him—they were all staring at the sea serpent with bulging eyes.

Even Dan'l Webster was shaken. He passed his hand for a moment across his brow and gave a sort of inquiring look at the jug of Jamaica by the hatch.

"Gentlemen," he said in a low voice, "the evidence—the ocular evidence would seem to be conclusive. And yet, speaking as a lawyer—"

"Thar she blows! I never thought to see her again!" yells Seth Peterson, half-driven out of his mind by the sight, as the sea serpent roiled the waters. "Thar she blows, by the Book of Genesis! Oh, why ain't I got a harpoon?"

"Quiet, Seth," said Dan'l Webster. "Let us rather give thanks for being permitted to witness this glorious and unbelievable sight." And then you could see the real majesty of the man, for no sooner were the words out of his mouth than the sea serpent started swimming straight toward the *Comet.* She came like a railway train and her wake boiled out behind her for an acre. And yet, there was something kind of skittish about her, too—you might say that she came kind of shaking her skirts and bridling. I don't know what there was about her that made you sure she was a female, but they were all sure.

She came, direct as a bullet, till you could count the white teeth shining in her jaws. I don't know what the rest of them did—though doubtless some prayers were put up in a hasty way—but Dan'l Webster stood there and faced her, with his brow dark and his eyes like a sleepy lion's, giving her glance for glance. Yes, there was a minute, there, when she lifted her head high out of water and they looked at each other eye to eye. They say hers were reddish but handsome. And then, just as it seemed she'd crash plumb through the *Comet,* she made a wide wheel and turned. Three times she circled the boat, hooting lonesomely, while the *Comet* danced up and down like a cork on the waves. But Dan'l Webster kept his footing, one hand gripping the mast, and whenever he got a chance, he fixed her with his eye. Till finally, on the third circuit, she gave one last long hoot—like twenty foghorns at once, it was, and nearly deafened them all—and plunged back whence she'd come, to the bottomless depths of the sea.

But even after the waters were calm again, they didn't say anything for quite a while. Till, finally, Seth Peterson spoke.

"Well, Mr. Webster," he said, "that one got away"—and he grinned a dry grin.

"Leviathan of the Scriptures! Give me paper and pen," said Dan'l Webster. "We must write this down and attest it." And then they all began to talk.

Well, he wrote an account of just what they'd seen, very plain and honest. And everybody there signed his name to it. Then he read it over to them again aloud. And then there was another silence, while they looked at one another.

Finally, Seth Peterson shook his head, slow and thoughtful.

"It won't do, Dan'l," he said, in a deep voice.

"Won't do?" said Dan'l Webster, with his eyes blazing. "What do you mean, Seth?"

"I mean it just won't do, Dan'l," said Seth Peterson, perfectly respectful, but perfectly firm. "I put it up to you, gentlemen," he said, turning to the others. "I can go home and say I've seen the sea serpent. And everybody'll say, 'Oh, that's just that old liar, Seth Peterson.' But if it's Dan'l Webster says so—can't you see the difference?"

He paused for a minute, but nobody said a word.

"Well, I can," he said. He drawled out the words very slow. "Dan'l Webster—Secretary of State—sees and talks to a sea serpent—off Plymouth Bay. Why, it would plumb ruin him! And I don't mind being ruint, but it's different with Dan'l Webster. Would you vote for a man for President who claimed he'd saw the sea serpent? Well, would you? Would anybody?"

There was another little silence, and then George Blake spoke.

"He's right, Dan'l," he said, while the others nodded. "Give me that paper." He took it from Dan'l Webster's hand and threw it in the sea.

"And now," he said in a firm voice, "I saw cod. Nothing but cod. Except maybe a couple of halibut. Did any gentleman here see anything else?"

Well, at that, it turned out, of course, that nobody aboard had seen anything but cod all day. And with that, they put back for shore. All the same, they all looked over their shoulders a good deal till they got back to harbor.

And yet Dan'l Webster wasn't too contented that evening, in spite of his fine catch. For, after all, he had seen the sea serpent, and not only seen her but played her on the line for twenty-seven minutes by his gold repeater, and, being a fisherman, he'd like to have said so. And yet, if he did—Seth was right—folks would think him crazy or worse. It took his mind off Lord Ashburton and the treaty with England—till, finally, he pushed aside the papers on his desk.

"Oh, a plague on the beast!" he said, kind of crossly. "I'll leave it alone and hope it leaves me alone." So he took his candle and went up to bed. But just as he was dropping off to sleep, he thought he heard a long low hoot from the mouth of Green Harbor River, two miles away.

The next night the hooting continued, and the third day there was a piece in the Kingston paper about the new government foghorn at Rocky Ledge. Well, the thing began to get on Dan'l Webster's nerves, and when his temper was roused he wasn't a patient man. Moreover, the noises seemed to disturb the stock—at least his overseer said so—and the third night his favorite gray kicked half the door out of her stall. "That sea serpent's getting to be an infernal nuisance," thought Dan'l Webster. "I've got to protect my property." So, the fourth night he put on his old duck-shooting clothes and took his favorite shotgun, Learned Selden, and went down to a blind at the mouth of Green Harbor River, to see what he could see. He didn't tell anybody else about his intentions, because he still felt kind of sensitive about the whole affair.

Well, there was a fine moon that night, and sure enough, about eleven o'clock, the sea serpent showed up, steaming in from ocean, all one continuous wave length, like a giant garden hose. She was quite a handsome sight, all speckled with the moonlight, but Dan'l Webster couldn't rightly appreciate it. And just as she came to the blind, she lifted her head and looked sorrowfully in the direction of Marshfield and let out a long low soulful hoot like a homesick train.

Dan'l Webster hated to do it. But he couldn't have a sea serpent living in Green Harbor River and scaring the stock—not to speak of the universal consternation and panic there'd be in the countryside when such a thing was known. So he lifted Learned Selden and gave her both barrels for a starter, just a trifle over her head. And as soon as the gun exploded, the sea serpent let out a screech you could hear a mile and headed back for open sea. If she'd traveled fast before, she traveled like lightning now, and it wasn't anytime before she was just a black streak on the waters.

Dan'l Webster stepped out of the blind and wiped his brow. He felt sorry, but he felt relieved. He didn't think she'd be back, after that sort of scare, and he wanted to leave everything shipshape before he went down to Washington, next morning. But next day, when he told Seth Peterson what he'd done, he didn't feel so chipper. For, "You shouldn't have done that, Mr. Webster," said Seth Peterson, shaking his head, and that was all he would say except a kind of mutter that sounded like "Samanthy was always particular set in her likes." But Dan'l didn't pay any attention to that, though he remembered it later, and he was quite short with Seth for the first time in their long relationship. So Seth shut up like a quahog, and Dan'l took the cars for Washington.

When he got there he was busy enough, for the British treaty was on the boil, and within twenty-four hours he'd forgot all about the sea serpent. Or thought he had. But three days later, as he was walking home to his house on Lafayette Square, with a senator friend of his, in the cool of the evening, they heard a curious noise. It seemed to come from the direction of the Potomac River.

"Must have got a new whistle for the Baltimore night boat," said the senator. "Noisy too."

"Oh, that's just the bullfrogs on the banks," said Dan'l Webster steadily. But he knew what it was, just the same, and his heart sank within him. But nobody ever called Dan'l Webster a coward. So, as soon as he'd got rid of the senator, he went down to the banks of the Potomac. Well, it was the sea serpent, all right.

She looked a little tired, as well she might, having swum from Plymouth Bay. But as soon as she saw Dan'l Webster, she stretched out her neck and gave a long low loving hoot. Then Dan'l knew what the trouble was and, for once in his life, he didn't know what to do. But he'd brought along a couple of roe herring, in a paper, just in case; so he fed them to her and she hooted, affectionate and grateful. Then he walked back to his house with his head bowed. And that very night he sent a special express letter to Seth Peterson at Marshfield, for, it seemed to him, Seth must know more about the business than he let on.

Well, Seth got to Washington as fast as the cars would bring him, and the very evening he arrived Dan'l sent him over to interview the serpent. But when Seth came back, Dan'l could see by his face that he hadn't made much progress.

"Could you talk to her, Seth?" he said, and his voice was eager. "Can she understand United States?"

"Oh, she can understand it all right," said Seth. "She's even picking up a few words. They was always a smart family, those Rocky Ledge serpents, and she's the old maid of the lot, and the best educated. The only trouble with 'em is, they're so terrible sot in their ways."

"You might have warned me, Seth," said Dan'l Webster, kind of reproachful, and Seth looked uncomfortable.

"Well, to tell you the truth," he said, "I thought all of 'em was dead. Nor I never thought she'd act up like this—her father was as respectable a serpent as you'd see in a long summer's day. Her father—"

"Bother her father!" said Dan'l Webster and set his jaw. "Tell me what she says."

"Well, Mr. Webster," said Seth, and stared at his boots, "she says you're quite a handsome man. She says she never did see anybody quite like you," he went on. "I hate to tell you this, Mr. Webster, and I feel kind of responsible, but I think you ought to know. And I told you that you oughtn't to have shot at her—she's pretty proud of that. She says she knows just how you meant it. Well, I'm no great hand at being embarrassed, Mr. Webster, but, I tell you, she embarrassed me. You see, she's been an old maid for about a hundred and fifty years, I guess, and that's the worst of it. And being the last of her folks in those particular waters, there's just no way to restrain her—her father and mother was as sensible, hardworking serpents as ever gave a feller a tow through a fog, but you know how it is with those old families. Well, she says wherever you go, she'll follow you, and she claims she wants to hear you speak before the Supreme Court—"

"Did you tell her I'm a married man?" said Dan'l. "Did you tell her that?"

"Yes, I told her," said Seth, and you could see the perspiration on his forehead. "But she says that doesn't signify—her being a serpent and different—and she's fixing to move right in. She says Washington's got a lovely climate and she's heard all about the balls and the diplomatic receptions. I don't know how she's heard about them, but she has." He swallowed. "I got her to promise she'd kind of lie low for two weeks and not come up the Potomac by daylight—she was fixing to do that because she wants to meet the President. Well, I got her to promise that much. But she says, even so, if you don't come to see her once an evening, she'll hoot till you do, and she told me to tell you that you haven't heard hooting yet. And as soon as the fish market's open, I better run down and buy a barrel of flaked cod, Mr. Webster—she's partial to flaked cod and she usually takes it in the barrel. Well, I don't want to worry you, Mr. Webster, but I'm afraid that we're in a fix."

"A fix!" said Dan'l Webster. "It's the biggest fix I ever was in in my life!"

"Well, it's kind of complimentary, in a way, I guess," said Seth Peterson, "but—"

"Does she say anything else?" said Dan'l Webster, drawing a long breath.

"Yes, Mr. Webster," said Seth Peterson, his eyes on his boots. "She says you're a little shy. But she says she likes that in a man."

Dan'l Webster went to bed that night, but he didn't sleep. He worked and worked those great brains of his till he nearly wore out the wheels, but he still couldn't think of a way to get rid of the sea serpent. And just about the time dawn broke, he heard one long low hoot, faithful and reminiscent, from the direction of the Potomac.

Well, the next two weeks were certainly bad ones for him. For, as the days wore on, the sea serpent got more and more restive. She wanted him to call her Samanthy, which he wouldn't, and she kept asking him when he was going to introduce her into society, till he had to feed her Italian sardines in olive oil to keep her quiet. And that ran up a bill at the fish market that he hated to think of—besides her continually threatening to come up the Potomac by day. Moreover, and to put the cap on things, the great Webster-Ashburton treaty that was to make his name as Secretary of State had struck a snag and England didn't seem at all partial to admitting the American claims. Oh, it was a weary fortnight and a troublesome one!

The last afternoon of the fortnight, he sat in his office and he didn't know where to turn. For Lord Ashburton was coming to see him for a secret conference that night at nine, and he had to see the sea serpent at ten, and how to satisfy either of them he didn't know. His eyes stared wearily at the papers on his desk. He rang the bell for his secretary.

"The corvette *Benjamin Franklin* reports—" he said. "This

should have gone to the Navy Department, Mr. Jones." Then he glanced at the naval report again and his eyes began to glow like furnaces. "By the bones of Leviathan! I've got it!" he said, with a shout. "Where's my hat, Mr. Jones. I must see the President at once!"

There was a different feeling about the house on Lafayette Square that evening, for Dan'l Webster was himself again. He cracked a joke with Seth Peterson and took a glass of Madeira and turned it to the light. And when Lord Ashburton was announced—a nice, white-haired old gentleman, though a little stiff in his joints—he received him with all the courtesy of a king.

"I am glad to see you so much restored, Mr. Webster," said Lord Ashburton, when the greetings had been exchanged. "And yet I fear I bring you bad news. Concerning clauses six and seven of the proposed treaty between Her Majesty's Government and the United States of America, it is my duty to state—"

"My lord, let us drop the clauses for a moment and take the wider view," said Dan'l Webster, smiling. "This is a matter concerning the future welfare and peace of two great nations. Your government claims the right to search our ships; that right we deny. And our attitude seems to you preposterous. Is that not so?"

"I would hesitate to use the word 'preposterous,' " said Lord Ashburton cautiously. "Yet—"

"And yet," said Dan'l Webster, leaning forward, "there are things which may seem preposterous, and yet are not. Let me put a case. Let us say that Great Britain has the strongest navy afloat."

"Britannia rules the waves," said Lord Ashburton, with a noble smile.

"There were a couple she didn't rule in 1812," said Dan'l

Webster, "but let that pass. Let me ask you, Lord Ashburton, and let me ask you solemnly, what could even the power and might of Britain's navy avail against Leviathan?"

"Leviathan?" said Lord Ashburton, rather coldly. "Naturally, I understand the Biblical allusion. Yet—"

"The sea serpent," said Dan'l Webster, kind of impatient. "What could all Britain's navy do against the sea serpent out of the Scriptures?"

Lord Ashburton stared at him as if he had gone mad. "God bless my soul, Mr. Secretary!" he said. "But I fail to see the point of your question. The sea serpent doesn't exist!"

"Doesn't he—I mean she?" said Dan'l Webster, calmly. "And suppose I should prove to you that it does exist?"

"Well, 'pon my word! God bless my soul!" said Lord Ashburton, kind of taken aback. "Naturally—in that case—however—but even so—"

Dan'l Webster touched a bell on his desk. "Lord Ashburton," he said, kind of solemn, "I am putting my life, and what is dearer to me, my honor and reputation, in your hands. Nevertheless, I feel it necessary, for a better understanding between our two countries."

Seth Peterson came into the room and Dan'l nodded at him.

"Seth," he said, "Lord Ashburton is coming with us to see Samanthy."

"It's all right if you say so, Mr. Webster," said Seth Peterson, "but he'll have to help carry the sardines."

"Well, 'pon my word! Bless my soul! A very strange proceeding!" said Lord Ashburton, but he followed along.

Well, they got to the banks of the Potomac, the three of them, and when they were there, Seth whistled. Samanthy was lying mostly under water, behind a little brushy island, but when she heard the whistle, she began to heave up and uncoil, all shining in the moonlight. It was what you might call a kind of impressive sight. Dan'l Webster looked at Lord Ashburton, but Lord Ashburton's words seemed sort of stuck in his throat.

Finally he got them out. "Bless my soul!" he said. "You Americans are very extraordinary! Is it alive?"

But then all he could do was goggle, for Samanthy had lifted her head, and giving a low friendly hoot, she commenced to swim around the island.

"Now, is that a sea serpent or isn't it?" said Dan'l Webster, with a kind of quiet pride.

"Indubitably," said Lord Ashburton, staring through his eyeglass. "Indubitably," and he kind of cleared his throat. "It is, indeed and in fact, a serpent of the sea. And I am asleep and in bed, in my room at the British Embassy." He pinched himself. "Ouch!" he said. "No, I am not."

"Would you call it sizable, for a sea serpent?" persisted Dan'l Webster.

Lord Ashburton stared again through his eyeglass. "Quite," he said. "Oh, yes, quite, quite!"

"And powerful?" asked Dan'l.

"I should judge so," said Lord Ashburton, faintly, as the sea serpent swam around and around the island and the waves of its wake broke crashing on the bank. "Yes, indeed, a very powerful engine of destruction. May I ask what it feeds upon?"

"Italian sardines, for preference," said Dan'l. "But that's beside the point." He drew a long breath. "Well, my lord," he said, "we're intending to commission that sea serpent as a regular and acknowledged war vessel in the United States Navy. And then, where's your wooden walls?"

Lord Ashburton, he was a diplomat, and his face didn't change expression as he stared first at the sea serpent and then at the face of Dan'l Webster. But after a while, he nodded. "You need not labor the point, Mr. Secretary," he said. "My government, I am sure, will be glad to reconsider its position on the last two clauses and on the right of search."

"Then I'm sure we can reach an agreement," said Dan'l Webster, and wiped the sweat from his brow." "And now, let's feed Samanthy."

He whistled to her himself, a long musical whistle, and she came bounding and looping in toward shore. It took all three of them to heave her the barrel of sardines, and she swallowed it down in one gulp. After that, she gave a hoot of thanks and gratitude, and Lord Ashburton sat down on the bank for a minute and took snuff. He said that he needed something to clear his mind.

"Naturally," he said, after a while, "Her Majesty's Government must have adequate assurances as to the good conduct of this—this lady." He'd meant to say "creature" at first, but Samanthy rolled her eye at him just then, and he changed the word.

"You shall have them," said Dan'l Webster, and whistled Samanthy even closer. She came in kind of skittish, flirting her coils, and Lord Ashburton closed his eyes for a minute. But when Dan'l Webster spoke, it was in the voice that hushed the Senate whenever he rose.

"Samanthy," he said, "I speak to you now as Secretary of State of the United States of America." It was the great voice that had rung in the Supreme Court and replied to Hayne, and even a sea serpent had to listen respectful. For the voice was mellow and deep, and he pictured Samanthy's early years as a carefree young serpent, playing with her fellows, and then her hard life of toil and struggle when she was left lone and lorn, till even Seth Peterson and Lord Ashburton realized the sorrow and tragedy of her lonely lot. And then, in the gentlest and kindest way you could ask, he showed her where her duty lay.

"For, if you keep on hooting in the Potomac, Samanthy," he said, "you'll become a public menace to navigation and get sat upon by the Senate Committee for Rivers and Harbors. They'll drag you up on land, Samanthy, and put you in the Smithsonian Institution; they'll stick you in a stagnant little pool and children will come to throw you peanuts on Sundays, and their nurses will poke you with umbrellas if you don't act lively enough. The U.S. Navy will shoot at you for target practice, Samanthy, and the scientists will examine you, and the ladies of the Pure Conduct League will knit you a bathing suit, and you'll be bothered every minute by congressmen and professors and visitors and foreign celebrities till you won't be able to call your scales your own. Oh, yes, it'll be fame, Samanthy, but it won't be good enough. Believe me, I know something about fame and it's begging letters from strangers and calls from people you don't know and don't want to know, and the burden and wear and tear of being a public character till it's enough to break your heart. It isn't good enough, Samanthy; it won't give you back your free waters and your sporting in the deep. Yes, Samanthy, it'd be a remarkable thing to have you here in Washington, but it isn't the life you were meant for and I can't take advantage of your trust. And now," he said to Seth Peterson, "just what does she say?"

Seth Peterson listened, attentive, to the hootings.

"She says the Washington climate isn't what she thought it was," he said. "And the Potomac River's too warm; it's bad for her sciatica. And she's plumb tired of sardines."

"Does she say anything about me?" asked Dan'l Webster, anxiously.

"Well," said Seth Peterson, listening, "she says—if you'll

excuse me, Mr. Webster—that you may be a great man, but you wouldn't make much of a sea serpent. She says you haven't got enough coils. She says—well, she says no hard feelings, but she guesses it was a mistake on both sides."

He listened again. "But she says one thing," he said. "She says she's got to have recognition and a husband, if she has to take this Lord Ashburton. She says he doesn't look like much, but he might get her introduced at Court."

A great light broke over Dan'l's face and his voice rang out like thunder. "She shall have them both," he said. Come here, Samanthy. By virtue of the authority vested in me as Secretary of State, and by special order of the President of the United States and the Secretary of the Navy, as witness the attached commission in blank which I now fill in with your name, I hereby attach you to the United States Navy, to rank as a forty-four-gun frigate on special duty, rating a rear admiral's flag and a salute of the appropriate number of guns, wherever encountered in American waters. And, by virtue of the following special order, I hereby order you to the South Seas, there to cruise until further orders for the purpose of seeking a suitable and proper husband, with all the rights, privileges, duties, and appurtenances pertaining to said search and said American citizenship, as aforesaid and Hail Columbia. Signed John Tyler, President. With which is subjoined a passport signed by Daniel Webster, Secretary of State, bidding all foreign nations let pass without hindrance the American citizen, Samanthy Doe, on her lawful journeys and errands." He dropped his voice for a moment and added reflectively, "The American corvette, *Benjamin Franklin*, reports sighting a handsome young male sea serpent on February third of the present year, just off the coast of the Sandwich Islands. Said serpent had forty-two coils by actual count, and when last sighted was swimming SSW at full speed."

But hardly had he spoken when Samanthy, for the last time, lifted her head and gave out a last long hoot. She looked upon Dan'l Webster as she did so, and there was regret in her eye. But the regret was tinctured with eagerness and hope.

Then she beat the water to a froth, and, before they really saw her go, she was gone, eaving only her wake on the moonlit Potomac.

"Well," said Dan'l Webster, yawning a little, "there we are. And now, Lord Ashburton, if you'll come home with me, we can draw up that treaty."

"Gladly," said Lord Ashburton, brushing his coat with his handkerchief. "Is it really gone? 'Pon my soul! You know, for a moment, I imagined that I actually saw a sea serpent. You have a very vivid way of putting things, Mr. Webster. But I think I understand the American attitude now, from the—er—analogy you were pleased to draw between such a—er—fabulous animal and the young strength of your growing country."

"I was confident that you would appreciate it, once it was brought to your attention," said Dan'l Webster. But he winked one eye at Seth Peterson, and Seth Peterson winked back.

And I'll say this for Dan'l Webster, too—he kept his promises. All through the time he was Secretary of State, he saw to it that the forty-four-gun frigate, *Samanthy Doe,* was carried on a special account on the books of the Navy. In fact, there's some people say that she's still so carried, and that it was her give Ericsson the idea for building the *Monitor* in the Civil War—if she wasn't the *Monitor* herself. And when the White Fleet went around the world in Teddy Roosevelt's time—well, there was a lookout in the crow's-nest of the flagship, one still calm night, as they passed by the palmy isles of the South Seas. And all of a sudden, the water boiled, tremendous and phosphorescent, and there was a pair of sea serpents and seven young ones, circling, calm and majestic, three times around the fleet. He rubbed his eyes and stared, but there they were. Well, he was the only one that saw it, and they put him in the brig for it next morning. But he swore, till the day he died, they were flying the Stars and Stripes.

TERROR IN CUT-THROAT COVE

BY ROBERT BLOCH

Sea serpents are not the only creatures of great size (and great malevolence) who might have taken up residence at the bottom of an ocean. Nor does such a creature have to be indigenous to the sea, or spawned in the mists of our prehistoric past. It could be from another dimension altogether, a thing so alien and terrible that we cannot even begin to understand the nature of its evil.

"Terror in Cut-Throat Cove" postulates the existence of just such a monster, hidden for centuries beneath the placid blue waters of the West Indies. A truly malefic monster, of the type created by H. P. Lovecraft in his classic horror fiction of the twenties and thirties. Indeed, Robert Bloch's story is part of Lovecraft's Cthulhu mythos (many other authors, notably August Derleth and Lin Carter, have perpetuated the mythos in the years since Lovecraft's death in 1936), and may even outdo the master in its portrait of those otherworldly creatures who

struggle to cross the gulfs between them and us for the sole purpose of destroying mankind. Perhaps you'll be able to sleep after reading it; some people can. If so—pleasant dreams . . .

Although he is best known as the author (both novel and screen versions) of Psycho, *Robert Bloch has been scaring the wits out of horror-story fans for close to fifty years. (His first story was published in* Weird Tales *in 1934, when he was just seventeen years old; that story was also a tribute to and a pastiche of Lovecraft's work.) He has published hundreds of short stories and two-score novels and collections, among them* The Scarf, The Dead-Beat, Nightworld, American Gothic, The Opener of the Way, Blood Runs Cold, *and* The King of Terrors. *He has also written and adapted innumerable radio plays, teleplays, and screenplays. A native Midwesterner, he now makes his home in Los Angeles.*

YOU WON'T find Cut-Throat Cove on any map, because that is not its real name. And you can search a chart of the West Indies thoroughly without locating the island of Santa Rita.

I have changed the names for obvious reasons. If those reasons are not obvious at the moment, they will be by the time you finish this account.

My own name is Howard Lane, and I lived on Santa Rita for almost a year without ever hearing of Cut-Throat Cove. That isn't too surprising, for it wasn't the lure of buccaneers and bullion that brought me here—in fact, you might say I left the United States just to get away from the atmosphere of piracy and plunder which dominates the modern commercial scene.

You might say it, but *I did* say it, night after night, in Rico's

Bar. Eventually, of course, I'd stop talking and fall down. Nobody ever paid much attention to me—before, or after.

Except on the night when I met Don and Dena. The teddy-bear and the Christmas-tree angel.

I had a little bit too much of Rico's rum that evening, and I admit it. But even after I got to know them I still thought my first impression was right.

Teddy-bear. That was Don, standing at the bar beside me; blonde, burly, his short arms thick and bare and covered with that soft golden fuzz; his nose splayed and pink, and his eyes like big brown buttons. I watched him order a drink, American beer. American beer, in cans, at a dollar a throw! And he was tossing American money on the bar—a twenty. That was enough to make me look twice. We seldom get strangers or tourists in Santa Rita, and the infrequent visitors never have any money. So I watched the teddy-bear as he carried the two cans of beer over to a table in the corner. And that's when I saw her sitting across from him.

The Christmas-tree angel. Her dress was white and wispy, her hair was spun gold, her eyes china blue. The complexion was peaches-and-cream, the peaches being slightly ripened by the sun. She laughed up at the teddy-bear as he approached, and I felt an unreasoning resentment.

Why is it always that way? Why does that kind of a girl always pick that kind of a man?

I'd asked myself that question a thousand times. I'd asked it ever since I'd come to Santa Rita a year ago. In fact, that's the real reason I *had* come; because once *I'd* picked just such a girl—only to find she picked that sort of man.

And I knew what he was, the moment I looked at him. He was the Muscle Beach Boy, the bushy-eyebrows type, the kind who shows up in all the cigarette ads with a tattoo on his hand. I made a little bet with myself about what would happen after he had poured out the beer. Sure enough, I won. He took hold of the empty beer can in one hamlike hand and squeezed, crushing it flat.

That made *her* laugh again, and I knew why. Because she wasn't a Christmas-tree angel, after all. She was just the kind of girl who fooled my kind of man into thinking that's what she was. So that we treated her that way: like a fragile, precious, enchanting ornament at the unattainable top of the tree of illusion. Until one of these crude animals came along to grab her with his furry paws, drink his fill, slake his lust, then squeeze her and toss her aside. But she liked that. Beer cans are made to be crushed. Laughing beer cans and tattoed teddy-bears.

Yes, I was drunk enough, I suppose, with my stupid similes and maudlin metaphors and the whole sickening mixture of cheap cynicism, sentimental self-pity, and raw rum.

Drunk enough so that when the teddy-bear returned to the bar and ordered another round, I pretended complete indifference. Even after he tapped me on the shoulder, I took my own ill-natured time before turning around.

"Care for a drink?" he asked.

I shrugged. "No, thank you."

"Come on, have a beer! Thought maybe you'd like to join us—we're strangers here, and we'd like to get acquainted."

That intrigued me. I knew the teddy-bear type, or thought I did. And while they're often full of false geniality at the bar, they *never* invite you to join them when they have a Christmas-tree angel in tow. Unless, of course, there's some ulterior motive involved.

Well, I had ulterior motives, too. American beer was a dollar a can—and I hadn't been able to lay a dollar bill down on the bar for a single drink in over eight months now.

I nodded. He held out a golden paw.

"My name's Don Hanson."

"Howard Lane."

"Pleased to meet you. Come on over, I'd like you to meet Dena, here. Dena, this is Howard Lane." He turned to me. "Dena Drake, my secretary."

I stared at her.

"It's really *Dinah*," she told me. "Like in the song. But Danny Kaye made a recording once, years ago, before I was born, and he pronounced it *Dena*, and that's what my older sister called me. So I guess I'm stuck with it. Everybody does a doubletake when they hear it."

I nodded, but not in agreement. It wasn't her name that caused me to stare. It was Don Hanson's description of her as his secretary. Their relationship was so obvious I couldn't imagine anyone except a child coming up with such an uninspired lie. Besides, it wasn't necessary here. Santa Rita isn't Santa Monica—only a newcomer would feel it necessary to apologize for the obvious. Still, this Don Hanson *was* a newcomer. In fact, that's what he was talking about now.

"Just got in before sundown," he was saying. "Little surprised to see how small this place—not even a hotel, is there? Doesn't matter, really, because I can sleep right on the boat."

"You came in your own boat?"

"It's a yacht," Dena said. "We sailed all the way from Barbados."

Don chuckled. "Pay no attention to her. It isn't much of a yacht, and besides, the crew did all the sailing. We couldn't be bothered, could we, honey?"

I would have liked it if Dena had blushed. But she didn't blush; she squealed as Don did his crushing act with the beer cans again.

Then he turned to me and grinned. "Lucky I ran into you this way," he said. "I was intending to look you up very soon."

"That's right," Dena chimed in. "We don't speak Spanish, either of us, but Roberto—that's the first mate of our crew—he does, and he talked to somebody here in town after we landed. That's how we found out you're the only white man on the whole island."

"Is that true?" Don asked. "Are you living down here all alone with these blacks?"

"No," I said.

"But they told Roberto—"

"No," I repeated. "It is not true. There are very few pure-blooded blacks on Santa Rita. The bulk of the population is of mixed blood; *mestizo* and *marino* and even more complicated combinations of African, Carib, Spanish, Portuguese, and French racial stocks. These people are for the most part simple and uneducated, but they have pride."

"Sure, I understand. I thank you for the tip. But you are the only white man."

"According to your interpretation of anthropology, yes."

"Dig him." Dena giggled. She gave me a melting sideways glance from beneath the long eyelashes—the kind of a glance such girls practice while sitting before a mirror and curling those eyelashes. "You'll pardon my curiosity, but just what are you doing way off here in this god-forsaken place?"

"I am drinking your employer's beer," I said, in a flat voice. "And for the past year I have been drinking rum. And this is not a god-forsaken place. It is an exotic tropical paradise, compete with cockroaches, beetles, bedbugs, mosquitoes, flies, and black widow spiders. Only one form of vermin is unknown here—the tax-collector. His absence more than makes up for the presence of the other insect pests, and also explains my own."

"You a tax-dodger, is that it?" Dena's voice held genuine interest. "A gambler on the lam, maybe?"

I shrugged. "I'm afraid it's not quite that romantic. I happen to be a free-lance writer with an unpredictable income. Having no family ties, I decided to look around for a place where the cost of living is low. Here in Santa Rita I have rented a roomy old furnished house built in the days of Spanish occupation, acquired a devoted couple as servants, and supplied myself with ample food—for less than I'd spend in such mainland paradises as Downhill, Oklahoma or Flyspeck, Utah."

"But don't you ever get lonely?"

"I was lonely long before I came to Santa Rita," I told her. "You can be lonely in New York."

"Brother, don't I know it!" Her smile seemed a little more genuine, but I didn't have an opportunity to analyze it.

Don put his hand on my arm. "Free-lance writer, eh? How's it going?"

"So-so. Some months good, some months not so good. It varies."

"Well. Maybe you'd like to earn a few bucks. I could use a little help."

"What doing?"

"Oh, sort of straightening things out with the local natives. You know these people, maybe you could smooth the way for me. I'd like to get a couple of permits, for one thing."

"Fishing? You don't need anything for that."

"Not fishing, exactly. Diving."

"He's a marvelous skindiver," Dena said. "Absolutely fabulous."

I nodded. "That won't require any official permission, either."

"Even if it's a salvage job?"

"Salvage?"

"Treasure," Dena said. "Why don't you level with him, darling?"

"Why don't you shut up?" Don scowled. He turned it into a grin for me. "All right, you might as well know. I've got a lead on something pretty big down here."

"Wait a minute," I said. "Did somebody sell you a map?"

"No, it isn't a map. It's a manuscript. An old manuscript."

I nodded. "And it describes how one of the galleons laden with bullion from the Inca mines was wrecked and sunk right here off the shoals of Santa Rita, in clear water. Is that it?" I gave him back his grin, with interest. "Why, that's one of the stalest yarns in the Indies! Somebody's always waiting to make a sucker out of the tourists with that gag. As far as I know, nobody has salvaged a Spanish treasure ship anywhere in Caribbean waters for years."

Don shook his head. "Perhaps we'd better get a few things straight," he said. "First of all, I know about the treasure ship dodge. I've knocked around these parts for a couple of years, mostly diving, and doing some fishing for kicks. A man can really live down here."

"The Hemingway bit," I said.

"Did you know Papa?"

"I spit in his milk. I'm a Beatrix Potter fan, myself."

"You don't say," Don muttered. "Well, anyway, I'm not a sucker fresh out of Miami. And I've gotten together a pretty good crew of boys. Five of them, including this mate of mine, Roberto. It was his father who had the manuscript."

"Don went after him when the sharks got him," Dena said. "He told me about it. He pulled him out, but his legs were gone and—"

"Knock it off. Maybe I should have left you on the boat. Or back in Barbados." He gave us each our portion of that frown-and-grin routine again, then continued. "Well, the father died, and Roberto came to me with this manuscript. He'd found it in with the old man's effects. Didn't know what it was–neither he nor the father could read English."

"You keep talking about a manuscript," I said. "Just what is it, really?"

"Actually, it's a sort of a journal."

"Written by an old prisoner on old Spanish parchment, and watermarked 1924, in Yonkers?"

"Nothing like that. And it isn't your treasure ship yarn, either." He leaned across the table. "Look here. I'm no brain, but I wouldn't sail a crew of five all the way down here to this crummy little island unless I was pretty sure there was something in it for me. So you needn't do the needling bit. You want to take a look at it for yourself, come aboard tomorrow morning. Then you can decide if you want in or not."

I hesitated, thinking of the teddy-bear and the Christmas-tree angel, and how I'd come all this way just to avoid playing with toys again. I had resolved that.

On the other hand, I could use some extra money—for eating, and for drinking, too. Drinking helped me to forget about teddy-bears and angels.

So I stood up and I bowed politely and I said, "Yes, it's a date," to the teddy-bear. And all the while I couldn't take my eyes off the angel . . .

At ten o'clock the next morning I sat on the forward deck of the *Rover*, reading *Isaih Horner, Hys Journal: Thyse Beeing A True Acct. Of The Voyage of The Black Star; 1711 Anno Domino.*

Don had told the truth. It wasn't a Spanish manuscript at all; it was written in the quaint and barbarous English of a semiliterate seaman in the first years of the eighteenth century. The crabbed handwriting was atrocious, the spelling and grammar worse, and no forger would have been inspired to disguise his bait with a long, rambling preliminary account of a sea voyage.

I'll make no attempt to reproduce the contents of the journal, but it was obviously genuine. Isaih Horner had been second mate of the *Black Star* during what he smugly described as a "trading voyage" to the Isthmus and the northern coast of Venezuela—but it took no great perception to realize that the principal business of the vessel was armed piracy. Indeed, Captain Barnaby Jakes, his commander, bears a name well known to anyone who has ever followed the history of the Brotherhood of the Coast; and there were a number of references to meetings with other gentlemen familiar to students of buccaneer lore. Moreover, the *Black Star* did no "trading"; instead, it "confiscated" the property of several Spanish and Portuguese ships which it intercepted en route from the Isthmus.

But the big prize was the *Santa Maria*—not Columbus's vessel, but a namesake, built well over a hundred years later in Spanish shipyards to convey the wealth of the new world to the coffers of His Most Christian Majesty.

The captain had learned that the *Santa Maria* was departing for Spain on its annual voyage, laden with a most unusual cargo of booty—the fruit of no less than three forays during which the conquistadores had penetrated far more deeply than ever before into the jungles south of Venezuela, in what is now known as the Amazon backwaters. A civilization had been ravished; not the Inca, but a valley people, worshiping a deity of their own and offering it sacrifice on an altar of beaten gold. The altar and the trappings of the temples constituted the sole "treasure"—but from rumored accounts, this was enough. There was, for example, a huge golden "chest" or "ark" which had been transported on the long march to the coast by no less than forty captured native slaves. Just why the gold had not been melted down into portable ingots on the spot was not made clear, except that the accounts mentioned a certain padre accompanying the expedition who insisted that the artifacts of pagan religion be kept intact. Indeed, there was some confusion as to whether or not he approved of removing the temple's contents at all; apparently there had been actual conflict with the commander of the expedition, and a number of men had died during the return journey to Spain.

But that was not important. What mattered was that the booty had been placed aboard the *Santa Maria,* in the deep hold designed for the conveyance of such cargoes, and the ship was sailing for Spanish waters, accompanied by a convoy of two lighter escort vessels, fully armed for protection against piratical marauders.

All this had Isaih Horner's commander learned; and so, apparently, had a number of other freebooters whose spies were active in the ports.

Normally, Captain Barnaby Jakes would not have acted upon this knowledge. The *Black Star,* with its twelve small guns and its mongrel crew of forty, preyed on smaller game; there were few members of the Brotherhood, even those equipped with a fleet of larger vessels, who ever dared attack a full-sized galleon, let alone one accompanied by an armed and alert escort. For pirates, despite the romantic lore and legend accumulating about their exploits through the centuries, were not lions in courage. They could more aptly be compared to jackals, or at best, hyenas. They sought out the defenseless, the crippled ships, the wrecks, and by the eighteenth century the days of the great early commanders—Henry Morgan, L'Olonnais and their like—were past.

The true "buccaneers" of the Indies had vanished; those who remained would seldom board an armed brigantine, let alone sack a city.

So Captain Barnaby Jakes had no intention of attempting to intercept the *Santa Maria* and her sister ships. Not until he heard of the storm.

A small sloop drifted up out of southern waters, and he rescued—and later slew—its two surviving crew members. But not before he had their eyewitness accounts of the great tempest in which they saw the *Santa Maria* riding the waves alone, after one of her escort ships foundered and the other was sent careering off its course.

The *Santa Maria,* crippled and alone, would have to put in at the nearest port now. And that would be the island of Santa Rita. If she could be caught in open waters—

The *Black Star* bore south for Santa Rita.

Isaih Horner, writing in his *Journal,* spoke piously enough of "the duties of a subject of Hys Mafestie" to harass the Popish Enemy and take legitimate spoils. But it was an expedition of piracy, impure and simple, and it might have succeeded, for they bore down on the *Santa Maria* just outside Santa Rita harbor.

The only trouble was, another "subject of Hys Mafestie" had found her first.

Closing in on her, cutting across her bows as she wallowed towards the safety of the shore, was a vessel which both Captain Jakes and mate Isaih Horner recognized immediately as the pride of one Ned Thatch, alias Edward Teach, alias Blackbeard. Because of a strict *punctilio* observed among the Brotherhood—and because Blackbeard's ship was easily twice the size and carried three times the guns of the little *Black Star*—there was nothing to do but stand by and watch the battle.

The *Santa Maria* had lost a mast in the storm, and its rudder did not function properly. Apparently most of its guns were out of commission, too, for while it fired defensive salvos as it lumbered along, there was not enough threat in its volleys to prevent Blackbeard from heading her off from the harbor entrance. The big galleon was forced to hug the shore and make for another opening along the coast of the island. Blackbeard followed, closing in without firing. That was ever his way—to hold his fire until almost alongside, and then let a direct volley rake the hull and then the decks.

Not until the *Santa Maria* had almost gained the shelter of the cove at the far side of the island did this opportunity occur. Blackbeard closed in quickly, then stood about for a direct broadside. It came, with a roar. The great galleon rocked and shuddered. The gunners reloaded for a second salvo, even more shattering than the first. The *Santa Maria,* riding low in the water, attempted to turn. A foremast toppled in a shroud of smoke. Now was the time to close in for the kill—grappling irons were ready, the boarding-pikes mustered. If enough shots had penetrated the vitals of the ship, it would sink within five or six hours; but a boarding party could secure surrender and transfer the treasure long before then. Blackbeard, presumably, was ready to lead the attack; as was his usual custom, he'd be lighting the candles he'd twisted into his beard, and carrying the pots of brimstone he hurled before boarding the enemy's deck. One more broadside, now—

It came. And the *Santa Maria* rolled with the blast, then careened tipsily to one side.

According to eyewitness Isaih Horner, watching from the deck of the *Black Star* at a distance of less than a mile away, the shots were directed at the top-deck of the galleon. But it was as though the entire discharge of thirty ship's cannons had simultaneously penetrated the vessel below the waterline, as if something had ripped the keel out of the Spanish ship.

For with a roaring and a roiling, with a great tidal tremor, the *Santa Maria* sank like a plummet before his very eyes. The water shot up from the opened hatchways, "lyke a verritable fountin" and Blackbeard, instead of boarding, hastily sheered off to avoid being caught in the almost instantaneous vortex of a whirlpool set up by the downward plunge of the great galleon. Within the space of two minutes the *Santa Maria* was gone. It had sunk into the waters of Cut-Throat Cove.

The journal did not end here. It told of how Blackbeard and Captain Barnaby Jakes made common ground in a salvage attempt, but were unable to send men down into the deep water to reach the vessel. There were several survivors whose accounts were reported and paraphrased—none of them could explain why the ship had so suddenly and inexplicably perished, except in terms of sailors' superstitions. It had been a "black voyage" and there was a "curse" upon the ship; they should not have carried the treasures of a "heathen temple." Isaih Horner had small patience with these notions—neither had Blackbeard or Captain Jakes. Being somewhat short of rations, and even more short of temper after the loss of such a prize, they merely slit the throats of the Spanish seamen and sent them down to follow their fellows.

It was impossible to land at Santa Rita—the Spanish garrison would undoubtedly be sending out vessels of its own against the intruders—so Blackbeard and the *Black Star* went their separate ways.

Isaih Horner's journal ended abruptly, a few pages later. He'd put in at Kingston, Jamaica, and was thinking of giving up "the life of a mariner."

"And that's just what he did," Don told me, as I laid the manuscript down on top of the oiled pouch in which it had been preserved. "I guess he turned to robbery on land. Anyway, when I tried to trace down what had become of him, I found out that an Isaih Horner was hanged for purse-snatching in the Government Docks in 1712."

"Then you checked on all this?" I asked.

"Of course I did. I told you I hadn't come down here on a wild goose chase. Found out everything I could. About the *Santa Maria,* the storm, the sinking. It's in the records."

"What about the treasure?"

"There isn't much. But it stands to reason that it existed. They never sent a galleon back to Spain with an escort unless it was loaded. Besides, this story of Horner's impressed me a lot more because it spoke about an altar and temple trappings instead of the usual guff—you know, gold bullion, chests of jewels, stuff like that. There wasn't any such thing anyway, except during the early days when the Spaniards went after the Aztecs and the Inca tribes."

"But if it's in the records, then why didn't others try salvaging the ship?"

"They did. Trouble is, it's in fairly deep water—I'd say somewhere between two hundred and three hundred feet. And up until a dozen years ago, it was impossible to dive that far safely, or to do any work at such a depth. Now we have the technique and the equipment. And we have the details we need. Five hundred yards offshore, just east of the cove entrance."

"How would you lift up an altar, or a heavy chest?"

"We'd have to go back for a big rig. What I want to do now is locate the wreck. That's a job in itself—have you any idea what happens to a boat that has been under water for almost two hundred and fifty years? Just finding its topmasts above the silt is hard enough to do." Don shrugged. "But that's no concern of yours. What I want is a little help from you in handling the local authorities. Explain what we're here for, that we're a research expedition, interested in salvaging historical relics. You don't need to mention the gold."

"I see."

Don eyed me. "Well, why should you? It isn't *their* property, is it? The laws of salvage—"

"According to the laws of salvage, you'd need a government permit to start work; not from here but from the mainland."

"All right, so I didn't make arrangements. Why can't you go to the mayor or whatever the head man calls himself and just get his okay? You can handle him. And I'm willing to spend a few bucks."

"How much?"

"How much do you think it will take?"

"Well, a hundred dollars is a fortune down here."

"That's pretty reasonable." He nodded. "I'll go another couple of hundred for you, if you can sew it up. What we want is permission to dive over at the cove, without any interference from the natives. Nobody should be allowed to hang around. Get it?"

"Got it!"

"How long do you think it'll take to line up the deal?"

"I can probably see Jose Robales this morning. He's the mayor of Santa Rita; the inland villages have *jefes* of their own, but they don't count. I should have word for you before the day is over."

"Make it in writing."

"Will do." I held out my hand. "He'll expect payment in advance."

"Right." Don reached into his jacket, pulled out his wallet. He extracted three one-hundred-dollar bills quite casually.

I was equally casual, an hour later, when I flipped one of the bills to Jose Robales in his little office near the waterfront. He signed the permit with a flourish.

"Remember," he told me, "I take your word for it that these people will not create problems here. You are to observe them as my representative and see that the crew keeps away from the village at the cove."

"I understand. I'll keep an eye on them, I promise."

"That is good. Then there will be no trouble, no?"

"There will be no trouble, no," I echoed.

But I was wrong . . .

The trouble came almost ten days later, when Don finally located the ship.

He'd moved to the area outside the cove immediately, of course, and anchored in fifty fathoms, five hundred yards out. Roberto and Juan Perez—another crew member—assisted him in the actual diving operations, while the other three attended to arrangements topside. They put down a heavy shot-line, with handholds, and it hit bottom at two hundred and sixty feet. Nobody got down that far until the third day; it takes time to get accustomed to such depths. And even when they managed to reach the ocean floor, that didn't locate the vessel for them. As Don explained, the ship itself would be covered with silt and almost undetectable. The shifting of the sands, the alteration of the shoreline itself through the long years; these factors added to the problem. It would take time and patience.

I came out every day; I beached a rowboat on the shore of the cove and it wasn't a long pull. I sat there and watched the operations. After they hit bottom, Don did most of the diving himself. Every second dive, he'd haul anchor and try a new location. By the time a week had passed they'd explored an area several hundred yards in circumference without finding a thing. But Don wasn't discouraged yet—just tired.

Dena was bored.

I'd sit with her on the deck of the yacht while Don was diving, and listen to her complain. She didn't care if Roberto and the others overheard her; actually, they were much too busy up forward to pay any attention to us.

"Pleasure trip!" she murmured. "He hauls me way off here to the middle of nowhere, and for what? To sit on my fanny out in the hot sun all day long while he's down there playing footsie with the fishes. Then at night he's tired, wants to turn in right away—not that there's anything else to do for excitement over on that crummy island of yours. A big nothing, that's all it is."

"Then why did you come along in the first place?"

Dena shrugged.

"Did he promise you a share of the treasure?"

"In a way." She scowled at me. "Not that it's any of your business."

"You in love with him?"

"That isn't any of your business, either."

"All right. I'm sorry."

"You don't have to be. I can take care of myself."

"So I notice."

"You notice a lot, don't you?"

"It's my business. I'm a writer, remember?"

"I'll bet you are." She lit a cigarette. "What would a writer want in a nowhere like this place?"

"Now *you're* getting personal," I told her. "But I *am* a writer. I've got books aaand stuff up at the house to prove it. Want to see them?"

"I've seen books already, thanks. Also etchings."

"That isn't what I had in mind."

"Don't kid me. I haven't met a man since I was fifteen who had anything else in mind. They always want to show me something. When I came aboard Don's boat back in Barbados, he was going to show me the portable bar."

"Then why did you accept his invitation, if you knew the way it would turn out?"

"Maybe I wanted it to turn out that way."

"Then you *are* in love with him."

"Shut up!" She turned away, tossing her cigarette over the side. It arced down and hissed into the waves. "All right, what's the sense of putting on an act? When I was eighteen I was singing with a band. I had a contract with G.A.C. and a chance to do a TV show, just a summer replacement deal on sustaining, but they told me it could build into something big if I got a few breaks. That was seven years ago, and I'm still waiting for the breaks. I haven't been with G.A.C. for a long time, and I haven't done any television, either. Six months ago I got a chance to play a night spot in San Juan. It wasn't a very good one, but the one in Port-au-Prince was worse, and the one in Trinidad was just plain lousy. I ended up in Barbados without a job, and without a dime. Then Don Hanson came along with his boat. I didn't care what kind of a guy he was or what kind of a boat he had. I wanted out. So, as the sun sinks in the west, we say farewell to beautiful Barbados. End of story."

"You don't really like him, do you?"

"I hate his guts. He's the kind of a guy who's always had plenty of money and is still greedy for more. He's the kind of a guy who always had plenty of muscles, but still has to use them to show off—and to push other people around. As far as

he's concerned, I'm not even a person; just another conven-
ience he wanted to take along on the trip, like his portable
bar."

"Then why don't you—"

"What? Ditch him and come with you to your island paradise? Don't give me that, chum. You've got nothing to offer.
But nothing." The blue eyes were level. "I didn't ask you for
your sad story, but I'll bet I already know it. There was a girl
in it, wasn't there? And another guy, who took her away,
while you sat mooning around. I've met your kind before—the
sensitive intellectual type, isn't it? Which is just another way
of saying you don't have any guts. I told you I hated Don's
guts, but at least he *has* some. Enough to go out after what he
wants. He'd never ask me to pull a sneak on another man;
he'd fight him for me. Would you fight Don? Not in a million
years!"

I sighed. "You're right," I said. "And very honest."

"I shouldn't have said that," she told me. "If I was really
honest, I'd admit I'm not worth fighting for. Not any more."

"Suppose I think differently. Suppose I'm willing to fight?"

"You couldn't win." She sighed again, and lighted another
cigarette. "Guys like you can never win. This is a money-
and-muscle world. Them as has, gits. Even if the prize is only
a beat-up bleached blonde with a bad case of the whim-
whams. Oh, let's forget it, shall we?"

I was going to tell her that I wouldn't forget it, that I
preferred an angel who admitted truthfully to a little tarnish,
and that maybe both of us were a bit too cynical and defeatist
for our own good.

But I never got the opportunity.

Because suddenly there was a commotion up forward, and
a babble of excited Spanish. Don was coming up—he was
clinging to the shot-line twenty feet down, spending five

minutes in stage decompression before being hauled aboard. His body was perfectly visible in the clear water; the weird fins, the goggles, the cylinder-assembly and regulator on his back all part of an eerie ensemble.

We waited patiently until he tugged three times, giving the signal for hauling up the line. Roberto and Juan hoisted him to the deck. He stood there, shivering slightly, while they unstrapped his equipment. Then he took off his goggles and grinned.

"I've found it," he said.

"No—are you sure?"

"Positive." He nodded, reaching for a towel. "And it's better than we could have hoped for. Went down on its side, right into a big rock crevice that protected the top-deck from silting. Part of the deck itself is still clear, and I could see what's left of the masts and forward cabin. We ought to be able to clear a path inside almost immediately—just chop a hole in the hull." He turned to Roberto. "But don't take my word for it! Here, I want you to go down and take a look for yourself, right now. And then Juan. The sooner all three of us have had a look at her and compared notes the better. Got your stuff?"

Roberto nodded, then hurried below. By the time Don had towelled himself back to warmth, taken a shot of brandy and accepted a cigarette, Roberto was already lowering himself over the side.

We watched him disappear along the shot-line, going down into the water.

Dena was excited. "What's it look like?" she asked. "Can you really see anything down there?"

Don lifted his head impatiently. "Of course you can," he told her. "It gets quite dark about halfway, but once you actually hit the bottom there's a lot of reflected sunlight; it seems to penetrate the dark, transparent area above. The light is bluish, but you can make out objects quite easily. I recognized the boat at once, even though it doesn't look much like a galleon any more."

"Everything's covered with slime, eh?" I asked.

"Slime? Whatever gave you that idea?" Don stared at me. "Trouble with you writers—you get everything out of books. Make a few dives yourself and you'd find out differently. There's no slime. The wood is just about eaten away and the metal structure is just a skeleton. Lots of little marine animals covering it. And fish everywhere—millions of 'em. You know, I may even have guessed wrong about the hull; maybe there's only the iron hasps and what I thought was wood was just a solid mass of fish. They like to swarm where there's some protection. Roberto should be able to tell us more when he comes back."

"It takes a long time to make a dive, doesn't it?"

"Going down is easy, if you're carrying a shot like he is. But coming back is slow work. You have to make at least three stops for decompression, to avoid the bends." There was a waterproof watch strapped to Don's wrist. He parted the golden fuzz and glanced at it. "I'd say he's due up again in about fifteen minutes. Should just be at the first stage of decompression now, about fifty feet under." He went over to the rail where the rest of the crew was gathered. "See anything yet?" he asked.

"No," Juan told him.

"Well, he ought to give the first signal soon."

We watched the rope, but it remained taut.

"Fifteen minutes," Don muttered to himself.

But it wasn't fifteen minutes. It was less than one minute later that Juan shouted, "Here he come!" and he wasn't pointing along the shot-line either, but far offside, beyond the rail.

"You're crazy!" Don grunted. "That's some damn fish, surfacing."

"No—is Roberto!" Juan said.

I stared. What broke water certainly wasn't a fish, for fish lack arms and legs, and they do not wear apparatus on their backs.

"Madre de Dios!" Juan cried. "Is Roberto!"

It was Roberto, all right, but I'd never have recognized him floating there in the water, his body swollen and distorted grotesquely by the change in pressure. Nor was that the worst of it.

Roberto's body had come up from the wreck below. But it no longer had a head . . .

"Of course it wasn't a shark," Don said. "No shark could bite like that. Besides, the way it was sheared off—"

He kept his voice low, even though Dena had gone below to her bunk.

"How about a squid?" I asked. "I've read about the way the big ones hole up in wrecks down there."

"You've *read!*" He gave me a pitying look. "Maybe you'd better read a little more. A squid isn't the answer, either. There isn't any kind of marine creature that could take a man's head off clean at the shoulders. And that includes whales, in case you also happen to have read *Moby Dick*." Don glanced at the body lying on the deck, covered with a tarpaulin. "No, the answer's not a fish or an animal, either. Roberto must have left the line and gone off to explore the wreck. And my guess about the fish is probably right. There is no solid hull left, only a framework. When Roberto reached the wreck, the fish swam off. My guess is that he tried to enter what's left of the ship, swimming between the ribs. And then—"

He drew a finger across his throat. It wasn't a pleasant gesture, but it was extremely graphic.

"But how could that do it?" I persisted. "I don't pretend to know the way those old boats were put together, but if they used iron, surely it was in big pieces. There wouldn't be any razor edges to worry about."

Don shrugged. "Do you know what happens to metal after it's been under water for a few hundred years? It wears down, eventually just crumbles away. Gold wouldn't, but old iron—"

"Then how could it be so sharp, and how would it hold up to slice a man's head from his shoulders just because he swam against it?"

"I don't know. But we'll find out tomorrow. Juan and I will go down."

He was only partially correct.

They buried Roberto at sunset, and I didn't stick around after the simple ceremony. That's just as well, because I heard about it the next morning.

If the sharks hadn't taken Roberto's head, they got their consolation prize. Even though the body had been carefully wrapped and weighted down with shot, they must have found him, because they had been swimming around the yacht all night, their long cold bodies gleaming as they surfaced and snapped their teeth in the moonlight. It hadn't been a pleasant evening.

I could tell when I looked at Dena's face the next day, and the crew's reaction was even more apparent.

As for Don, he was agitated only by anger.

"They're grumbling," he murmured, as he led me down

into the cabin, out of earshot of those on deck. "Want me to
turn back, chuck the whole thing. I don't know who started it,
but then these niggers are like children. Giving me a lot of
crap about curses and hoodoos." He sighed. "But that's not
the worst of it. Juan won't dive any more. He absolutely
refuses to go down."

"So what are you going to do?"

"Do? I can turn back, the way they want me to, and come
here again with a fresh crew. But that's a waste of time and
money. Dammit, I found the wreck! A few more trips down
and I'll have all the data I need on what it'll take to bring up
the treasure."

"If it's really there."

"That's just the point—I intend to find out. This is no time
to stop."

"You can still dive yourself."

"Yes, but it isn't a good idea to do it alone, at that depth,
unless there's someone else standing by in case of emergencies.
Not that there'll be any; now that I know what to expect, I
won't get caught the way Roberto was. Still, I need someone
to rely on."

"Have you tried offering Juan more money?"

"Certainly! I told him I'd pay him Roberto's wages in
addition to his own. But he's scared spitless."

Dena clambered down the ladder. "So what's the story?"
she asked, listlessly. "We leaving nature's wonderland?"

"Looks as though we'll have to," Don told her. "Unless—"
he paused, eyeing me. "Unless you could help out."

"Me?"

"Why not? You could learn to dive. I could teach you in
three days. Nothing to it, with a regulator, and we've got all of
Roberto's equipment. I'd make it worth your while—"

"No thanks," I said. "Don't mention money. I've got a poor

head for figures, but at least it's still on my shoulders. Which is more than you can say for Roberto's."

"I'd cut you in on the salvage," Don said. "We'd split on the gold. Think of it, a solid gold altar, and a golden chest so big it took half-a-dozen men to carry it."

Dena smiled. "Never mind the sales talk," she said. "Can't you see he just isn't the outdoor type?"

I don't know if it was *that* that did it, or the realization that unless I agreed she'd be sailing away. But all at once I heard myself saying, "Why not? At least I can give it a try."

That shut her up in a hurry, and it made Don start talking. Within a matter of minutes it was all arranged. He'd abandon his project for the next few days and devote all his time to instructing me. We'd start inland, near the beach at the cove, and then I'd get into deeper water. First with the shot-line and then alone, gradually learning how to handle myself in the depths.

And that's just the way it worked out.

There's no need to give a detailed account of what it's like to learn skindiving. The sea holds a lot of surprises, but your own body holds still more. I'd never have believed I could undergo the amount of pressure I experienced in the increasing scope of my descents, or endure the cold. I learned how to accomplish the necessary decompression, how to walk and swim and handle my limbs under weird gravitational alterations. And I learned, still more importantly, that I was not afraid. For the first time I really understood the fascination of skindiving as a hobby, or as the avocation or vocation of men like Clarke and Cousteau.

Don was a good, if impatient instructor. And more than his grudging praise, I relished the reluctant admiration of Dena. Thus stimulated, I underwent a rapid apprenticeship.

By the morning of the fifth day, I was ready to stand by and handle the line while Don dived. The crew seemed to have settled down into a state of morose resignation once more, and there were no difficulties.

I watched Don adjust his helmet and fins and clamber over the side. Dena leaned over the rail at my elbow and we traced the trail of bubbles rising through the translucent water. Then we waited.

Almost an hour passed before Don reappeared on the line at the twenty-foot decompression stage. He stayed so long that I went down myself, gesturing to him in the water. He signaled for me to leave, with a wave of his hand. I came up again.

"Is he all right?" Dena asked.

"I guess so. But he's certainly in no hurry to come up."

Finally, though, he emerged. The fins, the tanks, the helmet came off. He took a towel, sank into a deck chair, and his usually ruddy face was unnaturally pale in the midday sun.

"What's the matter?" I muttered.

"Nothing. Nitrogen narcosis."

I nodded. He'd explained it to me—the nitrogen intoxication which sometimes affects the central nervous system after one relies on the air supply from the tanks during long dives to great depths. It brings on anesthesia, hallucinations, and all sorts of odd reactions, but disappears when the diver decompresses.

"Took a long time to wear off," Don continued. "Hit me so suddenly I wasn't really aware of it. At first I thought the men were right about their squid, or whatever they think is down there in the wreck."

"You reached it?"

"Yes. And there is no hull, as I suspected; just masses of fish clustering almost solidly around the crevice where the ship settled. Inside there's bits of wood and metal still leaving a partial skeleton, but all the heavy stuff—the guns and the spars—is sunken into the sand. Over at one side there's a big bulge. I'd swear it's the altar and the chest we're looking for, but I never got to examine them.

"Because that's when I began to feel funny. The water seemed to be turning black. The first idea I had was about the squid, so I scuttled out of there. And when I turned around to take a look, the whole area seemed to be not only black, but boiling. Clouds of bubbles. Fish, of course, returning to the spot. And they'd churned up the silt. But at the time I would have sworn there was some big animal coming up from under the wreckage. Then, when I saw Roberto's head bobbing around the center of the black stuff, I realized what was wrong with me. I was drunk as a coot. So I came back up on the rope. I was so woozy I almost forgot to let go of the weights."

"Did you find the place where Roberto had his accident?"

"No, I didn't. Maybe you can when you go down."

"You mean—?"

"Why not? No reason why you shouldn't get used to it. I won't tackle it again today, so it's your turn. Maybe you can get closer than I did. Just remember to watch out for the nitrogen when it hits you. Chances are it won't, though."

Dena shook her head. "He shouldn't risk it," she said. "After all, he's just learning, and it's over two hundred feet. You told me yourself it calls for an experienced diver—"

"Only one way to get experience, isn't there?" I said. "I'm ready."

And I was, the moment I heard the veiled concern in Dena's voice.

I lowered my mask over the side, dipping it in the water so that no mist would cloud the inner surface of the goggles.

Juan strapped the cylinlder blocks of the regulator to my back
and looped the hose over my head as I fitted the rubber mask
until it molded tightly to my face. I gripped the mouthpiece
between my lips as Juan hung ten pounds in weights to my
belt. I adjusted my fins, picked up a spear, then went over the
side, grasping the rope with my left hand as I lowered myself
into the water.

It was cold. Gradually I felt my body adjusting to the
temperature and the pressure, just as my eyes adjusted to the
deeper gloom. Bubbles burst around me and fish swam past.
My lungs ached. I straightened to a horizontal position so
that intake and exhaust were equalized at the same pressure
level and the regulator would function properly. It was hard
not to panic; to remember, in effect, that the demand
regulator was doing my breathing for me, or at least supply-
ing the air which my constricted lungs needed as I flailed my
way down. The pressure grew stronger, my movements
correspondingly slower. Here in the deeper darkness I began
to feel drunk—nitrogen narcosis was not the cause, merely the
gravitational change. My ears and sinuses ached, and I swallowed until the pain eased. A school of small fish glided by. I
was tempted to abandon the shot-line and follow them. But
no, the line was my guide to the treasure below. I went down,
deeper into the darkness.

Not enough nitrogen had entered my bloodstream to
produce any side effects. All I had to worry about was the
pressure. How far down was I? Close to two hundred feet,
probably. It was hard to move, now; hard to hold the spear. I
wanted to rest for a while, to float.

The water here was dark. Only the bubbles from the
regulator retained any color—they were round and yellowish,
like beads of amber strung endlessly upwards from here to the
surface. So far to the surface up there. So cold down here.

And getting colder now. Because I was descending again. Deeper and Deeper. Darker and darker. Colder and colder. *Down went McGinty—*

Drunk. All right, so I was drunk. But that was good, because I couldn't feel the pain any more. My ears had stopped hurting. The cold didn't bother me, now. And it was easy to continue, to go all the way down. All the way down to where the treasure lay—the golden altar.

And then I saw the rock crevice, saw the great solid swarm of fish packed in a writhing mass and rising up like the dim drowned outline of a ghostly galleon. And I left the line and wriggled forward, moving like a fish myself. A swordfish, with a spear. They fled before me, these little ones. I was Neptune, scattering my subjects. Make way for the king! *King of the Sea.*

Drunken diver, rather. Or was it drunken driver? Could they arrest you for drunken diving? Fine you twenty clams?

I tried to clear my mind. Mustn't go on like that. Had to be careful, avoid running into whatever it was that sheared off poor Roberto's head. Funny way to die. Most men lost their heads over a woman—

And then I *saw* her.

I saw the woman.

She was standing perhaps fifty feet to my left, away from the crevice and the wreck. It was the glint of light that first caught my eye; a reflection brighter than anything else here in the murky dimness. I thought it might be the sunlight glinting from the scales of a large fish, and I turned my head, and I saw her.

Saw the black hair floating free in a mane that masked the face. Saw the sudden movement of her body as she turned and waved the cutlass. The gleaming cutlass, razor-sharp—

Women do not walk the ocean floor brandishing cutlasses. I realized that, but my awareness was only partial. Because another part of me was whispering, *Now you know. Now you know what cut off Roberto's head.*

And then *she* saw *me,* and the black mane whipped back, revealing her face. It was a blob of greenish white gristle with four gaping holes: two black sockets, a jagged nasal septum, and a grinning maw that parted now as a tiny fish wriggled *out.*

And it wasn't the skull that frightened me, it wasn't the sight of a corpse walking here at the bottom of the sea. It was just the hideous, grotesque inconsequence of the little fish swimming out of the dead mouth.

That's what I was afraid of, and that's what I remembered as I pulled in panic for the shot-line. As I struggled to release the weights I dropped my spear and stared. The figure wavered off in the distance, disappearing into the crevice where the ship lay. And now the black bubbles were rising, cascading in clouds from the spot. Through the turbulence I could see the skull face melting and blending, and I saw another face that could have been Roberto's, and yet others—brown, bearded, grimacing faces that formed out of bubbling blackness and disappeared in inky incoherence.

Then I was going up the line, not remembering to move slowly, but propelled by the panic, flailing forward in frantic fear.

At the fifty-foot level I forced myself to stop and wait. The water below was clear and no inchoate ichor rose about me. I counted slowly, then climbed again. Twenty feet now—another five minutes and I'd be free. Free and safe. But what if I waited, and something came after me? *What if it was following me, crawling along the line?*

My lungs were bursting. My head was bursting. Not with pressure, but with fright. I couldn't wait any more, I couldn't stand it, I had to get out, I *had* to—

I kicked and released myself, straining upwards, striving for the sun. My head broke water and I could see the light, feel it all about me.

Then it dissolved into darkness and I went down again, down into the black bubbles . . .

It was Don who hauled me out. I learned it later, when I opened my eyes and found myself lying on the deck.

"Don't try to talk," Dena said.

I nodded. I had neither the strength nor the desire. It was a good twenty minutes and two shots of rum later before I was able to sit in a deck chair and tell my story.

Don shook his head. "Nitrogen narcosis," he said. "You had it worse than I."

"But the corpse with the cutlass—Roberto's head—"

"Hallucinations."

"Yes, but how?" I thought about it for a moment. "Was it the manuscript that set me off? The part about the pirates? Did I subconsciously remember Mary Read and Anne Bonney and the other females who sailed in Blackbeard's day?"

"You must have," Don told me.

"But we both saw Roberto."

"We were both thinking about him, and what happened down there."

"Well, what *did* happen, do you suppose."

Don sighed. "Perhaps we can find out tomorrow."

"You're not going down again?" Dena asked.

"Of course I am. One more trip and I should be able to locate that altar, and the chest. A few fish churning up the silt aren't going to scare me away." He grinned at me. "Tell you what. If you're so concerned about my welfare, I'll take Howard along tomorrow for a guardian. We'll both go down. Whatd'ya say?"

What could I say, with Dena watching me? I nodded, reluctantly. I didn't really want to go down into that deeper darkness again.

And that night, when the dreams came, I was left with still less desire to return to the wreck.

The dreams came, and I lay tossing in my bed in the old house on the hillside above the winding waterfront of Santa Rita. I knew I was there, in my bed, but at the same time I was once again writhing in deep waters.

In my dreams I swam down to the wreckage, wriggled into the crevice where the black bubbles churned, and scraped at the sand with my spear until the point wedged against a solid object. It was the chest, of course, and I could detect the outline of the heavy lid set solid on the massive golden container. I sought to brush away the encrustation of corrosion and fungoid growth and gaze upon the gold beneath, but as I reached out the lid began to rise. It swung open slowly, and the blackness seeped out; the black bubbles burst like bloating blossoms. And they were not bubbles, but heads, and each head had a face, and each face had a mouth, and each mouth was gaping wide to greet me with a grotesque grimace. Yet these were only smoky bubbles, ghost faces floating there in the water—the broad, flat faces of savages, the bearded faces of *hidalgos* and Spanish mariners, the seamed and pitted countenances of corsairs; yes, and here was Roberto again, and the woman. The dark cloud floated forth, and it was like a great black bush bearing heads for fruit; a strange undersea growth waving there in the dim depths, growing before my eyes. And now the bush put forth fresh branches, and the branches were long and waving; a writhing mass of titanic tentacles. Still the smoke poured out, and billowed forth, and now I perceived that there was a body beneath the nightmare nebulosity of faces and feelers; a black body that was like a squid, a sea serpent, a reptilian monster spawned in the dawn of prehistory when nature shaped strange simulacra from primeval slime. And beneath the seething, shifting smokiness of that amorphous and polymorphous presence there were real eyes—real eyes that glowed and glared and glinted at me. But they were *more* than eyes; they were mouths as well. Yes, they were mouths, for I could see the pupils gape and the lids rolled back like lips, and I knew that the eyes would devour me, they would ingest me in their hunger, incorporate my essence into the black being of that incredible body so that I too would take my place as one of the scores of shifting shapes in the smoke which emanated from it.

It was one and it was many, it was a composite creature of an incorruptible corruption; it was insanity incarnate.

I screamed and fled from it, but the faces and the feelers flowed forth to envelop me in ichorous essence, so that I drowned in the bubbling blackness of its being. I was consumed by it.

And then there was no fear, and no revulsion, for in its place came an overwhelming expansion of awareness, so that I became a part of *it* and I knew. My memory was *its* memory, my knowledge was *its* knowledge. And my hunger was *its* hunger—

Memory.
Deep in the jungle they built the temple and reared a golden altar of worship. And behind the golden altar was the great golden ark in which I rested and waited for the sacrifice. Nor did I wait too long, for they came frequently to attend

me, bringing me the captives of their warfare, trussed on poles like pigs. And when there were no captives they brought me slaves, and when there were no slaves they brought me children, and when there were no children they brought me their choicest virgins. All I devoured in the darkness, incorporating far more than flesh—for I took from living things the continuity of their consciousness and added their awareness to mine. So that I grew and grew, eternally enlarging. For I was that which is known in all legends; the creature of darkness which devours the world. And if I were not fed, if my appetite were not appeased, I would flow forth to raven freely as I had—long eons ago, or was it yesterday, or would it be tomorrow? But if they kept me sated, I was content to dwell in the temple. And when they built the ark I entered it willingly, nor did I try to leave, for it was pleasnt to curl and coil and coalesce in the darkness and wait for them to bring me fresh fare. I remembered, now . . .

Knowledge.
Time is a rushing river that flows endlessly, yet never reaches the sea. And it is pleasant to drift upon the stream, drift drowsily and content. So that when I coiled compactly in the golden chest, I willed myself to satiated sleep. And it was then that they hammered down the lid, so that I could not escape; hammered it fast to hold me captive, and put an end to sacrifice. But I was still aware; I knew when the armored white strangers came and prevailed over my worshipers, and I endured as they sought to pry open the lid of the great chest, and then abandoned their vain effort to talk of fire and of melting down. Finally there was talk of a golden gift to their ruler and in the end the chest was borne away to the ship, together with the altar of sacrifice. I did not stir or

struggle, for I anticipated the nearing moment when the chest *would* be opened again, and I could feast. Feast on flesh, feast on spirit. Yes, I knew, now . . .

Hunger.

I drowsed in the darkness, and then the thunder came, and the shattering sound awakened me. I felt the shock and the shudder as the sinking ship gave way and I fell into the depths; the lid of the chest burst and I was free. Yet I did not come forth, for there was no reason. Not until the bodies drifted down, sinking slowly. Then I put forth a portion of myself, bubbling out from the lid and groping until I grasped the floating forms and drew them to me. I feasted until replete, then slept once more. There was no need to emerge from the chest until the opportunity came to feed again. Time means nothing, for I endure forever. I have but to wait. I neither dwindle nor grow; nothing grows except the hunger.

But the hunger is there, and lately I have stirred, heeding its pangs. The other day I took a man—it was curious, in that he came to me willingly and saw the chest with its lid ajar. He could not lift it, of course, because of the weight of the water, but he felt along the edges. Then I bubbled forth, grasping him and pulling him down, and he threshed mightily so that the lid fell, decapitating him. The body floated away, but I did not pursue. I do not have to pursue. I am aware of his awareness now, and with it I know that there are others of his kind in a ship, just above me. They will follow him down, for they are seeking the chest and the altar. Yes, they will come to me, and soon I shall feast again.

In the feasting there is great pleasure. To taste the memories, to savor the surge of every emotion, to know the nuances of all desires; there is the richness of rage, the pungency of passion, the fine, full flavor of frantic fear. I eat it all, and I digest it, and I retain it, and that is *my* ruling need. Most of all I want the woman, the golden woman. And I will engulf her with my eyes, and I will take her whiteness into my blackness, and drain her body of all delight—

"No!" I was screaming now, it was my own voice that was screaming, and it was my own sweat-drenched body that threshed in ultimate fright there upon the bed in the moonlight as I awoke.

It had been a nightmare. I knew that now, and yet I *believed.* No subconscious fantasies can evolve without stimulation, and my stimuli had come from beneath the sea. *I believed.*

But when the harsh sun rose, my certainty wavered. By the time I rowed out to the yacht, I was half-ashamed to even speak about the dream. And when I started to tell Dena and Don of what had shattered my sleep, I was more than apologetic.

"Sure you weren't hitting the rum again?" Don asked.

"No, I didn't touch a drop. But even if it was just a nightmare, I'm convinced there's *something* behind it. That business of the lid coming down to decapitate Roberto—"

"You know yourself what it would weigh, and how slowly it would move in water at that depth."

"Yes, but if something were holding him—"

"What could hold him? Your mysterious monster, made out of black bubbles? The one who lives inside the chest?"

"We saw the bubbles, remember?"

"Sure we did. And we saw the fish that made them, churning up the silt down there in the crevice." Don wiped his forehead with a hairy arm. "Personally, I think you cooked up this yarn because you'd like to chicken out of making a dive with me. You were pretty shook up yesterday, weren't you? Sure you were."

"Leave him alone," Dena said. "The poor guy almost drowned. If he doesn't want to go back down, I don't blame him."

"I'll go," I said. "Don't worry about me."

"Then come on," Don snapped, "Juan has our gear laid out. The sooner we get started, the better."

We stripped down to our trunks, and I followed the teddy-bear over to the rail in silence. Juan helped us into our equipment. And then it was time to lower ourselves along the shot-line, lower ourselves into the drowned domain of darkness and seek what waited there . . .

Don reached the bottom before me. Spear in hand, he jackknifed through the gloom in the direction of the crevice, then waved a flipper to urge me forward.

The fish did not swarm here today, and we could see the ribs of the skeleton ship wavering weirdly in the water. And Don swam between them, then lowered himself to the sand as he groped forward, digging his spear into the bulky, buried outline of a shape set against the side of the rocks. Suddenly he flung up a flipper again, gesturing impatiently as I held back. The spear scraped over the encrustations and bubbles rose.

Then I saw the glint and hurried forward. He *had* found something—it was the altar!

There was no way of determining if it had fallen flatly or upended itself in the sand—in either case it was huge; far larger than I'd expected. And its surface, beneath the silt, was hammered, gleaming gold. I peered into Don's face, beneath the goggles, and read the exultation in his eyes.

We'd found what we were looking for.

The cost of rigging up a winch and windlass to raise it from the depths would be tremendous, but the reward was worth the effort. This was a prize surpassing the dreams of any treasure-seeker. And there was still the chest—

Again, it was Don who moved forward, deeper into the debris centered between the ribs of the hulk. He stooped and groped and probed, then rounded a rocky outcropping in the wall of the crevice and literally stumbled across the rectangular lid of the great chest sunken in the sands.

I was beginning to feel faint. Part of it was residual fear, of course, but most of it was sheer excitement at the realization of our discovery.

Whatever the cause, I was conscious of a growing giddiness, and I moved back, not wanting to stray too far away from the shot-line. Don waved at me, but I shook my head and continued to retreat. Only when I saw the line slanting before me did I halt and gaze off into the crevice.

Don had stopped over the imbedded outline of the lid and now he was digging at it with his spear. I remembered his own remarks about the weight of the water and knew his puny efforts would be futile; perhaps he was beginning to suffer from nitrogen narcosis too.

But no, his attempts were *not* useless! Because even as I watched, the lid was rising. Slowly, very slowly, the sand began to slant and shift beneath the spear. And now I could see an opening inch up, and there was a blackness and a bubbling. It was like the blackness and the bubbling I'd encountered yesterday, during my dive, but there were no fish about to churn the silt. Yet the lid continued to rise, and the darkness flowed forth.

The darkness flowed forth, just as it had in my dream.

And then Don was backing away, and he flailed the spear before him; flailed frantically at the faces that seethed and surged in shapeless shadows. And out of the faces emerged the feelers, coils of twisting tentacles that shrouded him in smoke. I thought of the legends of the huge *djinn* imprisoned by Solomon in tiny bottles, and I thought of how lambent gases are compressed in minute containers, and I thought of protoplasm that proliferates instantaneously in response to the blind, insensate forces which spawned life out of the insane vortex of chaos when the world began. But this was not *djinn* or gas or protoplasm; it was nightmare. Black nightmare, boiling out of a golden chest at the bottom of the sea, black nightmare that emerged now in sudden, shocking solidity; ozzing obscenely aloft until it towered titanically amidst its twining tendrils.

And I saw the central coils part to reveal the eyes, the eyes which were like mouths—which *were* mouths, because they were swallowing Don. The coils whipped him aloft, forced him against the openings, and the lid-lips came down. I could see Don's legs threshing in a blur of bubbles; one of his flippers had come off.

I forced myself forward, spear in hand. But the chest was closing; the tentacles were forcing it down from within. The black, threshing mass disappeared, carrying the white mass of Don's body with it, and the lid clanged shut. Behind it floated a mass of bubbles, and a tangle of reddish skeins, and something small and curiously white. Don's foot, sheared off at the ankle by the closing lid—

I blacked out.

Half an hour later I found myself gasping and retching on the deck in the warm sunlight. I had no memory of how I came to the surface; apparently Juan had seen me ascend and came down to hold me through the decompression stages. He bent over me, and his brown face was almost as pale as Dena's.

I told them about Don.

In Dena's face I could read only doubt and incredulity, plus a strange compassion. But Juan nodded, slowly.

"We must leave this place," he said.

I shook my head. "But you can't leave now—there's the gold, it's really down there, and it's worth a fortune—"

"What is gold to a dead man?" he murmured. "We will go back to Barbados."

"Wait!" I begged. "We've got to think things over. Dena, you understand—"

"Yes." She turned to Juan. "We can't decide anything now. Can't you see he's exhausted? Look, let me take him ashore. Tomorrow we can decide what must be done. There's no sense talking any more. And no reason to get all excited over hallucinations."

"Hallucinations!" I sat up, shaking.

She put her hand on my shoulder. "Never mind. We'll discuss it later, when you're rested. Come on, I'll go in with you. Juan can have one of the men row us ashore."

I was silent. It took all my strength to get over the side and into the rowboat. When we landed, about a mile down from the cove, Dena and the crewman helped me walk up the steep, winding path which led to the old house I occupied on the hill. Looking down, I could see the yacht riding out there on the waters, silhouetted against the sunset.

The crewman went back, but Dena stayed. My serving couple, Felipe and Alicia, prepared a meal for us. Then I sent them away. The food and a few drinks restored me. By the time darkness came I was ready to talk. And Dena was ready to listen.

We sat on the terrace outside the house. The sky was bright, and I had the feeling that, if I wished, I could reach out and grasp the moon and the stars. But I was content merely to sit there and watch the play of moonlight and starlight in Dena's golden hair.

Dena filled our glases and sank back.

"All right," she said. "What really happened down there?"

I stared out at the water. "But I already told you."

"We're alone now. You aren't talking for Juan's benefit, or the crew's."

"I realize that."

She sipped her drink. "Can't you remember? Was it really all hallucination?"

I leaned forward. "Dena, none of it was hallucination. It happened just the way I told you. We found the treasure. And that creature down there. I dreamed about it, but it's real, it actually exists. Maybe it's not the only one, either—what about all these legends of sea serpents and monsters? What happened to the crew of the *Marie Celeste*? I've read about such things on land, too; jungle villages, whole primitive civilizations which had been apparently destroyed instantaneously without warning. Suppose there *are* lifeforms we know nothing about, spawned when the earth was young and still surviving—or spawned even *before* the earth evolved? What about the beings that might have come here from the stars, the alien entities that never die? Those legends—"

"Legends!" Dena brushed the hair back from her forehead, frowning. "I'm interested in the truth."

"But I'm trying to explain—"

"You don't have to explain." She stared at me levelly. "I know what happened. You and Don went down to the wreck. You found the altar, perhaps you even found the chest. And they were gold, all right."

"Yes. I wasn't lying. Those objects would be worth a fortune if we raised them."

"Of course. You thought about that, didn't you? And you

thought how wonderful it would be to have that fortune, keep it for yourself. So you got hold of Don's spear, and you killed him. And then you came back up with your crazy story about the monster, knowing it would frighten Juan and the others, keep them from going down to look. Now you'll wait until they go, get your own crew, and salvage the treasure. That's the way it was, wasn't it? You killed Don."

"No.

She came closer, her voice low. "I understand. It wasn't just for the sake of the money, was it? You wanted me. You knew you'd have to get Don out of the way, first. And you remembered what I said, about not having the guts. So it's my fault, too. I'm not afraid to face the truth—I'm partly responsible."

"You don't know what you're saying."

"Yes, I do. I'm saying that I'm sorry, but it's happened now and I can live with it. We can both live with it. We will get the treasure together. You and I. And then, if you still want me—"

Then she was in my arms and I looked down at my tarnished angel, at the golden toy, mine now for the taking. And I smiled, and I pushed her away.

"It's too late. I don't want you. Now, or ever."

"I'm not good enough for you any more, is that it?" She stood up quickly. "Now that you know about the gold, you think you can keep it all for yourself and you won't need me because you can buy other women."

"I don't need you. And I don't need other women any more, either."

"Oh, yes you do! You need me all right! Because all I have to do is go to that precious mayor of yours here on the island and tell him who murdered Don."

"Go ahead," I said. "We'll see what happens when he tries to pit himself against a god. For it *is* a god, you know. Stronger and stranger than any entity of earth."

Dena stepped back, still staring. "You're crazy," she whispered. "That's it. You've gone crazy."

"Because I don't want you as a woman any more? Because I'm through with sentimental daydreams about teddy-bears and angels? Oh, no, Dena. I'm not crazy. I *was* crazy, perhaps, until I gazed on the ultimate realities. What I saw was not pretty, but its truth transcends terror. I've gazed on something far more powerful than the petty forces that rule our little lives and our little lusts. There is a power stronger than all earthly desire, a hunger greater than all earthly hunger. And when I saw it today, when I recognized it down there, I did the only thing a mortal may do. I bowed down and worshiped, do you hear, Dena? I remember now what happened after Don died. I sank to my knees on the ocean floor and worshiped!" I rose and faced her. "And then I went over to the chest and I opened the lid. I was not afraid any longer, because I knew *it* was aware of my emotions. I could realize that. And I could release it without harm, because it understood I meant to serve it. Dena, I opened the lid!"

"I don't believe you, I don't believe anything you're saying—"

"*They* believed me." I gazed out at the moonlit waters of the cove beyond.

She followed my stare. "Don't you see what's happening?" I said, softly, "The yacht is moving. Juan raised the anchor. He believed what I told him. And he and the crew must have made up their minds. They aren't going to wait until tomorrow. They aren't waiting for us at all. They remember what happened to Roberto and to Don and they want to get away."

Dena gasped. "You're right—the yacht *is* moving! What can we do?"

"We can watch," I told her, calmly. "They want to get

away. But they won't. They don't know what you know now—that I opened the lid. And its hunger is growing. Look!"

The moon was very bright over the water. And even at the distance of a mile we could see the bubbles rising, see the waves churning and boiling as something broke the surface just before the vessel. It was like a wave, like a waterspout, like a giant cuttlefish. And the tentacles tossed and twisted and twined about the prow, and the little yacht tilted, and then a black bulk emerged from the waters an swept across the deck. In the distance we could hear faint screams, and then Dena was screaming too as the boat careened over on its side and the huge black blob enveloped its white hull and bore it down, down—

The black bubbles disappeared, and there was only the soft and shimmering surface of the sea, glittering in the cold silver moonlight.

"The *Mary Celeste*," I murmured. "And countless other ships. Countless other mortals in all climes, in all times. When the appetite waxes, it awakens. When it wanes, it subsides. But now the hunger grows again and it will come forth to feed. Not on the bodies alone, but on the *being*. It will glut on soul-substance, feast on the emotions and the psyche. First a ship, then a village, then a town, perhaps an entire island. And what is comparable to that knowledge? Does that slimy gold under the water or the tarnished gold of your body hold any allure for one who realizes his true destiny at last? His destiny to serve a god?"

"Get away from me—I'll go to Robales—"

I pinned her arms. "You will not go to Jose Robales. You will come with me. And I will summon it to the sacrifice."

She screamed again, and I hit her with the heel of my hand across the back of the neck. It silenced her, but did not bruise her mouth or face. I knew it would be better if she was not marked. One does not bring spoiled fruit or withered flowers as an offering to the gods.

I carried her down to the beach, then, in the moonlight. And I stripped her and staked her out upon the sand there at the water's edge. She was silver and gold in the moonlight, and for a moment I coveted the treasure of her body's richness. But I had spoken truly; this was as nothing to the knowledge of my destiny. I had found myself at last—I was meant to serve. To serve, and to summon.

I sent my thoughts out across the water and deep down. It was not difficult, not since I had opened the chest and let the blackness therein meet and mingle with my being. For already I was a part of it and it was a part of me. And I knew this was what it was searching for—not the crew, but the golden woman.

Now it would come to slake all hunger and all thirst. And my own appetite would be appeased in the sacrificial act.

I did not have long to wait. The bubbles burst near the shore and then it flowed forth. Larger now—for as it feasts, it grows. The black blur became a black cloud, the black cloud became a black blot, the black blot became a black body; a thousand writhing arms to caress her nakedness, a thousand pulsing lips to drink, a thousand hungry mouths to savor and to swallow.

And the blackness flowed over her whiteness and it was like an exploding ecstacy in which I was the ravisher and the ravished, the eater and the eaten, the victor and the victim, the watcher and the watched, and it was better than seeing Don, it was better than seeing the crew, and I knew it would keep getting more wonderful each time, the sensation stronger still as *we* kept feeding and growing, feeding and growing.

Yes, *we*.

Because when it was finished, and the blackness melted back into the rolling waters, leaving the beach bare before it in the moonlight, I knew that *we* would go on together.

There had been no altar this time, but that did not matter. *We* know nothing, care nothing for altars of gold. The bed is not the bride, the plate is not the meal. Anywhere and anytime, all that is necessary is soul and substance for the sacrifice. So that *we* can swallow and grow, swallow and grow.

I made *our* plans.

Jose Robales had warned me to keep the crew away from the natives in the little village behind the cove. They were only ignorant savages, after all—probably not much better than the jungle natives who had reared the golden altar to a god. But they lived—and that is enough to *we* who drink life.

So I would summon the god again, tomorrow, the next day, soon. And it would come in its strength and take nourishment. Perhaps the villagers would bow down to it and then raise an altar of their own. Perhaps not. In the end, it couldn't matter. Because in the end *we* would take them all.

And perchance Jose Robales might come to us. If not, in due season *we* would go to him.

Yes, in due season *we* would visit everyone on the island of Santa Rita. And our awareness would grow as we incorporated all the lives and all the learning and all the lusts. And our appetite would increase. And *we* would grow; grow in size, grow in power, grow in strength to satisfy our dark desires.

There need be no end. It is a small distance from island to island. And as *we* grow we can travel faster, seize more swiftly and surely. With us there is no time and no death—nothing to halt or to hinder.

The creature that swallows the world.

Why not?

From island to island, always growing. Then on to the mainland, to the swarming cities. It will feast and I will share, it will search and I will lead, it will rule and I will serve, forever and ever.

And I have written it down now so that all may know the truth and decide whether to join in worship or serve us in another way—as subjects, sustenance for sacrifice.

The choice is yours, but make it swiftly. For I feel the urging of that black appetite, and soon *we* must go forth to ravage and raven across the world . . .

(*Statement of Jose Robales, mayor.*)

In the matter of the man Howard Lane, presently confined to await trial on the charge of murder, these facts are known.

The foregoing account was found, in the prisoner's own hand, upon the desk in the study of his home, by Felipe and Alicia Martino, his servants.

The statement was handed to me when I visited his house early this morning, together with Officer Valdez, seeking to question him concerning the sinking of the yacht *Rover,* which event had been reported to me by certain natives of the village near Cut-Throat Cove.

Howard Lane being asleep, I first examined the above statement and then awakened him, formally charging him with the murder of Roberto Ingali, Donald Hanson, and the woman Dena Drake.

This he of course denied, but in such a manner as to permit of only one supposition—that this account he had written truly represents his own belief as to what occurred.

It is evident that the prisoner suffers from a severe mental derangement, and I shall make it a point to see that he undergoes a complete examination before formally bringing him to trial. At the moment one can only conclude that he performed the crimes while in a state of unbalance, and—although it is not easy to determine the method—arranged for the sinking of the yacht.

Unfortunately there are as yet no witnesses who can testify to actually seeing the vessel go down, but the sudden disappearance of a seaworthy boat anchored in calm waters, coupled with the discovery this morning of timbers and bits of wreckage washed ashore in the cove, permits of no other conclusion. It was undoubtedly Hanson's boat.

The prisoner's statement seems obviously the work of a mind obsessed with guilt, and it is to be hoped that he will recover sufficiently to make a full and sensible confession.

Before wiring to summon a physician, I shall make it my business, as an official and as a former friend of Howard Lane, to visit him in the jail and urge that course upon him.

Indeed, I would have done so today, had it not been that the reports of the wreckage washed ashore occupied my time and attention until late this afternoon.

As it is now well into the evening, I will put off my interview until tomorrow morning.

It is to be admitted that one is shaken by this sad turn of events.

The spectacle of Howard Lane, my former friend and now my prisoner, in the grip of his delusions—shrieking threats and curses like an hysterical woman—disturbs one far more than I can indicate. Even now I can hear him moaning in his cell below.

And it is sorrowful indeed to reflect upon the sudden tragedy which has visited our peaceful island.

As I sit here and gaze out across the calm waters of which the prisoner has written so vividly, I cannot reconcile this scene with such a chaos of murder and violence. As for the statement itself, absurd as it may seem to one still in full possession of his reason, there is a certain powerful if irrational logic about it—

Wait. The prisoner below is not moaning. He is shouting again, in measured cadences. It is as though he were *chanting*.

And the waters of the bay—

The moonlight is clear and I can see the black bubbles rising. They are moving closer to the shore, moving swiftly. And now I hear the screaming from the waterfront. They see it, they see it coming out of the water. It is black and immense, and it is slithering forward, it is coming to feast just as he said it would, it is coming to devour the w—

PART III

OTHER CREATURES STRANGE AND WONDERFUL

NOTES LEADING DOWN TO THE EVENTS AT BEDLAM

BY BARRY N. MALZBERG

There are, perhaps, an infinite number of other creatures strange and wonderful, some of which we suspect exist and some of which we know nothing about. One of the former is the changeling, the creature who is able to take the form of a human and dwell among us—and in one way or another prey on us as well. The werewolf is one form of changeling; but there are other forms too, creatures even stranger and more subtly malignant than the loup garou.

One such changeling is that which the narrator of "Notes Leading Down to the Events at Bedlam" meets and, to his eternal anguish, falls in love with. But chilling though it is, this is not just a simple horror story; it is one of complexity and ambition, which the author himself considers "a lovely equation of sex and death . . . I have written little with the conviction of the last page or so."

243

Barry N. Malzberg (born 1939) has been a polemical figure in science fiction circles—and elsewhere—since he began publishing in the late 1960s. His style and his vision are unique, and whether his work is liked or reviled (it seems to divide about equally), few can deny its power. Such novels as Screen, Oracle of the Thousand Hands, Underlay, Beyond Apollo, Herovit's World, Destruction of the Temple, *and* The Last Transaction *are intense and caustic indictments of modern society's ills and future legacies. (It is tempting to add two novels,* The Running of Beasts *and* Acts of Mercy, *to that list; but since these were written in collaboration with your editor, a certain modesty forbids.) Malzberg has published close to six million words during his thirteen years as a professional writer, including some eighty novels and two hundred and fifty short stories—a remarkable total in today's contracting fiction market. He makes his home in New Jersey.*

GENTLEMEN:

So here I sit, pen in hand, and I will try to comply with your request, that is to write an explanation of my condition and why I think I am here to the best of my ability although I do not know if I am capable of doing this or what purposes it will serve even if this dismal task were accomplished. Gentlemen! Gentlemen! You are so *solemn* with your posturings and rubbings of hands, your mumbling of strange words like *dementia* which I can barely understand and I do not know how I can reach past this solemnity to strike to the core of truth because I am not myself a solemn man; I am a man, you will find it hard to believe this, known until fairly recently for the merriment of his disposition, his *joie de vivre*, his *je ne sais quoi* which insouciantly carried him larking through all the passageways of life. And no more now, no more.

I know that you have discussed all of this with my wife, Wilhemina. This memoir may well be her idea and not yours. I tell you, I tell you at the outset, do not believe a word she says, gentlemen. There is no credibility in her. She merely wishes to know how well I know her secrets.

Nevertheless, I will write this memoir or at least a brief set of notes leading toward a memoir. There are so few matters to occupy my valueless time in these rather grim surroundings and I know that my failure to cooperate will only make my confinement more indefinite than it is already. Also these notes are sure to amuse me. Also I appreciate what one of you called your "new view of madness," madness as being caused by external facets of one's history and not necessarily being a mere investiture of demons. I know that I am not mad even though you take me for this but if I do not cooperate with your proposed "cure" by explaining to you how and why I feel I am in these rather dismal environs you will conclude, will you not, that the demons are inviolable and I will be here through eternity.

(Do not listen to a word my wife says. She is treacherous, deceitful, filled with hypocrisy and as the cause of these events will lie to protect herself. Dismiss her, gentlemen!)

At least if I am here through eternity I will be separate from Wilhemina; this the only good to be wrenched from the horrible pass to which I have come. I know that in your naïveté and innocent, stumbling lust, you cannot understand why I would feel this way, for Wilhemina is a lovely woman, twenty-four years old at this time and at that tantalizing point where the frivolities of the girl and the true, darker sensuality of the woman merge to a depth of temptation. Without your solemnity in her presence where would you be? At her veritable knees, gentlemen, you do not need to apologize. This is simple truth.

I met and married Wilhemina, the daughter of friends of my business partner, in the fall of 189—, just seven scant months ago although it now seems that a different man must have made this tragic error. Beautiful she was and mysterious in the way of all beautiful women, nor was I ever able to find out much of her background. "I am a mystery to everyone," she said, "often enough even to myself, just believe in me," and I believed in her, gentlemen, I took her from her parents without dowry and in my large if cheerless unfurnished apartment and after a wedding trip to Spain about which I can only seem to recall a series of rooms and carriages swept by heat and lust, groveling and connection (I have no recollection whatsoever of landscape) we began our life together. Soon I found that she was an adopted child who had wandered into her parents' lives through ways remarkable and devious in 187— and never a word about her background, but there was no more information to be derived from this couple, an ancient and embittered pair who had attended our wedding in ecstasy and had then left their dwellings for a long trip to Scotland, no return date posted, no forwarding address yielded. My partner at this time also found obscure business in the North which caused him to place the firm in my hands for an indefinite period and the last I had heard of him, the police were unable to ascertain his activities or location since he had checked out of a small hotel in the Netherlands four months ago.

Nevertheless business prospered. The elixir of the gods is being paid for in the most mundane (but most profligate) of coin and the winery at that time had been expanded to take in not only a large number of new distillers but a kind of sub-partner whose competence with accounts was stunning and who left me virtually unlimited free time to pursue my new life with my twenty-four-year-old bride, who opened up layers of knowledge for me, night after night . . . until I became a man quite dazzled, fascinated and entrapped.

I had waited until middle life to marry. As is common with so many men of my class I believed that I should not marry until I had reached a position of financial and professional stability and although I was fully forty-seven years old when I met and married Wilhemina—I blush to confess this, gentlemen, but complete frankness was demanded in these memoirs and I am beyond self-delusion *no matter what your diagnosis*—I was greatly inexperienced in matters of the flesh, having channeled my energies to the establishment of a businessand finding substantiation, so to speak, in life.

Now I know what had been stolen from me in small pieces throughout all those empty years but even in the early months with Wilhemina I did not know it then. I thought that joy forestalled was joy twice gained, and I would now find in the last twenty years of my life a magnitude of joy well eclipsing the deprivations of the first forty-seven years, and Wilhemina, I do say, assisted me in this insane endeavor. (Now, you see, I know it was insane; one can never atone for what has been lost.)

I was very much possessed by her. Gentlemen, I was very much possessed by her. Even at this moment I feel that necessity, the desire to drive myself against her, to touch her, to entwine myself with her in the night . . . I cannot go on. A certain delicacy must infuse these memoirs, owing to the conventions of the day, and conventions to one side, to be explicit about what happens to us in private has always struck me as evil and disgusting. What we do with ourselves or with one another alone is none of anyone's business. You will forgive me; I know of the more modern researchers who feel that sexuality is a legitimate area of discussion but I will have nothing to do with their bizarre ideas. You will forgive me.

You will forgive me, gentlemen. Solemn as all of you might be with your beards and heavy coats, even an alienist must have known passion in his time and I like to think that outside of these walls, far from the needs of the patients, outside these walls as I say and in private as I was once in private with my young wife . . . you commit secret acts out of honesty and passion. And that you understand. And that you understand.

In the fifth month of our marriage after a long and tumultuous night with Wilhemina I awoke at one of those off-hours of the morning where time itself seems shuffled and dispersed: two o'clock, four o'clock, perhaps five-fifteen. It does not matter the time; I awakened with that peculiar and startled awareness which so many of us know only at those strange hours when something within us throws off the cloak of sleep to confront the unspeakable . . . and found, as I turned instinctively to my dear wife for comfort, that lying next to me in the bed was not her but a beast, a beast of such awful description—

—A beast neither human nor inhuman, skin like scales, the tint like no color in the universe, features that were neither hers nor those of any animal I have seen: the whole cold, cold, emitting a cold breath like fog which engulfed me and as I retreated from the beast in horror it moved, apparently in its own sleep, nearer to me, and we *touched*. I touched the skin and scales of the beast, my body galvanized to an intensity I had never before known, literally contracted and I must have screamed then.

I must have screamed, something peculiar and terrible pouring from me, a vaulting, a congelation of self, leaping from the sheets, groaning and gasping, and the beast screamed too, a sound less a shriek than a cry, and then as I uncovered my eyes (for being human means that in all of our perversity we wish to confront the unspeakable even as we flee it) I saw the beast shudder, waves and rivulets running, and it assumed again the shape of Wilhemina—

—Wilhemina reaching toward me from the bed as I cowed in a corner. Wilhemina uttering soothing words. Wilhemina extending comfort and moving toward me and, gentlemen, I could not stand it, you must believe this, I could not stand it as my wife came upon me, her eyes lit with desire and pain, I feared that her touch was that of the beast and I would have fled the room, seizing what clothing I needed from a closet, and run across the moors like a lunatic (this the only time, admittedly, that I did approach lunacy; otherwise your diagnosis is false) but my limbs did not have the strength to move me and then she came upon me, put her hands on mine and it was the familiar, sweet, dark touch of her flesh against mine. "Come," she said. "Come back into the bed. What's wrong with you? Why are you cowering like that?"

I allowed her to lead me shaking back to the sheets. I did not have the strength of a child, gentlemen, or its diction, being able only to sputter incoherent sounds which may have made me sound bestial myself. "Great God," I was finally able to say or some similar religious expletive, "God help me," and made another effort to leave the bed but Wilhemina, now shorn of her bedclothing, clambered over me like the night and held me fluttering, mouth against neck, gently biting, and I did not have the strength to move or to resist as she spoke to me.

And speak to me she did as we lay wrapped that way in the bed. She said something like this, I must have seen her Condition. I must have seen her Symptom, she said, she had had it all her life, it did not happen very often, there was no explanation for it, she had never seen it herself because she was *not* herself when it happened, but a few times, when there had been poor luck she had been seen by others: her parents, who might have seen her in her sleep.

(She will deny all of this when you bring the point to her, gentlemen. She is cunning in ways I could not have understood. She will say that I have lied out of dementia but I do not care for I know what I have seen and where I have been now and what I am in a way which you never will.)

Some might have seen her in the dark, she said, but it meant nothing. I was barely able to listen. I can hardly recount it now. Her explanation as placed against what I had seen was like a solitary weak flower in a storm. What did it matter? What could it measure? And shrinking, retreating, I fell from her, without the strength now to flee, but feeling my skin beginning to glaze under her touch. It was uncontrollable, she said sadly. She did not even know what happened to her during these periods of sleep. Could I tell her? The others had only babbled. Would I explain? Could I give her details? She could not obtain medical counsel on her own, of course, because she would be institutionalized for dementia (I trust, gentlemen, that you note the irony of this!), but perhaps if I, a credible, etsablished businessman not to say her husband, were to attend to the doctors and—

I stayed with her. That was my fundamental error although not the cause of my condition as you will see. She was my wife, I loved her (and love her, God help me, yet), what I had seen was so incredible that in retrospect it diminished to the easy, fuzzy representation of nightmare like the masks of children on All Hallows Eve and the only condition I placed was that we did not speak of it again and that no recollection of that first night be shared.

(Why *did* I not leave her? Why did I not abrogate the

marriage as a man of my position and influence could well have done with legal ease? Why did I not evict her from my quarters without settlement? I could have done this. It would have been accomplished with facility. I told myself that the reason I would not evict her was that she was my wife and what we had known together was irreplaceable; that I might have been hallucinating despite her confirmation of her "condition," that the "condition" itself might not reappear due to the Love of a Good Man . . . oh, I told myself many things. You will see through the center of this, gentlemen, as you claim erroneously to see through so much else . . . although never Wilhemina. Deny, deny. She will deny all.)

And life passed placidly enough for some days or weeks. No recurrence of the "condition." No indication that it had ever happened. A total, blissful denial. Until I awoke once again in that bellows hour of the night, body tensed as if for culmination or collapse, and found beside me—

—Ah, but this time it was not nearly so bad. I had been this way once before, you see, also I could gauge my own reaction more closely and look with objective interest upon the beast which lay like a human in the bed, breathing in palpitation, scales fluttering like feathers, and I found that I was able to confront it straight on without hysteria. Anything, I learned, *anything* could be confronted if you were willing to face it and it was only when the beast's horrid "eyes" opened and it looked at me with a stare both luminescent and somehow pained—

—that I screamed and the thing shuddered. Wilhemina returned in an instant (the transition was so quick as to be almost unnoticeable) and clutched me to her saying impossible, this was impossible, the "condition" was a phenomenon which occurred only once in a while and now it had appeared twice within a short time and how terrible, terrible this must be for you, Gerald, her fingers floating up and down my body, horror in the touch but horror turning once again into its kind companion lust . . . and so I allowed myself to be taken by and to take her, the two of us grasping in the darkness and it was not so bad, gentlemen, not so bad at all and we said nothing more, did not remark upon what had happened the next day or the next but the night after that—

—awakening yet again, just three days later I saw the beast and the beast, two of its eyes open, was looking at me, had obviously been looking at me for a long time, a woe and acceptance in that dreaming gaze which I cannot describe, and then, grumbling and gasping, it closed the gap between us, put its "hands" upon me, the skin glinting like a dead animal under the moon and that touch, only that touch must have restored my voice. Is it true that I screamed? No, I did not scream, I fairly died—

—and Wilhemina returned and I fell into her as if she were the earth, her return the only reassurance that the horror beside me was not the exact quotient of my past and future life, the life after death too, and she whispered to me words of comfort yet again but I did not want to hear them. The "condition" could not possibly recur, she said, perhaps if it did she would seek assistance. She could not live this way. She saw in my eyes the horror she had induced. And I took her and took her and nothing more of this and the next day between us without comment as it had always been and the next night—

—the beast was upon me, wrapped against me, I could find the smell now, a harsh scent like teak and vomit intermingled, pulled up through my nostrils, pleadings in the grumblings of the beast as it wrapped me in and I could not scream, being held so tightly until at last, released, I shouted and blessed Wilhemina—

—reappeared against me and I took her and there was no difference in the taking as between her and the beast. This is what I came to understand, gentlemen, with my eyes closed, fulminating against her. It was not one but the other, the two together, my dear wife, the beast, have not one but both because this was what had been created and this was what I had married and my confusion was great, oh gentlemen, it was great as was my horror but underneath, beneath the horror, another perception was growing and it is of this perception which I think you now want me to speak so we will get at the roots of this and hasten my cure. She brought me here under false pretenses. It is not me but *she* who is mad, not me but she who needs treatment, not she but me you must attend, night after night the clutchings and the shifting in the bed beside me, the straining acuteness, the knowledge of what I had married—

—but you wanted the perception, gentlemen, so I give you the perception. I give you this: the realization that it was not annulment of beast I wanted after that first horrid moment of confrontation, not the death of the beast but its continuation, the intermingling if you will and that in wanting the one, my wife, I wanted the other, the beast, and it had always been this way, this was why, the real reason, I had waited so long to marry, knowing unconsciously what was within me, the desires of the fiend. Now I will never know, the two of them so mingled together. I am losing control: *it was not her I wanted but the other.*

I must have had intimations before our marriage, I must have suspected this but I wanted I wanted I wanted I can no longer control this put the leeches on me or the ropes if you will put me in a cage in the square and batter on the bars. I will not continue with this yea though I be in Bedlam for fifty years more dying a shrunken old man than to continue these notes do not listen to her she is treacherous and cunning will say anything you wish to hear, listen to me, no do not listen to me.

For I have gauged and measured now my madness and know myself to be madder by far than even the least solemn of you oh God the *scent* of it coming against me in the night—

IN THE STRAW
BY EDWARD D. HOCH

The second kind of "other creature strange and wonderful" is that which we do not even suspect exists until, suddenly and frighteningly, it appears. What is it? Where has it come from? And most important, what does it want from us, the so-called dominant species?

These are just some of the questions posed by the sudden emergence of the creature from "In the Straw," Edward D. Hoch's startling short-short. And the shivers it generates are as much the result of the continuing unknown—what we do not see and do not learn—as of what we do see and learn about this particular beast. For it has intentions toward humans somewhat different than other creatures, hungers made all the more terrifying because they are close to some basic appetites of our own . . .

Widely considered today's foremost writer of mystery and detective short stories, Edward D. Hoch makes frequent side trips into the realm of the macabre and always with surprising results (cf: his shorts in two previous volumes in this series, Voodoo! *and* Mummy!*). His Simon*

Ark stories have long been favorites among fantasy/horror enthusiasts for their effective mixture of the weird-and-supernatural and the formal detective story. Among his novels are the science fiction—detective hybrids The Transvection Machine, The Fellowship of the Hand, *and* The Frankenstein Factory, *and a straight mystery,* The Shattered Raven. *He has also published four collections of short stories (the most recent being* The Thefts of Nick Velvet), *and for the past several years has edited the popular anthology series,* Best Detective Stories of the Year.

BERT," HIS wife called, seeing him come in from the field. "Bert, I think there's something in the barn, in that big pile of straw. An animal of some sort."

Bert Jenkins adjusted the strap on his overalls and put down the rake he was carrying. "Probably that coon again. Thought I'd chased it away."

He followed her into the barn and stood by the big pile of straw that he kept for the cows. It filled all of one section, towering over his head, and it could have hidden a dozen raccoons with ease. "Don't hear anything now," he said.

"Keep quiet and listen!"

They stood still for a full minute, straining their ears to hear any rustling in the straw. But there was nothing. Finally Bert Jenkins said, "Doris, you been dreaming again. There's nothing in the straw."

"I tell you I heard something!"

He poked at the straw with a handy pitchfork and listened again. Still there was nothing. "Come on," he told her. "It's almost time for supper."

They left the barn and walked together to the farmhouse.

At the door to her kitchen Doris Jenkins glanced back, a look of puzzlement on her face, but she said nothing.

It was not until a week later that Bert Jenkins became aware of the odd behavior of his wife. He'd been running the tractor over in the south field, preparing the ground for a spring planting of oats. When he returned in the late afternoon he found the house empty. Doris was not in the garden nor anywhere in sight, yet the car was still parked in the rutted driveway next to the house.

"Doris!" he called out. "Doris, are you back in the barn?"

There was no reply, but after a moment she appeared, walking fast, glancing back at the barn door. "Doris, what in hell were you doing in there?"

"I . . ." Her face was dead white, and her hands were trembling. "Bert—that thing in the pile of straw! It's still there, and I think it's growing!"

"What nonsense is this?" He went into the sitting room and lifted his shotgun from the rack. He slipped two shells into the chambers and snapped the weapon shut. "We'll see about it," he mumbled, and walked past her into the yard. Doris was at the age when women sometimes had problems, he knew, but she'd never shown signs of imagining things before.

The barn door was standing open, swinging gently in the afternoon breeze. He walked in and stared hard at the pile of straw. It did seem different to him somehow, but in a way he couldn't define. Larger, perhaps—but that made no sense at all. He'd added nothing to the straw since late summer of the previous year.

"Bert . . . ."

"Stand back. I'm going to shoot into the straw. If anything's there, a load of buckshot should bring it out in the open."

He pulled both triggers of the gun as Doris covered her ears against the sound. The straw jumped and flew from the force of the buckshot, but nothing stirred within the pile.

"Well," he said, glancing at her, "whatever it was seems to be gone now."

She did not reply immediately. Instead she simply stood staring at the pile of straw. "Yes," she said finally, and turned and left the barn.

During the weeks that followed, Bert Jenkins grew increasingly aware of his wife's strange activities. Several times, returning unexpectedly from the fields, he found her in the barn. When he questioned her about it, she would make up some transparent excuse for her presence there.

Once, coming right to the point, he asked, "Is it that animal again? The one in the straw?"

"No," she said and turned quickly away.

After that he did not mention the straw again, but as her trips to the barn became more frequent his own troubled curiosity grew. He took to sneaking into the barn himself, often when she was resting or gone to town. The pile of straw was indeed there, and it seemed each time to be larger than he remembered it. It was almost as if it were growing—or something beneath it were growing.

Finally, one day when he could stand it no longer, he attacked the straw with his pitchfork, spending the entire morning moving it from one side of the barn to the other. He found nothing beneath it but soft, muddy earth. As he left the barn to return to his plowing, Doris came out on the back porch of the farmhouse. "Do you think that will stop it?" she asked.

"Stop it?"

"Stop it from *growing*."

He glanced quickly away. There was something like madness in her eyes, and he did not want to face it.

After that she spent much of her time in the barn. He avoided the place as much as he could, and especially the area where the straw was piled. But on those occasions when he did look in on it, he had to admit that the pile was indeed growing. If anything, it was growing more rapidly than before, and soon it would fill the entire barn.

"I'm padlocking the place," he told her one night after supper.

"What?"

"I'm padlocking the barn. You're not to go out there again."

"Then you believe me at last?"

"I didn't say I believed you or not. I just said I was padlocking the barn. You have enough things in here to keep you busy. No need to look for trouble."

And the next morning he kept his word. A stout padlock was put on the barn door. Of course she could still get in through the cow pasture if she really wanted to, but that side faced the fields where he worked and he did not think she would try it.

When he returned in the evening from the plowing, she was busy in the kitchen, humming a little tune to herself. For the first time in weeks everything seemed normal. It was not until she was setting the table for the evening meal that he happened to notice the bit of straw that clung to her skirt on one side.

He rushed from the kitchen, down the back steps, and across the yard to the barn door. The padlock was still closed, but the hasp had been yanked from the wood, pulled free as if by some terrific force. His heart pounding, he examined the door more closely. There were marks on it, deep scratches in the old wood. But they were on the *inside* of the door.

The force that had pulled the hasp from the wood had come from *inside* the barn.

He let the door swing free and took a gentle step inside. "All right, whoever you are! I know you're in here!"

He listened but no answer came, no movement.

"You may have bewitched my wife, but I'm something different. I can handle you, whoever you are."

Waiting, listening, straining to see some movement in the dimness of the barn's interior, he wished he'd brought his shotgun. Whoever it was—

His ears picked out a sound, soft, almost nonexistent. But a sound.

Regular.

Like a very soft, muffled heartbeat. A heartbeat beneath a pile of straw.

"*Who are you?*" he shouted. "*What are you?*"

There was a movement behind him and he whirled to face Doris standing in the barn doorway. "It's big," she said, speaking so softly he could barely hear her. "It's bigger than you already, and it's growing every day."

"Get out of here," he told her. "Get back to the house."

"You can't kill it. Not before it kills you."

"Get back to the house," he repeated. Her voice sent a chill down his spine.

When she was gone, he wasted no more time. Whether the thing in the straw was real or a product of her tortured imagination, he wanted no more of it. He brought a five-gallon can of gasoline from the tool shed and emptied it into the pile of straw. Then he lit a match and stepped back. In a flash the straw was ablaze, sending flames licking high to the roof of the barn, lighting the interior as he'd never seen it before.

He retreated before the flames, taking time only to release the cows and steers to the pasture outside. Then he headed back to the farmhouse. Doris appeared on the back porch, the glow from the flames already reflected in her face. "You think that can stop him?" she challenged. "All you've done is burn down a barn needlessly."

"Call the volunteer fire department," he told her. His voice sounded tired, even to his own ears. She spoke now of *him* instead of *it*, and he wondered when that change had taken place. Perhaps it only was in her mind after all. The fantasy of a childless woman, imagining the biggest child of them all growing larger out there in the straw.

By the time the firemen arrived, the barn was burnt almost to the ground. Bert Jenkins watched it with a certain sadness, and his wife refused to watch it at all, retreating instead to her bedroom.

After it was over, and the firemen had gone, he went upstairs to be with her. "You haven't killed him," she said quietly, sitting in the darkness.

"Doris . . ."

"He'll come for us now. Soon."

"Stop talking like that, Doris. There was nothing in the barn."

"Then why did you burn it down."

He sighed and fell silent. He could no longer talk to her. She was like a stranger in his house.

He awakened from sleep with the odor of burnt timber still strong in his nostrils. Though it was not yet dawn, the bed was empty at his side. He slid out, quietly, and went downstairs to the kitchen, but Doris was not there.

He found her at last in the back yard, searching among the water-logged embers of the barn. She was sobbing when he led her back to the house.

He was determined that day to call a doctor, but in the end he did nothing. There were no psychiatrists closer than the city, and he knew old Doc Rogers could do nothing for her. All through the day he stayed close to her side, and he noticed many times that she would cock her head as if listening for something he could not hear. Only once during that day did she speak, in a seemingly rational moment. "Bert," she pleaded, "lock the bedroom door tonight."

"Of course, dear. Don't you worry."

"*Lock* it!"

"I will," he promised.

She was shivering in bed that night, after he'd locked and bolted the door. He tried to warm her with his body, but it was useless. He lay there, dozing fitfully, wondering what the morning would bring.

He'd been in bed for some hours when he heard it. The same regular beating sound that had come from the barn. But louder now, as if the straw no longer muffled it, or the thing itself had grown larger.

Doris sat up in bed at his side. He could not see her face in the darkness, did not know if her expression was one of terror or relief.

"It's coming closer," he said, more to himself than to her. "It's in the house! My God, Doris—what is it?"

"Something," she mumbled. "Something that just happened, out there in the straw. Beneath the straw, where it's warm and damp and dark."

Then he heard it, the scratching on the other side of the bedroom door, a sound made by long fingernails or the claws of some animal. He remembered the marks on the barn door.

"My god!" he screamed. "It's come for me!"

Then she was out of bed, facing him in the darkness, and he was almost glad he could not see her face. "No," she said. "He's come for me."

And she unlocked the door.

He snapped on the bedside light, holding it as a weapon above his head, and saw the creature that suddenly filled the doorway. The straw was still sticking to its moist body, the odor of fire still clinging to it like an aura. At first he thought it was some sort of mutant bear. But then he saw the claw, and before he could move it was upon him.

"Doris!" he screamed. "Get the shotgun!"

And then it was ripping at his flesh.

The state police came to the farmhouse two days later, after a neighbor reported that neither Jenkins nor his wife seemed to be around. They found Bert Jenkins in the upstairs bedroom, his body ripped and crushed and thrown aside like an old rag.

"What do you think could have caused that?" the trooper asked his partner.

"Animal of some sort. Look at those claw marks!"

They found Doris Jenkins downstairs, her body huddled behind a sofa. She'd blown away part of her head with a blast from her husband's shotgun.

"Whatever it was didn't attack her," the trooper observed.

"But why did she shoot herself? Why didn't she use the gun on the animal, whatever it was?"

The first trooper shrugged. "We'd better get help up here anyway. The thing left a trail out toward the ruins of that barn."

"Footprints?"

"No. Bits of straw with some goo on them."

"That's odd," his partner said, straightening up from Doris Jenkins's body. "She's got that same straw all over her nightgown, and her arms."

The first trooper scratched his head. "It almost looks as if she didn't shoot herself till after the thing left her. Till after she was safe."

"That doesn't make any sense."

The trooper stared out at the trail of straw leading back to the barn. "No," he agreed. "I guess it doesn't."

WHERE DO YOU LIVE, QUEEN ESTHER?
BY AVRAM DAVIDSON

The creature which appears in "Where Do You Live, Queen Esther?" may not properly fit within the perimeters of this anthology. Or then again, it may fit quite well. It all depends on your point of view, and on how much credence you place in things—literally, things—*of magical origin.*

A great many people believe in the powers of magic, and in particular that of voodoo magic. Queen Esther, a simple woman working in a cold foreign place who yearns for the warmth of her native West Indies, is such a believer. But unlike other believers, she is not afraid of the creatures of her native magic. No, not her. Her never feared no ugly old duppy . . .

Avram Davidson was born in 1923 and began publishing fiction in his late twenties. Over the past three decades he has given readers of science fiction, fantasy, and short mysteries a distinguished body of literate, witty stories and novels. Nearly all of his book-length works are science fiction, some of the best of which are Mutiny in Space *(1964),* The Phoenix and the Mirror *(1969), and* Peregrine: Primus *(1971). Most critics agree, however, that his finest work is in the story form—the best of which (including the macabre classic "The Golem") may be found in such outstanding collections as* What Strange Stars and Skies, Strange Seas and Shores, Or All the Seas with Oysters, *and* The Enquiries of Dr. Esterhazy. *He is the only writer ever to win major awards in three separate fields: a 1958 science fiction Hugo for* Or All the Seas with Oysters; *a 1961 Mystery Writers of America Best Short-Story Edgar for "The Affair at Lahore Cantonment"; and a 1975 World Fantasy Award for* The Enquiries of Dr. Esterhazy.

COLD, COLD, it was, in the room where she lodged, so far from her work. The young people complained of the winter, and those born to the country—icy cold, it was, to them. So how could a foreign woman bear it, and not a young one? She had tried to find another job not so far (none were near). *Oh, my, but a woman your age shouldn't be working,* the ladies said. *No, no, I couldn't really.* Kindly indeed. Thank you, mistress.

There was said to be hot water sometimes in the communal bathroom down the hall—the water in the tap in her room was so cold it burned like fire: so strange: hot/cold—but it was always too late when she arrived back from work. Whither she was bound now. Bound indeed.

A long wait on the bare street corner for the bus. Icy winds and no doorways, even, to shelter from the winds. In the buses—for there were two, and another wait for the second—if not warm, then not so cold. And at the end, a walk for many blocks. The mistress not up yet.

Mistress . . . Queen Esther thought about Mrs. Raidy, the woman of the house. At first her was startled by the word—to she it mean, a woman live with a man and no marriage lines. But then her grew to like it, Mrs. Raidy did. Like to hear, too, mention of the *master* and *the young master,* his brother.

Both of they at table. "That second bus," Queen Esther said, unwrapping her head. "He late again. Me think, just to fret I."

"Oh, a few minutes don't matter. Don't worry about it," the master, Mr. Raidy, said. He never called the maid by name, nor did the mistress, but the boy—

As now, looking up with a white line of milk along his upper lip, he smiled and asked, "Where do you live, Queen Esther?" It was a game they played often. His brother—quick glance at the clock, checking his watch, head half-turned to pick up sounds from upstairs, said that he wasn't to bother "her" with his silly question. A pout came over the boy's face, but yielded to her quick reply.

"Me live in the Carver Rooms on Fig Street, near Burr."

His smile broadened. "Fig! That's a fun-ny name for a street. . . . But where do you live at home, Queen Esther? *I* know: Spahnish Mahn. And what you call a fig we call a bah-nah-nah. See, Freddy? *I* know."

The older one got up. "Be a goodboynow," he said, and vanished for the day.

The boy winked at her. "Queen Esther from Spanish Man, Santa Marianne, Bee-Double-You-Eye. But I really think it should be Spanish *Main,* Queen Esther." He put his head seriously to one side. "That's what they used to call the Caribbean Sea, you know."

And he fixed with his brooding, ugly little face her retreating back as she went down to the cellar to hang her coat and change her shoes.

"The sea surround we on three sides at Spanish Man," she said, returning.

"You should say, 'surrounds *us,*' Queen Esther. . . . You have a very funny accent, and you aren't very pretty."

Looking up from her preparations for the second breakfast, she smiled. "True *for* you, me lad."

"But then, neither am I. I look like my father. I'm *his* brother, not *hers,* you know. Do you go swimming much when you live at home, Queen Esther?"

She put up a fresh pot of coffee to drip and plugged in the toaster and set some butter to brown as she beat the eggs; and she told him of how they swim at Spanish Man on Santa Marianna, surrounded on three sides by the sea. It was the least of the Lesser Antilles. . . . She lived only part of her life in the land she worked in, the rest of the time—in fact, often at the same time—she heard, in the silence and cold of the mainland days and nights, the white surf beating on the white sands and the scuttling of the crabs beneath the breadfruit trees.

"I thought I would come down before you carried that heavy tray all the way upstairs," said the mistress, rubbing her troubled puffy eyes. Her name was Mrs. Eleanor Raidy—she was the master's wife—and her hair was teased up in curlers. She sat down with a grunt, sipped coffee, sighed. "What would I ever do without you?"

She surveyed the breakfast-in-progress. "I hope I'll be able to eat. And to retain. Some mornings . . ." she said darkly. Her eyes made the rounds once more. "There's no pineapple, I suppose?" she asked faintly. "Grated, with just a little powdered sugar? Don't go to any extra trouble," she added, as Queen Esther opened the icebox. "Rodney. *Rodney?* Why do I have to shout and—"

"Yes, El. What?"

"In *that* tone of voice? If it were for my pleasure, I'd say, Nothing. But I see your brother doesn't care if you eat or not. Half a bowl of—"

"I'm finished."

"You are not finished. Finish now."

"I'll be *late*, El. They're waiting for me."

"Then they'll wait. Rush out of here with an empty stomach and then fill up on some rubbish? No. Finish the cereal."

"But it's *cold*."

"Who let it get cold? I'm not too sure at all I ought to let you go. This Harvey is older than you and he pals around with girls older than he is. Or maybe they just fix themselves up to look—eat. Did you *hear* what I say? Eat. Most disgusting sight I ever saw, lipstick, and the *clothes?* Don't let me catch you near them. They'll probably be rotten with disease in a few years." Silently, Queen Esther grated pineapple. "I don't like the idea of your going down to the museum without adult supervision. Who knows what can happen? Last week a boy your age was crushed to death by a truck. Did you have a—*look* at me, young man, when I'm talking to you—did you have a movement?"

"Yes."

"Ugh. If looks could kill. I don't believe you. Go upstairs and—Rod*NEY!*"

But Rodney had burst into tears and threw down his spoon and rushed from the room. Even as Mrs. Raidy, her mouth open with shock, tried to catch the maid's eye, he slammed the door behind him and ran down the front steps.

The morning was proceeding as usual.

"And his brother leaves it all to me," Mrs. Raidy said, pursuing a piece of pineapple with her tongue. She breathed heavily. "I have you to thank, in part, I may as well say since we are on the subject, for the fact that he wakes up screaming in the middle of the night. I warned you. Didn't I warn you?"

Queen Esther demurred, said she had never spoken of it to the young master since that one time of the warning.

"One time was enough. What was that word? That name? From the superstitious story you were telling him when I interrupted. Guppy?"

"Duppy, mistress." It was simply a tale from the old slave days, Queen Esther reflected. A cruel Creole lady who went to the fields one night to meet she lover, and met a duppy instead. The slaves all heard, but were affrighted to go out; and to this day the pile of stones near Petty Morne is called The Grave of Mistress-Serve-She-Well. Mistress Raidy had suddenly appeared at the door, as Queen Esther finished the tale, startling Master Rodney.

"Why do you tell the child such stories?" she had demanded, very angry. "See, he's scared to death."

"*You* scared me, El, sneaking up like that."

Queen Esther hastened to try to distract them.

" 'Tis only a fancy of the old people. Me never fear no duppy—"

But she was not allowed to finish. The angry words scalded her. And she knew it was the end of any likelihood (never great) that she might be allowed to move her things into the little attic room, and save the hours of journeying through the cutting, searing cold.

Said the mistress, now, "Even the sound of it is stupid. . . . He didn't eat much breakfast." She glanced casually out the window at the frost-white ground. "You noticed that, I suppose."

Over the sound of the running water Queen Esther said, Yes. She added detergent to the water. He never did eat much breakfast—but she didn't say this out.

"No idea why, I suppose? No? Nobody's been feeding him anything—that you know of? No spicy West Indian messes, no chicken and rice with bay leaves? Yes, yes, I know, not since that one time. All right. A word to the wise is sufficient." Mrs. Raidy arose. A grimace passed over her face. "Another day. And everything is left to me. Every single thing . . . Don't take all morning with those few dishes."

Chicken and rice, with bay leaves and peppercorns. Queen Esther, thinking about it now, relished the thought. Savory, yes. Old woman in the next yard at home in Spanish Man, her cook it in an iron caldron. Gran'dame Hephsibah, who had been born a slave and still said "wittles" and "vhisky" . . . very sage woman. But, now, what was wrong with chicken and rice? The boy made a good meal of it, too, before he sister-in-law had come back, unexpected and early. Then shouts and tears and then a dash to the bathroom. "You've made him sick with your nasty rubbish!" But, for true, it wasn't so.

Queen Esther was preparing to vacuum the rug on the second floor when the mistress appeared at the door of the room. She dabbed at her eyes. "You know, I'm not a religious person," she observed, "but I was just thinking: It's a blessing the Good Lord didn't see fit to give me a child. You know why? Because I would've thrown away my life on it just as I'm throwing it away on my father-in-law's child. Can you imagine such a thing? A man fifty-two years old, a widower, suddenly gets it into his head to take a wife half his age—." She rattled away, winding up, "and so now they're both dead, and who has to put up with the results of his being a nasty old goat? No. . . . Look. See what your fine young gentleman had hidden under the cushion of his bedroom chair."

And she riffled the pages of a magazine. Queen Esther suppressed a smile. It was only natural, she wanted to say.

Young gentlemen liked young ladies. Even up in this cold and frozen land—true, the boy was young. That's why it was natural he only looked—and only at pictures.

"Oh, there's very little gets past *me*, I can assure you. Wait. When he gets back. Museum trips. Dirty pictures. Friends from who knows where. No *more!*"

Queen Esther finished the hall rugs, dusted, started to go in to vacuum the guest room. Mrs. Raidy, she half-observed in the mirror, was going downstairs. Just as the mistress passed out of sight, she threw a glance upward. Queen Esther only barely caught it. She frowned. A moment later a faint jar shook the boards beneath her feet. The cellar door. Bad on its hinges. Queen Esther started the vacuum cleaner; a sudden thought made her straighten up, reach for the switch. For a moment she stood without moving. Then she propped the cleaner, still buzzing, in a corner, and flitted down the steps.

There was, off the kitchen, a large broom closet, with a crack in the wall. Queen Esther peered through the crack. Diagonally below in the cellar was an old victrola and on it the maid had draped her coat and overcoat and scarf; next to it were street shoes, not much less broken than the ones she wore around the house.

Mistress Raidy stood next to the gramophone, her head lifted, listening. The hum of the vacuum cleaner filtered through the house. With a quick nod of her head, tight-lipped in concentration, the mistress began going through the pockets of the worn garments. With little grunts of pleasurable vexation she pulled out a half-pint bottle of fortified wine, some pieces of cassava cake. "That's all we need. A drunken maid. Mice. Roaches. *Oh,* yes." A smudged Hektographed postal card announcing the Grand Annual Festivity of the St. Kitts and Nevis Wesleyan Benevolent Union, a tattered copy of Lucky Tiger Dream Book, a worn envelope . . .

Here she paused to dislodge a cornerless photograph of Queen Esther's brother Samuel in his coffin and to comment, "As handsome as his sister." There were receipts for international postal orders to Samuel's daughter Ada—"Send my money to foreign countries." A change purse with little enough in it, and a flat cigarette tin. This she picked at with nervous fingers, chipping a nail. Clicking her tongue, she got it open, found, with loathing large upon her face—

—a tiny dried frog—a *frog?*—a—surely *not!*—

"Oh!" she said, in a thin, jerky, disgusted voice. "Uh. *Uh!*" She threw the tin away from her, but the thing was bound with a scarlet thread and this caught in her chipped fingernail.

"—out of this *house!*" she raged, flapping her wrist, "and never set foot in it *again,* with her *filthy-ah!*" The thread snapped, the thing flew off and landed in a far corner. She turned to go and had one unsteady foot on the first step when she heard the noise behind her.

Later on, when Queen Esther counted them, she reckoned it as twenty-five steps from the broom closet to the bottom of the cellar stairs. At that moment, though, they seemed to last forever as the screams mounted in intensity, each one seeming to overtake the one before it without time or space for breath between. But they ceased as the maid clattered down the steps, almost tripping over the woman crouched at the bottom.

Queen Esther spared she no glance, then, but faced the thing advancing. Her thrust she hand into she bosom. "Poo!" her spat. "You ugly old duppy! Me never fear no duppy, no, not me!"

And her pulled out the powerful obeah prepared for she long ago by Gran'dame Hephsibah, that sagest of old women half-Ashanti, half-Coromanti. The duppy growled and drivvled and bared its worn-down stumps of filthy teeth, but retreated step by step as her came forward, chanting the words of power; till at last it was shriveled and bound once more in the scarlet thread and stowed safely away in the cigarette tin. *Ugly old duppy . . . !*

Mr. Raidy took the sudden death of his wife with stoical calm. His young brother very seldom has nightmares now, and eats heartily of the savory West Indian messes that Queen Esther prepares for all three of them. Hers is the little room in the attic; her chimney passes through one corner of it, and Queen Esther is warm, warm, warm.

WRIGGLE
BY JOHN LUTZ

Creatures, like many good things (and a few not so good things), sometimes come in small packages. Take worms, for instance. They are among the smallest of all known creatures; they are also not especially pleasant to look at or to handle. Of course, slippery and squirmy though they may be, they're quite harmless. None of us has anything to fear from an ordinary worm.

But how about an extraordinary worm? Like the one Ann and Ron Craig discover lying dormant in a bottle of tequila during their vacation in Mexico City—a tiny grayish wriggling thing of unknown origin. It may well be the most extraordinary of all worms, if not of all creatures large and small. And the most deadly . . .

Born in 1939, John Lutz sold his first short story in 1965 and has followed it with well over a hundred more during the past fifteen years. Most of his work is in the mystery/suspense category (he is a regular contributor to Ellery Queen's Mystery Magazine *and* Alfred Hitchcock's Mystery Magazine, *among other periodicals), but his occasional excursions into fantasy are very good and make one wish he would take the trip more often. His first novel,* The Truth of the Matter, *was published in 1971; his most recent,* The Outside Man, *appeared early this year. Of those which came between are the* roman à clef *political thriller,* Lazarus Man *(1979), and one of the best creature novels of recent years,* Bonegrinder *(1977), about a legendary beast which terrorizes a small community in the Ozark Mountains. A full-time writer for the past several years, Lutz lives with his wife and family not far from those same Ozarks, in a suburb of St. Louis.*

A third case worthy of note is that of Isadora Persano, the well-known duellist, who was found stark raving mad with a match box in front of him which contained a remarkable worm said to be unknown to science.

—Sir Arthur Conan Doyle,
The Problem of Thor Bridge.

"THEY SAY that when the worm dies, the tequila is sufficiently aged." As he spoke, Ron Craig poured a generous measure of tequila into his glass to strengthen the margarita he was drinking.

The four of them—Ron and Ann Craig and Deke and Miriam Waterman—were sitting in the Craigs' room at the Hotel Reforma in Mexico City, getting quietly drunk.

Ann Craig stared at the tiny curled object at the bottom of the green-tinted bottle. "Then it really is true," she said to her husband. "There actually is a dead worm in each bottle of tequila."

Ron winked a conspiratorial male wink across the table at Deke. "She never knows when to believe me."

Deke flashed his handsome, jury-winning smile. "They like to be kept off balance," he said, licking some of the salt from the rim of his glass. His wife Miriam glanced blearily at him. She was not as pretty as the elfin, raven-haired Ann and was acutely aware of the fact.

Ann also was aware of it. Though the two couples were the best of friends, bridge foursomes and tennis doubles competitors in the Cleveland subdivision where they lived, Ann was sure that Miriam wondered in weak moments about Deke and her. Deke had the reputation and looks of a Lothario.

Not that it mattered much now. Deke and Miriam were going back to Cleveland after only a week in Mexico. This was the vacation the two couples had long planned for, but Deke, who was a junior partner in a corporate law firm that demanded a great deal of its lawyers, had been called back for an important trial. Ann and Ron would stay in Mexico by themselves for another week. Ron wanted to see a bullfight, and Ann wanted to go to the famous anthropological museum and the Aztec pyramids.

Tonight was the last time the couples would see each other in Mexico. Deke and Miriam had reservations on an early Mexicana flight the next morning.

It was when Ann and Ron, who was himself almost as handsome as Deke and much loved by Ann, were saying good night and goodbye to Deke and Miriam at the door, that Ann happened to glance at the nearly empty tequila bottle near the lamp on the desk.

"It moved," she said.

Ron turned to her, gazing quizzically from beneath the S-shaped lock of blonde hair that had tumbled down on his tanned forehead. "What?"

"The worm in the bottle," Ann said. "I saw it move."

Ron laughed. Deke and Miriam laughed too.

"You're tired, baby," Ron said, kissing Ann's forehead. "It was a trick of the light."

"Don't be too sure," Deke said with a grin. "Where did you buy that tequila, Ron?"

More laughter. Deke knew where Ron had bought the tequila. At the Juanita Mercado, a spacious indoor marketplace wherein were sold raw fish, live lobsters, unevenly plucked chickens with wrung necks, and tons of produce trucked in by Mexican farmers. Near the exit had been a small display of liquor presided over by an old man with a beard, wearing a ragged, poorly made poncho of the type sold to tourists outside hotels. His prices were cheaper than at the shops that catered to wealthy Americans and Europeans, so Ron had bought a bottle of tequila and Deke had picked up some Mexican vodka and bourbon to take with him back to the States.

"I hope you two aren't too sick to make your flight in the morning," Ron said jokingly.

"If the worm can survive that tequila, so can we," Miriam told him.

"I hope they *do* miss their flight," Ann said. "Then we can have more time together."

"But no way to pay for it when I'm unemployed," Deke said.

They finished their goodbyes, and Ron and Ann were alone.

Ron smiled at Ann and wearily wiped his eyes. It was past midnight after a long day. He began unbuttoning his shirt and walked toward the bathroom. As he passed the desk, he picked up the tequila bottle, held it to the light, gazed at it and pronounced, "Dead." He dropped the bottle into the wastebasket by the desk and continued into the bathroom.

Ann undressed quickly, put on her silk nightgown she had bought in Zihuatanejo, and waited for Ron beneath the covers on the hard bed with its strange coarse sheets. She had planned on their making love, but he was a long time in the bathroom and she fell asleep.

Ann opened her eyes just before dawn, not knowing what had awakened her. The drapes weren't completely closed, and moonlight or light from the neon advertising outside lanced palely into the room, illuminating the half of the bed where Ron lay breathing deeply and evenly. Ann felt a quiet, indefinable uneasiness, as if something dreadful had penetrated her consciousness just far enough to make its presence but not its identity known. She was cold. Her flesh tingled oddly. And when she ran a hand along her arm she felt goose bumps.

For a moment Ann considered waking Ron. But that was silly. Nothing actually was wrong. She was merely haunted by a dream she couldn't quite remember, a subtle nightmare. And now she was awake and not alone.

She turned her head to look at Ron for reassurance, and her body instantly became rigid with horror. In the pale light she could see quite clearly something small and luminous writhing in his right ear. As she watched in silent revulsion, the glistening thing seemed to become even smaller, then disappeared.

She raised her head and stared with wide eyes. There was nothing on the pillow near Ron's head.

He opened his eyes and looked at her. "What's wrong, baby?"

"I . . . I thought I saw something!" Her heart seemed to be struggling to the irregular rhythm of mad music.

"What do you mean, 'something'?"

"It was in your ear. I saw it for just an instant." She couldn't tell him what she really thought she'd seen. "An insect of some kind, maybe."

Ron blinked at her. "So where did it go?"

Ann swallowed. "I don't know. I don't see it now." *Had* she seen it?

Ron reached over and patted her shoulder. "You've been seeing things lately that aren't there, baby. You're tense and have been for days. A vacation's supposed to relax you, so why don't you just let that happen and stop worrying?"

He moved to her side of the bed, coiled a long arm about her and began caressing her. She felt his lips like two warm writhing things on the nape of her neck, and quickly she moved as far from him as possible, to the very edge of the mattress.

"No," she said, simply and with finality.

There was something fierce and brittle in her voice. He didn't try to change her mind.

Ron was himself the next morning. Ann didn't know what she had expected after the tiff last night. What she got was normality.

On a whim she lifted the empty tequila bottle from the wastebasket.

The worm was gone.

Ann wiped her forehead with the back of her hand. Maybe the air had withered the tiny worm to nothing. Maybe it had slipped from the bottle when Ron had dropped it into the wastebasket. Maybe it was down along the curved edge of the bottle's bottom and she couldn't see it. She replaced the bottle and said nothing.

After breakfast in the hotel's bustling coffee shop, Ann and Ron and two other couples went on a guided tour of the

National Museum of Anthropology. The guide was an old man named Pablo, who wore a black beret and his national pride with equal aplomb. Pablo explained to them that many of the artifacts they were seeing came from a civilization that predated the Aztecs, a civilization about which almost nothing was known that had disappeared—when and how no one could accurately say. When the Aztecs came they had vowed to settle where their priests saw an eagle devouring a snake. That place was the ancient city that they found. It became the Aztec city of Tenochtitlán in the year 1325, and Mexico City itself rests on its ruins.

The Aztec religion demanded blood sacrifice, and many huge stone figures contained hollows used to hold blood or the hearts torn from the breasts of sacrificial victims.

"The people before the Aztecs," Ann asked, "were they also so bloodthirsty?"

Pablo shrugged, his seamed face blank. "That I cannot say, señora."

On the way out of the museum, as they passed one of many enigmatic totems, Ann thought she saw engraved in ancient stone a number of small figures with coiled bodies and elongated, flattened heads. Immediately a spiraling weight seemed to drop through her. The simple configuration of those interlocking small curves on stone rang cold and familiar in her mind. She stared at them again, but they were, she told herself, merely a series of designs wrought by a hand long dead.

"No one knows when or how they disappeared," Ann muttered, back at the Hotel Reforma. "It's one of the world's great mysteries."

"What?" Ron's eyes were dark slits of irritability as he stared across the room at her.

"There's no reason to be angry," Ann said. "I was just

thinking about the civilization that predated the Aztecs, about what might have happened to them."

"If you're so interested in that museum," Ron said acidly, "why don't you go back there by yourself tomorrow and leave me alone?"

"I don't want it to be that way, Ron." She walked to him, rested a hand on his arm. She could feel the heat of his body through his cotton shirt. "What's wrong with you today? You've been picking on me. You act sometimes as if you hate me."

He knocked her hand away. Then he shook his head slightly yet vigorously. He smiled at her. "You're right," he said, "and I'm sorry." He touched her elbow gently. "Why don't we go out and have some dinner?"

They kissed. Ron pulled away from Ann rather roughly.

They left to walk to the Zona Rosa and a restaurant that the tour book recommended.

Dinner at a place called Lejania (their second choice, since the restaurant they had set out for was closed for remodeling) wasn't very pleasant. Ann and Ron argued over what to order, how tasty it was, how to figure the tip in pesos and how to return to the hotel.

They decided to walk, and they did so by the most direct route and silently. Even now, back in their room, Ron wasn't speaking to Ann. She felt eerily alone, estranged from her husband, in a foreign city full of people whose language she didn't speak and whose heritage she couldn't understand.

Ron was staring at her from where he sat on the bed, his fingertips pressed to his temples, his face contorted in pain.

"Do you have a headache?" she asked, bewildered.

He stood up. His eyes were odd. They didn't blink, not once. They held Ann in fascination, froze her were she stood.

"Ron? . . ." she said, plea and question, as he moved toward her.

His hands shot upward with a terrible mechanical motion and clamped about her neck, squeezing, squeezing. His breath rasped loudly, blew hot and sour on her face. The room danced in a reddish haze and a terrible weakness entered her knees, a weakness she knew she must fight. She flailed her arms, attempting screams that lodged soundlessly in her strictured throat. She could hear and feel the crunch of cartilage.

Then her right hand closed on something beside and behind her. The heavy brass desk lamp! Hardly knowing what she was doing, she swung the lamp in a tight, lethal arc, feeling it strike something solid, over and over again.

The pressure about her neck lessened, then was gone completely, and she heard a distant thud. Ron striking the floor. Another Ron in another room in another world. It had to be!

Gagging, drawing her breath agonizingly through her bruised windpipe, Ann stared down at her husband's misshapen, bloody head and at the lamp clutched in her hand.

She fainted before she could sit down.

The maid found Ann Craig the next morning lying on the floor near her dead husband, then screamed and fled to notify the manager. The manager investigated and phoned the police. The police, in the persons of Lieutenant Federico Ramirez and Sergeant Juan Avilla, were alone now in the suite's small sitting room with Ann. On the other side of the wall, Ron Craig's body was at last being prepared for removal. There would be, as a matter of routine, an autopsy, but there was little doubt as to the cause of death. Ramirez and Sergeant Avilla had listened to Ann's story. She was under arrest on suspicion of murder.

Ramirez, a short, heavy man of middle age who had been a policeman twenty-four years, sighed as he stood and stared down at the suspect. This was a lovely woman who seemed genuinely confounded by her crime and whose story made no sense at all. Yet she was found alone in the room with the victim, her hand still gripping the murder weapon. Further questioning might reveal the true story. Perhaps she was innocent after all. Ramirez hoped so.

"I'll go downstairs and make sure the way is clear," he said to Avilla. "Wait ten minutes, then bring Señora Craig down."

Avilla nodded. His lean features suggested nothing of the workings of his mind. The perfect policeman's face.

Ramirez, seeing with satisfaction that the corpse finally had been removed, left the room and took the elevator to the lobby.

Ten minutes later Ramirez stood outside the Hotel Reforma near a patrol car and waited for Avilla to arrive with the suspect. He was leaning against the car's fender, gazing at a colorful display of magazines hung with metal clips at a nearby newsstand, when his attention was diverted by some sort of commotion inside the Hotel Reforma's lobby. Quickly Ramirez motioned to the armed patrolman seated behind the car's steering wheel, and both men entered the lobby at a brisk walk.

A knot of people stood in front of the elevators. The expressions on their faces were of horror and shock. Ramirez approached the elevators, identified himself as a policeman, and elbowed through the onlookers.

Avilla was leaning against the back wall of the elevator. At his feet was Ann Craig. The front of her dress was bloody and her eyes were open and fixed in death. There was a crescent of gore on the wall near Avilla.

The patrolman pushed the crowd back. Ramirez entered

the elevator, smelled the scent of gunpowder, so like the scent of human feces.

"She tried to kill me," Avilla moaned. "I don't know why. Suddenly she went wild and clawed for my revolver, tried to turn it on me. There was no warning, lieutenant, I swear! I had no choice!"

Sirens growled reluctantly to angry silence outside the hotel. More uniformed policemen arrived.

"Go outside and sit in the car," Ramirez told his long-time sergeant. "Wait for me there, my friend."

Avilla handed his revolver to Ramirez and obeyed, moving with dreamlike slowness. Ramirez nodded to the driver of the car, who accompanied Avilla.

Ramirez shook his head and stared down at the beautiful woman who lay dead before him. The wide spectrum of aberrant human behavior often amazed and saddened him.

Heads turned. The crowd was parting. The professionals who had recently finished with the husband's corpse were returning with their equipment to shape chaos into some sort of order with which the police might cope.

Ramirez noticed on the floor of the elevator a small, grayish worm of some kind wriggling near the victim's head.

He was about to step on the worm, casually grind it to oblivion with the toe of his shoe, when the police photographer tapped him on the shoulder and nudged him aside so he could squeeze past with his bulky camera gear. A second later Ramirez stepped from the elevator to provide room for the doctor who had arrived to make official the grotesquely obvious fact of Ann Craig's death.

No one noticed the tiny curled object clinging to the side of Ramirez's right shoe.

Ramirez made sure that the law was well-represented at the scene and left the lobby to join Avilla outside in the car.

He sat silently beside the sergeant as their driver maneuvered them out into the swift flow of traffic.

They were riding along the Paseo de la Reforma toward headquarters when Ramirez felt a faint tickling sensation in his right ear. Then he winced slightly as he experienced a brief, flaring headache.

At that moment Ramirez saw in a dark recess of his mind the rage-distorted, dead face of Ann Craig. He knew that probably her actions would never be explained. And that neither her guilt nor that of her husband could be established by law.

There are some cases that are never closed, Ramirez told himself as his headache worsened. Some mysteries that are never solved.

THE POND
BY NIGEL KNEALE

Frogs, like worms, are basically innocuous creatures. They live in swamps or rivers—or ponds—and bother no one. But humans, for some reason, refuse to return the favor. Frogs are among the most oppressed of creatures: reviled because their skin is green or warty brown and their eyes bulge and their bodies are often slimy; hunted for food, sport, and/or profit, and dissected in biology labs everywhere.

Some men, the old man in "The Pond" being one of them, have even nastier reasons for hunting and killing the poor frog. Reasons which would stretch the limits of endurance of any creature alive. But what such men forget is that frogs, like worms, can turn. And that every frog can have his day . . .

Nigel Kneale's little gem is one of the finest and creepiest horror tales ever penned—an amazingly neglected story that any anthologist should be proud to reprint. It is also a fitting final selection for this book, in that it presents an edifying moral for us all: "It's not nice, and may be very dangerous, to mess with Mother Nature."

An actor-turned-writer, Nigel Kneale has achieved considerable acclaim in England (much as Rod Serling did here) for his original teleplays based, more often than not, on traditional science fiction and fantasy themes. He is the author of the critically heralded Quatermass series, both the initial television versions and the later expansions into feature Hammer films (The Quatermass Xperiment, *a.k.a.* The Creeping Unknown; Quatermass and the Pit, *a.k.a.* Five Million Years to Earth). *Among his other well-known teleplays are* The Year of the Sex Olympics, The Stone Tape, *and* The Road, *all three of which were collected under the title* The Year of the Sex Olympics and Other TV Plays *(1976). His screenplays in addition to the Quatermass series include adaptations of* Look Back in Anger *and* The Entertainer. *In the late 1940s, before he turned to visual media (media), Kneale wrote a number of short stories (and was the recipient of the Somerset Maugham Literary Prize in 1950); the best of these tales, many of which are as mordant and macabre as "The Pond," may be found in his single prose work,* Tomato Cain and Other Stories *(1950).*

IT WAS deeply scooped from a corner of the field, a green stagnant hollow with thorn bushes on its banks.

From time to time something moved cautiously beneath the prickly branches that were laden with red autumn berries. It whistled and murmured coaxingly.

"Come, come, come, come," it whispered. An old man, squatting froglike on the bank. His words were no louder than the rustling of the dry leaves above his head. "Come now. Sssst—ssst! Little dear—here's a bit of meat for thee." He tossed a tiny scrap of something into the pool. The weed rippled sluggishly.

The old man sighed and shifted his position. He was crouching on his haunches because the bank was damp.

He froze.

The green slime had parted on the far side of the pool. The disturbance traveled to the bank opposite, and a large frog drew itself half-out of the water. It stayed quite still, watching; then with a swift crawl it was clear of the water. Its yellow throat throbbed.

"Oh!—little dear," breathed the old man. He did not move.

He waited, letting the frog grow accustomed to the air and slippery earth. When he judged the moment to be right, he made a low grating noise in his throat.

He saw the frog listen.

The sound was subtly like the call of its own kind. The old man paused, then made it again.

This time the frog answered. It sprang into the pool, sending the green weed slopping, and swam strongly. Only its eyes showed above the water. It crawled out a few feet distant from the old man and looked up the bank, as if eager to find the frog it had heard.

The old man waited patiently. The frog hopped twice, up the bank.

His hand was moving, so slowly that it did not seem to move, towards the handle of the light net at his side. He gripped it, watching the still frog.

Suddenly he struck.

A sweep of the net, and its wire frame whacked the ground about the frog. It leaped frantically, but was helpless in the green mesh.

"Dear! Oh, my dear!" said the old man delightedly.

He stood with much difficulty and pain, his foot on the thin rod. His joints had stiffened and it was some minutes before he could go to the net. The frog was still struggling desperately. He closed the net round its body and picked both up together.

"Ah, big beauty!" he said. "Pretty. Handsome fellow, you!"

He took a darning needle from his coat lapel and carefully killed the creature through the mouth, so that its skin would not be damaged, then put it in his pocket.

It was the last frog in the pond.

He lashed the water with the net rod, and the weed swirled and bobbed: there was no sign of life now but the little flies that flitted on the surface.

He went across the empty field with the net across his shoulder, shivering a little, feeling that the warmth had gone out of his body during the long wait. He climbed a stile, throwing the net over in front of him to leave his hands free. In the next field, by the road, was his cottage.

Hobbling through the grass with the sun striking a long shadow from him, he felt the weight of the dead frog in his pocket, and was glad.

"Big beauty!" he murmured again.

The cottage was small and dry, and ugly and very old. Its windows gave little light, and they had colored panels, dark blue and green, that gave the rooms the appearance of being under the sea.

The old man lit a lamp, for the sun had set; and the light became more cheerful. He put the frog on a plate, and poked the fire, and when he was warm again, took off his coat.

He settled down close beside the lamp and took a sharp knife from the drawer of the table. With great care and patience, he began to skin the frog.

From time to time he took off his spectacles and rubbed his eyes. The work was tiring; also the heat from the lamp made them sore. He would speak aloud to the dead creature, coaxing and cajoling it when he found his task difficult. But in time he had the skin neatly removed, a little heap of tumbled, slippery film. He dropped the stiff, stripped body into a pan of boiling water on the fire, and sat again, humming and fingering the limp skin.

"Pretty," he said. "You'll be so handsome."

There was a stump of black soap in the drawer and he took it out to rub the skin, with the slow, over-careful motion that showed the age in his hand. The little mottled thing began to stiffen under the curing action. He left it at last, and brewed himself a pot of tea, lifting the lid of the simmering pan occasionally to make sure that the tiny skull and bones were being boiled clean without damage.

Sipping his tea, he crossed the narrow living room. Well away from the fire stood a high table, its top covered by a square of dark cloth supported on a frame. There was a faint smell of decay.

"How are you, little dears?" said the old man.

He lifted the covering with shaky scrupulousness. Beneath the wire support were dozens of stuffed frogs.

`All had been posed in human attitudes; dressed in tiny coats and breeches to the fashion of an earlier time. There were ladies and gentlemen and bowing flunkeys. One, with lace at his yellow, waxen throat, held a wooden wine-cup. To the dried forepaw of its neighbor was stitched a tiny glassless monocle, raised to a black button eye. A third had a midget pipe pressed into its jaws, with a wisp of wool for smoke. The same coarse wool, cleaned and shaped, served the ladies for their miniature wigs; they wore long skirts and carried fans.

The old man looked proudly over the stiff little figures.

"You, my lord—what are you doing, with your mouth so

glum?" His fingers prized open the jaws of a round-bellied
frog dressed in satins; shrinkage must have closed them.
"Now you can sing again, and drink up!"

His eyes searched the banqueting, motionless party.

"Where now—? Ah!"

In the middle of the table three of the creatures were fixed
in the attitudes of a dance.

The old man spoke to them. "Soon we'll have a partner for
the lady there. He'll be the handsomest of the whole company, my dear, so don't forget to smile at him and look your
prettiest!"

He hurried back to the fireplace and lifted the pan; poured
off the steaming water into a bucket.

"Fine, shapely brain-box you have." He picked with his
knife, cleaning the tiny skull. "Easy does it." He put it down
on the table, admiringly; it was like a transparent flake of
ivory. One by one he found the delicate bones in the pan,
knowing each for what it was.

"Now, little duke, we have all of them that we need," he
said at last. "We can make you into a picture indeed. The
beau of the ball. And such an object of jealousy for the lovely
ladies!"

With wire and thread he fashioned a stiff little skeleton,
binding in the bones to preserve the proportions. At the top
went the skull.

The frog's skin had lost its earlier flaccidness. He threaded
a needle, eyeing it close to the lamp. From the table drawer he
now brought a loose wad of wool. Like a doctor reassuring his
patient by describing his methods, he began to talk.

"This wool is coarse, I know, little friend. A poor substitute
to fill that skin of yours, you may say: wool from the hedges,
snatched by the thorns from a sheep's back." He was pulling
the wad into tufts of the size he required. "But you'll find it

gives you such a springiness that you'll thank me for it. Now, carefully does it—"

With perfect concentration he worked his needle through the skin, drawing it together round the wool with almost untraceable stitches.

"A piece of lace in your left hand, or shall it be a quizzing-glass?" With tiny scissors he trimmed away a fragment of skin. "But—wait, it's a dance and it is your right hand that we must see, guiding the lady."

He worked the skin precisely into place round the skull. He would attend to the empty eye-holes later.

Suddenly he lowered his needle.

He listened.

Puzzled, he put down the half-stuffed skin and went to the door and opened it.

It was dark now. He heard the sound more clearly. He knew it was coming from the pond. A far-off, harsh croaking, as of a great many frogs.

He frowned.

In the wall cupboard he found a lantern ready trimmed, and lit it with a flickering splinter. He put on an overcoat and hat: the evening was chilly. Lastly he took his net.

He went very cautiously. His eyes saw nothing at first, after working so close to the lamp. Then, as the croaking came to him more clearly and he became accustomed to the darkness, he hurried.

He climbed the stile as before, throwing the net ahead. This time, however, he had to search for it in the darkness, tantalized by the sounds from the pond. When it was in his hand again, he began to move stealthily.

About twenty yards from the pool he stopped and listened.

There was no wind and the noise astonished him. Hundreds of frogs must have traveled through the fields to this spot; perhaps from other water where danger had arisen, perhaps, or drought. He had heard of such instances.

Almost on tiptoe he crept towards the pond. He could see nothing yet. There was no moon, and the thorn bushes hid the surface of the water.

He was a few paces from the pond when, without warning, every sound ceased.

He froze again. There was absolute silence. Not even a watery plop or splashing told that one frog out of all those hundreds had dived for shelter into the weed. It was strange.

He stepped forward, and heard his boots brushing the grass.

He brought the net up across his chest, ready to strike if he saw anything move. He came to the thorn bushes, and still heard no sound. Yet, to judge by the noise they had made, they should be hopping in dozens from beneath his feet.

Peering, he made the throaty noise which had called the frog that afternoon. The hush continued.

He looked down at where the water must be. The surface of the pond, shadowed by the bushes, was too dark to be seen. He shivered, and waited.

Gradually, as he stood, he became aware of a smell.

It was wholly unpleasant. Seemingly it came from the weed, yet mixed with the vegetable odor was one of another kind of decay. A soft, oozy bubbling accompanied it. Gases must be rising from the mud at the bottom. It would not do to stay in this place and risk his health.

He stooped, still puzzled by the disappearance of the frogs, and stared once more at the dark surface. Pulling his net to a ready position, he tried the throaty call for the last time.

Instantly he threw himself backwards with a cry.

A vast, belching bubble of foul air shot from the pool. Another gushed up past his head; then another. Great patches of slimy weed were flung high among the thorn branches.

The whole pond seemed to boil.

He turned blindly to escape, and stepped into the thorns. He was in agony. A dreadful slobbering deafened his ears: the stench overcame his senses. He felt the net whipped from his hands. The icy weeds were wet on his face. Reeds lashed him.

Then he was in the midst of an immense, pulsating softness that shielded and received and held him. He knew he was shrieking. He knew there was no one to hear him.

An hour after the sun had risen, the rain slackened to a light drizzle.

A policeman cycled slowly on the road that ran by the cottage, shaking out his cape with one hand, and half-expecting the old man to appear and call out a comment on the weather. Then he caught sight of the lamp, still burning feebly in the kitchen, and dismounted. He found the door ajar, and wondered if something was wrong.

He called to the old man. He saw the uncommon handiwork lying on the table as if it had been suddenly dropped; and the unused bed.

For half an hour the policeman searched in the neighborhood of the cottage, calling out the old man's name at intervals, before remembering the pond. He turned towards the stile.

Climbing over it, he frowned and began to hurry. He was disturbed by what he saw.

On the bank of the pond crouched a naked figure.

The policeman went closer. He saw it was the old man, on his haunches; his arms were straight; the hands resting between his feet. He did not move as the policeman approached.

"Hallo, there!" said the policeman. He ducked to avoid the thorn bushes catching his helmet. "This won't do, you know. You can get into trouble—"

He saw green slime in the old man's beard, and the staring eyes. His spine chilled. With an unprofessional distaste, he quickly put out a hand and took the old man by the upper arm. It was cold. He shivered, and moved the arm gently.

Then he groaned and ran from the pond.

For the arm had come away at the shoulder: reeds and green water-plants and slime tumbled from the broken joint.

As the old man fell backwards, tiny green stitches glistened across his belly.

BIBLIOGRAPHY

NONFICTION

Baumann, Elwood D. *The Loch Ness Monster.* New York: Franklin Watts, 1972.

Brown, Charles Edward. *Sea Serpents: Wisconsin Occurrences of These Weird Watery Monsters.* Madison, Wisconsin: Wisconsin Folklore Society, 1942.

Buehr, Walter. *Sea Monsters.* New York: Norton, 1974.

Burton, Maurice. *The Elusive Monster.* London: Hart-Davis, 1961.

Clark, Jerome, and Coleman, Loren. *Creatures of the Outer Edge.* New York: Warner Books, 1978.

_____. *The Unidentified.* New York: Warner Books, 1975.

Costello, Peter. *In Search of Lake Monsters.* New York: Coward McCann, 1974.

Dart, Raymond A. *Adventures with the Missing Link.* London: Hamish Hamilton, 1959.

Digby, G. B. *The Mammoth and Mammoth-Hunting in Northeast Siberia.* London: H. F. & G. Witherby, 1926.

Dinsdale, Tim. *The Leviathans.* London: Routledge & Kegan Paul, 1966.

_____. *Loch Ness Monster.* London: Routledge & Kegan Paul, 1961.

Gould, R. T. *The Loch Ness Monster and Others.* London: Geoffrey Bles, 1934.

Green, John. *On the Tracks of the Sasquatch.* New York: Ballantine, 1973.

Heuvelmans, Bernard. *In the Wake of the Sea Serpents.* New York: Hill & Wang, 1968.

297

_____. *On the Track of Unknown Animals.* New York: Hill & Wang, 1965.

Holiday, F. W. *The Great Orm of Loch Ness.* London: Faber & Faber, 1968.

Izzard, Ralph. *The Abominable Snowman Adventure.* London: *Daily Mail,* 1954.

Keel, John A. *Jadoo.* New York: Messner, 1957.

_____. *Strange Creatures from Time and Space.* New York: Fawcett Gold Medal, 1970.

Lee, John, and Moore, Barbara. *Monsters Among Us: Journey to the Unexplained.* New York: Pyramid, 1975.

McEwan, Graham J. *Sea Serpents, Sailors and Sceptics.* Boston: Routledge & Kegan Paul, 1978.

Napier, John. *Bigfoot: The Yeti and Sasquatch in Myth and Reality.* New York: E.P. Dutton, 1972.

Patterson, Roger. *Do Abominable Snowmen of America Really Exist?* Yakima, Washington: Northwest Research Association, 1966.

Sanderson, Ivan T. *Abominable Snowmen: Legend Come to Life.* Philadelphia: Chilton, 1961. Revised edition published by Jove Books (New York), 1977.

_____. *"Things."* New York: Pyramid, 1967.

_____. *More "Things."* New York: Pyramid, 1969.

Slate, Ann B., and Berry, Alan. *Bigfoot.* New York: Bantam, 1976.

Smith, Warren. *Secret Origins of Bigfoot.* New York: Zebra Books, 1977.

_____. *Strange Abominable Snowmen.* New York: Popular Library, 1970.

Snyder, Gerald S. *Is There a Loch Ness Monster?* New York: Messner, 1977.

Stonor, C. *The Sherpa and the Snowman.* London: Hollis & Carter, 1955.

Tchernine, Odette. *The Yeti.* London: Neville Spearman, 1970.

Tenzing, Norgay (with Ullman, J. R.). *Tiger of the Snows.* New York: Putnam, 1955.

Whyte, Constance. *More Than a Legend.* London: Hamish Hamilton, 1957.

Witchell, Nicholas. *The Loch Ness Story.* London: Penguin Books, 1975.

Wolf, Leonard. *Monsters.* San Francisco: Straight Arrow Books, 1974. Brief essays on twenty famous types of creatures.

FICTION:

Adams, Samuel Hopkins. *The Flying Death.* New York: McClure, 1908.

Arthur, Robert, ed. *Monster Mix.* New York: Dell (Mayflower), 1968. Collection of short stories.

Bogner, Norman. *Snowman.* New York: Dell Books, 1978.

Burroughs, Edgar Rice. *At the Earth's Core*. Chicago: McClurg, 1922.

————. *Back to the Stone Age*. Tarzana, California: Burroughs, 1937.

————. *Land of Terror*. Tarzana, California: Burroughs, 1944.

————. *The Land That Time Forgot*. Chicago: McClurg, 1924.

————. *Pellucidar*. Chicago: McClurg, 1923.

————. *Tanar of Pellucidar*. New York: Metropolitan Books, 1930.

————. *Tarzan at the Earth's Core*. New York: Metropolitan Books, 1930.

————. *Tarzan the Terrible*. Chicago: McClurg, 1921.

Case, David. *The Cell: Three Tales of Horror*. New York: Hill & Wang, 1969. Collection of three original novellas.

Davenport, Basil, ed. *Famous Monster Tales*. Princeton, New Jersey: D. Van Nostrand, 1967. Collection of short stories.

Dicks, Terrance. *Dr. Who and the Abominable Snowman*. London: Target Books, 1974.

————. *Dr. Who and the Loch Ness Monster*. Los Angeles: Pinnacle Books, 1979.

Doyle, Sir Arthur Conan. *The Lost World*. New York: Doran, 1912.

Dreadstone, Carl. *The Creature from the Black Lagoon*. New York: Berkley Books, 1977. Novelization of the film.

Hulke, Malcolm. *Dr. Who and the Cave Monsters*. London: Target Books, 1974.

Lewis, Richard. *The Spiders*. New York: Signet Books, 1980.

Lovelace, Delos. *King Kong*. New York: Grosset & Dunlap, 1932. Reissued 1976. Novelization of the film (conceived by Edgar Wallace and Merian C. Cooper).

Lutz, John. *Bonegrinder*. New York: Putnam, 1977.

MacKenzie, Compton. *The Rival Monster*. London: 1952.

Masson, Richard. *Creatures*. New York: Pocket Books, 1979.

Nesvadba, Josef. *In the Footsteps of the Abominable Snowman*. London: Gollancz, 1970.

Page, Thomas. *The Spirit*. New York: Rawson Associates, 1977.

Sarac, Roger. *The Throwbacks*. New York: Belmont Tower, 1969.

Seltzer, David. *The Prophecy*. New York: Ballantine, 1978.

Sheldon, Walter J. *The Beast*. New York: Fawcett Gold Medal, 1980.

Smith, Guy N. *Killer Crabs*. New York: Signet Books, 1979.

————. *Night of the Crabs*. London: New English Library, 1977.

————. *The Slime Beast*. London: New English Library, 1975.

Tremayne, Peter. *The Curse of Loch Ness*. London: Sphere Books, 1979.

Vercors. *You Shall Know Them*. Boston: Little Brown, 1953. Also published as *Murder of the Missing Link*. New York: Pocket Books, 1955. Translation of *Les Animaux Denatures*.

Verne, Jules. *Journey to the Center of the Earth*. London: Griffth & Farran, 1872.

_____. *Twenty Thousand Leagues Under the Sea*. London: Sampson Low, 1873.

FILMS

Abominable Snowman of the Himalayas, The (British, 1957). Forrest Tucker, Peter Cushing, Maureen Connell.

Attack of the Crab Monsters (1957). Richard Garland, Pamela Duncan.

Attack of the Giant Leeches (1959). Ken Clark, Yvette Vickers.

Beast from the Haunted Cave, The (1959). Michael Forrest, Sheila Carol.

Beast from 20,000 Fathoms, The (1953). Paul Christian, Lee Van Cleef.

Beast of Hollow Mountain, The (1956). Guy Madison, Patricia Medina.

Bigfoot, The Mysterious Monster (1975). John Carradine, John Mitchum, Chris Mitchum.

Creature from Black Lake, The (1976). Jack Elam, Dub Taylor.

Creature from the Black Lagoon, The (1954). Richard Carlson, Julia Adams, Richard Denning.

Creature from the Haunted Sea (1955). Anthony Carbone, Betsy Jones-Moreland.

Creature Walks Among Us, A (1956). Jeff Morrow, Rex Reason.

Curse of Bigfoot, The (1972). William Simonsen, Robert Clymire.

Dinosaurus (1960). Ward Ramsey, Paul Lukather.

Gargoyles (Made-for-TV, 1972). Cornel Wilde, Jennifer Salt.

Giant Behemoth, The (British, 1959). Gene Evans, Andre Morell.

Godzilla (Japanese, 1956). Raymond Burr.

Godzilla Versus the Sea Monster (Japanese, 1966). Akira Takarada, Toru Watanabe.

Gorgo (British, 1961). Bill Travers, William Sylvester.

It Came from Beneath the Sea (1955). Kenneth Tobey.

King Kong (1933). Fay Wray, Bruce Cabot, Robert Armstrong.

King Kong (1976). Jeff Bridges, Charles Grodin, Jessica Lange.

King Kong Versus Godzilla (Japanese, 1962). Michael Keith, James Yagi.

Legend of Boggy Creek, The (1973). Semi-documentary written, directed, and produced by Charles B. Pierce.

Man Beast (1956). Rock Madison, Virginia Maynor.

Monster from the Green Hell, The (1957). Jim Davis, Barbara Turner.

Monster from the Ocean Floor, The (1957).

Monster from the Surf (1965). Jon Hall, Sue Casey.

Monster of Piedras Blancas, The (1961). Les Tremayne, Jeanne Carmen.

Monster That Challenged the World, The (1957). Tim Holt, Audrey Dalton.

Prophecy (1979). Talia Shire, Robert Foxworth.

Reptilicus (European, 1962). Carl Ottosen, Ann Smyrner.

Revenge of the Creature (1955). John Agar, Lori Nelson.

Secret of the Loch, The (Scottish, 1934). Seymour Hicks.

Skullduggery (1970). Burt Reynolds, Chips Rafferty, Edward Fox.

Snowbeast (1977). Bo Swenson, Yvette Mimieux, Clint Walker.

Snow Creature, The (Japanese-American, 1954). Paul Langton, Leslie Denison, Teru Shimada.

Tarantula (1956). John Agar, Mara Corday, Leo G. Carroll.

Them (1954). James Arness, James Whitmore, Edmund Gwenn.

Trog (1970). Joan Crawford, Michael Gough.

Valley of the Gwangi (1969). James Franciscus, Richard Carlson, Gila Golan.